HEART OF THE WISH

Maggie Alexandrite

~Nightfall Curses Press~

Copyright © 2026 by Maggie Alexandrite

Published by Nightfall Curses Press

All rights reserved.

No part of this publication may be reproduced, distributed, or transmitted in any form or by any means, including photocopying, recording, or other electronic or mechanical methods, without the prior written permission of the publisher or author.

The story, all names, characters, and incidents portrayed in this book are fictitious. Any resemblance to actual persons (living or deceased), places, buildings, or products is purely coincidental.

Book Cover by Aimeé Fôrémar

First Edition: May 2026

ISBN (paperback): 978-1-0674148-0-1
ISBN (ebook): 978-1-0674148-1-8

For Mom. For Papa. For Jeter and Rocco.

And for anyone who has ever felt less than human.

WISH

*N*ot a stitch of blood escaped out of the cut on the end of Mina's left forefinger. The reddened skin around her new wound only shed deceit.

Mina tossed the pink card that had accidentally cut her onto the table. It landed with the others, all displaying best wishes to her love, Davian, in a range of fancy to clumsy handwriting. The wonderful words got cut off as the near hundred cards overlapped each other. No amount of reorganizing fixed the problem.

The pink card seemingly laughed at Mina from atop the pile. It gloated the fact that if it sliced a normal person, they wouldn't be in as much danger as she was now. Davian fought so hard to keep her nature disclosed. She'd never forgive herself if she ruined him because of the smallest cut.

She internally sneered at the card and pivoted from it. Lifting her hand in front of her face, she studied the diagonal, scarlet, slash on her jaundiced skin. No magic, peeked through the tiny opening. A sigh unwound her tight jaw. Today was not the day for exposure. She curled her finger into her palm and tossed the card onto the table with the others.

Far off movement in the corner of her eye grabbed her attention. A blessing for her brain ached from organizing and reorganizing the cards.

She looked through the streamers and lanterns hanging from the wooden rafters of the courtyard. She peered past the finer details on their surfaces, illuminated by the sinking golden sunlight. She stared over the rows of picnic tables lined up perfectly over the verdant green of the square space with covered dishes of steaming food, shiny utensils, and white plates carefully set up on the light blue table clothes. Homing in on the courtyard's proscenium entrance, she focused on the distracting movement of a person climbing the ladder at the center of the opening, their shadow slanting across the ground.

Mina had no heart, but the cold way the magic she was made out of bundled in her chest made her feel a little human. The cause of such a sensation always came from the same source: Davian. Her greatest and only love. He'd know how to organize the cards.

She weaved through the tables easily. Later, when every guest arrived, they'd clog up the space and make it harder to move anywhere. She'd invited everyone from the village of Virvin to Davian's celebration, plus an extra guest as a secret surprise—one of his oldest friends.

However, having the village folk, plus an old friend, hadn't felt grand enough. If Mina could've invited the entire world, she would've. Davian deserved all the reverence he could get.

"Lumina would have found a way," Mina mumbled to herself.

"What are you speaking of?" the man himself asked.

Mina's face snapped up.

Davian squinted down at her from atop the ladder, a single piece of sunlight hitting his hardened but handsome face. He had one arm stretched above his head, holding a welcome wreath against the proscenium's top wooden beam.

"I spoke of nothing," she said. "Nothing of importance."

He awkwardly shrugged on his outstretched side. "All right."

"I did have a question, though."

The smallest frown formed on his lips. "How about you help me first?" He wiggled the wreath. "Come hold this in place."

Mina's question died at his request. She rushed to the other side of the ladder, her emerald skirt swishing at her legs while she climbed.

"Stop being so heavy with your feet, or you'll knock us over," he said, chuckling lightly. It almost distracted her from the harshness in his tone.

Mina slowed. She placed herself one step lower than him, though he still could've moved up one. It would've made pinning the wreath easier and taken the sunlight out of his eyes.

"I have the perfect spot, but I didn't realize I put the nails in my pocket, and the hammer at my feet," he said. "Hold it while I sort myself out."

Mina reached through the wreath, brushing Davian's fingers. Clutching the ladder with her opposite hand, she held the wreath in place, pressing harder as his hold on it slithered away. Bright red dots from its twigs burned his skin. If they bit Mina as hard as they did him, she couldn't feel it. The sense of touch made no sense to her. She could smooth a blanket over her bed, never truly feeling its texture. She knew it was there, pressing against her skin, but a whirlpool of magic spun in her head, making her blank out on the blanket's true sensation. A flaw imparted to her by her nature. One flaw of many.

Davian shook out his marked-up hand. He grabbed the hammer and produced the nails from his pocket. Mina tracked him, loving how he made mundane movement extraordinary.

"Move your fingers to the left a little," he instructed, lifting a nail. "I don't want to hurt you."

Mina stared at him.

"I am joking, of course." He aligned the nail with the wreath. "You can't feel anything," he muttered, clearing his throat. "Still, your hand could get squashed. It's better not to test your limits."

"Even if I felt pain, you could never hurt me." She longed to smile for him. But her lips didn't even twitch.

His own stretched into a wan smile. "Just move your fingers."

Mina did.

He pulled back the hammer and slammed it against the nail. Cracks pierced the air. Broken twigs fell to the ground.

Mina stiffened. She wanted to blink and hide from the sound of the second and third hits. Her muscles were too weak to flinch. They only tensed, never letting her produce normal expressions.

Where she could clench her jaw and grind her teeth, she couldn't frown, blink, raise or furrow a brow. By all matters, speaking should've hurt her, but it didn't when her lips stayed in a neutral position. Her body had a set of rules on what she could and couldn't do, yet those rules blurred together in the middle, leaving her at a boiling point of frustration. Why should she be able to speak but never smile?

All she knew was tension. Tightness on her features and around her body that did not change the eternal statue she was on the outside. Every now and again she painfully twitched and painfully changed her voice with a hiccup. Those signs which showed a little bit of humanity should've been triumphs. All they did was build misery on frustration as they reminded her that she was only a body. A body floating from place to place, doing whatever was best for Davian.

Davian's visage blurred in the scope of Mina's unblinking eyes.

The hammer had stopped. The cracks persisted in her ears.

Crack. Crack. Crack.

"You can let go now."

Mina couldn't move.

Crack. Crack. Crack.

"Mina. Let go."

She removed her hand from the twigs. The blurriness slowly cleared. Vibrant red marks dotted her skin.

Taking a step down, the world swayed. Mina clung to the ladder. Her magic balled up in her head along with the echoing cracks.

"Scared? Don't be," Davian said. "It's not that far..." His forehead wrinkled and his hand snapped around her wrist. "What's this?"

The coldness in her chest spread. The loving care she knew it held for Davian vanished when she realized which hand he'd shackled to his.

He pressed his fingers into her flesh. She sensed them, desiring to know how soft and warm they were. They crawled to the wound she'd been certain wouldn't be a problem. He pried open her skin, letting airy blackness with violet streaks flow out of her.

"Mina." His brows settled low on his forehead. "Why are you cut?"

Throat closed off, she struggled for words. "I...got it from a card. A gift from a gift," she said, trying to punch some humor into her voice. Nothing broke her flat tone. "It was an accident. That's why I came over here, not to show you this, but to ask you how you'd like your cards organized."

"You need to be careful," he snapped. He lifted her hand, shaking it in her face. "Think of all the explaining I'd have to do if someone saw this magic. People get curious when someone uses their one grand wish."

"Wishes are marvelous," Mina told him.

He ignored her remark. "If someone besides me told Lumina, then"—his voice grew softer, dreamlike—"she'd call me a silly boy in a glorious way." He shook his head and swallowed. "She's the only one who can know what you are. If that time comes, of course. I just don't want anybody else prying into our affairs."

Sharpness sliced far beneath Mina's skin, from her heartless chest down into her empty abdomen. The magic in her head heated.

That name. Lumina. It created illness. Years of hearing it had done nothing to create immunity. At least the inability for expression saved Mina from many potential arguments about Lumina and never bringing her up again. About how it made her uncomfortable to hear the name of the woman she resembled, the woman who'd broken Davian's heart and drove him to wish for a replacement from the Wishmaker.

"You are being silly," Mina informed him. She wiggled her wounded finger. "Nobody will see it, and Lumina will never know." Davian flinched at the name. Struck as if he were a child caught lying. "Besides, the wreath *you* asked me to hold could've cut me deeper."

He pushed her hand away, drawing his lips together. His gaze stayed firmly away from her. Crossing his arms, he fell into a pit of silence.

Mina wished she could mock his childish pout in order to show him how ridiculous he looked.

"Just know I'm not trying to upset you," she said. He didn't move nor say anything. She sighed, reaching up to touch the side of his face. "I promise I'll be more careful for you."

Davian recoiled from her just as her fingers nearly grazed his cheek. His feet clanked heavily down the ladder, rocking Mina at the top while her palm caressed the air he once occupied.

"There's someone here," he mumbled, almost sounding relieved.

Cluttered footsteps grew louder and closer to them. A melody of erratic panting filled the air. The disappointment that filled Mina at the interruption was replaced by excitement when she saw the black tail swinging behind their first guest. The surprise invite. *Irvin.* His appearance would cheer Davian up and maybe he'd finally show some appreciation for her thoughtfulness.

"How late am I?" Irvin asked, setting a hand on his chest. He kept his other behind his back, clearly holding something.

"You're early," Davian said. "Early enough to help us with the finishing touches."

Mina lowered her arm. Although he smiled, the elation she'd hoped for wasn't on Davian's face or in his voice. If she were Irvin, she would've marched back down the hill from the unwelcomeness.

Irvin straightened his tie and slicked back the turbulent fur on his head as best he could. The ends of his whiskers curled down and tapped his chin, all tangled and crooked.

"Wait, Davian, what happened to your birthday being a surprise?" As he spoke, his sharp teeth glinted from within his mouth, whiter than a sheet of untouched snow.

Mina carefully made her way down the ladder and arrived at Davian's side. He kept his focus on Irvin, leaning away from her.

"How can I be surprised about my own birthday?" Davian asked Irvin. "It's been the same day my whole life."

Irvin narrowed his eyes. "That's not what I meant, and you know it."

Hearty laughter spilled out of Davian. Mina scanned him, stunned. Had he just become sick? She never heard him laugh so fully before. Not even when they first met and he'd been at his happiest with her. Perhaps Irvin's arrival *had* touched him deeply.

Davian jerked his head at Mina.

Irvin's gaze landed on her. He flinched.

"She's hopeless," Davian said. "When it comes to keeping secrets, of course. She chose the largest spot in Virvin for a surprise. It was only a matter of time before I found out." He tapped his temple and lowered his voice, pretending she couldn't hear him. "Sometimes I wonder if she has a brain or..." He glanced at her.

"Or what?" Mina asked. Her magic thickened into a flow of lava.

His face dulled, upper lip furling. "Maybe there's nothing but magic stuffed in there."

Irvin laughed, clapping his hands. "Great joke. Imagine it, a terrible way to live. Magic without a brain."

"Yes, I know it is," Davian whispered. He cleared his throat, lighting up as he turned to his friend. "Anyway, I'm glad I knew about the party. I don't like surprises."

Mina stilled. From what she knew, Davian expressed the opposite view about surprises. That was why she planned the party as one in the first place, and had done so last year, and the year before, and the year before that, and the many, many before that. He should've told her they weren't up to his fancy and saved her the trouble.

Irvin scratched the back of his head. "You know, I rushed here not wanting to be late for the surprise, and even if it existed, I'd still be guest number one. Who would've thought my unintended punctuality was the real surprise? As I always say, in dire times, you have to keep trying. That's what made me the first guest, I guess."

Mina eyed him for a moment.

He cleared his throat. "Well, anyway, if I'm going to help you, where should I put this?"

He shifted his hand out from behind his back and held up a poorly wrapped gift.

"You didn't need to bring that." Davian clapped a hand on Irvin's back. "Seeing you is enough."

"Ah, but I did need to. Those who save brothers together must bring gifts for each other."

Davian smirked. "Is this a hint that I must get you a gift for your birthday?"

Blush lit up Irvin's cheeks. He wiggled his cat ears atop his head. "What would make you say that?"

"Nothing, nothing," Davian said. "Your gift is more than appreciated."

"Yes," Mina chimed in, startling Irvin. "It's a kind gesture."

He handed her the gift, avoiding her fingers. "Yes, I guess it is."

Holding it, Mina knew that *poorly wrapped* improperly described the gift. It was a disaster. Irvin had wrapped the simple, small box in too many layers of paper on one side, making it bulge, and not enough on the other, exposing an entire corner. If he and Davian weren't so near, she would've torn it open and fixed the atrociousness.

"Come over and have a drink with me," Davian said to Irvin.

They strolled into the courtyard, bursting into an upbeat conversation that said they wouldn't remember to get around to the finishing touches. At least there weren't many, though a few more streamers would've been nice. Mina guessed she'd have to quickly hang them on her own if she had time.

On her way back into the courtyard, she glanced at the wreath, noting its off-center placement. Any eye, up close and faraway, would've caught the mistake. She tried to reason that mistakes weren't always bad, and the wreath's placement could've worked. *But it's badly off-center,* she thought.

She made her way to the card table, and cleared a small portion of them aside, setting the gift in the space. Now she'd have to organize the cards around the gift.

Davian and Irvin stood with drinks, the streamers hanging around them. The space between them brightened as they spoke in a natural flow. They'd been friends for a long time, having once set out to save a young boy together, Lumina's brother.

Lumina.

The third member of their little group, all having known each other since childhood. Davian said she was the responsible one and the bravest of the bunch. From what Mina gathered, she wouldn't have struggled to organize a pile of cards.

Digging her nails into her palm, Mina refrained from smacking the cards off the table and trampling on them until they blended in with the grass.

"I can't do *anything*," she said.

"Mina," Davian called out. "I hear more guests coming. Go greet them."

"You should do it," she muttered as she hurried to the entrance. "This is your party."

The ladder remained where Davian left it, right in the way. She cursed inwardly, dragging it to the side and kicking away as many fallen twigs as she could. Her energy depleted, and she hardly caught her breath as she began cordially greeting the guests.

Unfortunately, everyone in Virvin came all at once, walking into the courtyard in small batches that kept Mina constantly speaking and trying hard to be upbeat.

Regular humans, like Davian, strode in confidence. Butterflies swept by her, shouting, "Hello!" A bush of roses, the Ovy family, trudged over the ground, leaving a long crater behind—one of many the Ovy family left in Virvin. They always got in trouble for it by the mayor, Mister Rains, a man always in a neat, green suit and had a watering can for a head. He swept past Mina without greeting her back, his eyes set on Davian.

Out of every person here, only she and Davian knew she was the most magical one. Every living being had magic in them, but Mina was made of it, though she couldn't grip its power and harness it for anything. Its only ability was to keep her alive as Davian's wish for someone like Lumina to love him fully.

She tried to smile with each greeting, her nature holding her back. Her lips didn't want to do more than speak disinterested-sounding words. She kept her left fist tight, hiding her cut and chiding her unfixable lack of enthusiasm.

"Where do you think we put gifts?" an older woman asked the friend she towered over as they sauntered onto the grass. Her body was made of bark and branches full of green leaves matching the stark eyes sticking out of her head.

Mina flexed all over. *Gifts.* She hadn't made space for gifts, and she didn't get Davian a gift from herself. Of all the simple things she had to do, she'd forgotten the most obvious, important one.

"I'm unsure," the woman's friend responded, placing a finger on her chin. She was an older human woman. White hair puffed on her shoulders, matching the clouds. She contrasted her friend with soft features and a delicate voice. "Perhaps we should ask Davian."

"Gifts," Mina blurted, whipping and barreling towards the women. "Space. I hadn't—"

The two women huddled close together, eyes wide, each clutching the gifts they held.

Mina pointed. "Table. Put them around the card table, and don't go near it after that. Ever."

The women whispered to one another. They weren't the only ones wrinkling their foreheads, scoffing, and cupping their hands over their mouths to weakly hide their snide remarks. Others around them paused, arching their brows. A few people questioned Mina and who she thought she was, speaking as if she hadn't lived with Davian in the same village as them for the past two decades.

Mina remained by the entrance, looking between the next bundle of guests and the ones making themselves comfortable at the tables, popping open the dishes of food. She managed to stay steady in her final greetings, her voice lowering until it turned into a whisper. Once the last guest passed through, her voice dissipated, and so did her presence. No one spared a glance her way. The only reminder of her existence were the comments about the lack of a surprise party. Each time someone approached Davian, Mina swallowed regret. She should've sent addendum invitations to save him from being bombarded.

Voices circled the air. Mina pulled her white shawl close around herself, listening. Two familiar ones stood above the rest—the pair who had questioned where the gifts went.

"I wonder if Lumina will come?" the tree woman asked.

Mina gripped her shawl tighter, nearly ripping it in half.

"I don't know," the other woman replied. "She is Davian's oldest friend; it would only make sense for her to be here."

The other woman nodded. "Seeing her after so long would be nice."

Mina couldn't move. Not when she knew neither woman, nor anyone at all, would see Lumina tonight.

With the chatter, bustle, and dance, she hoped nobody would notice. If someone did, she'd lie and say Lumina didn't accept her invitation. There would be no further questions, and Mina would never have to admit she didn't send an invitation. That she didn't make one at all.

"Davian doesn't need her anyway," Mina said. "He has me."

His wish from the Wishmaker. A copy of Lumina, the human woman who had rejected his love long ago. Mina held a striking enough resemblance to her from what she saw in an old painting, only differing by the yellow tint of her fair complexion, the gray ends on her curly, straw-like hair, and the rippling black scars around her right eye. She might've been broken as Lumina's living reflection, but she loved Davian more than anything. More than Lumina ever could.

"Excuse me," a woman said from behind.

Mina turned to greet her, only for her words to die as she took in a familiar face. The smooth face of a woman gracefully entering her middle-aged years.

I'm seeing things, was Mina's first thought. *I thought about her too much. Now my mind is playing a trick on me.*

Mina turned away for a few seconds. When she turned back, the woman was still there, the corners of her lips lifting in amusement.

"Could you tell me where Davian is?" the woman asked. She held a delicately wrapped gift with a card tied to the top. Mina didn't need to read the name inside to know who stood before her, not an apparition, not a ghost, but a guest. The only uninvited guest. What was supposed to have been a perfect celebration exploded into flames all because of one thing: Lumina was here.

REFLECTION IN FLESH

*M*ina always avoided mirrors. The less she saw of her dead face, the better. But every now and again she'd give into the pull of the glass, peering into her own reflection and attempting expressions. A smile stretched the corners of her lips uncomfortably, a stabbing sensation lancing her cheeks. Burning pressure exerted into her sinuses when she scrunched her nose.

Failed expressions haunted her. Pain arrived when she tried being human for a moment, yet if someone took a knife to her arm, she wouldn't feel it—a horrible trade.

Lumina smiled easily, giving Mina the first glimpse as to how a proper one looked on her face. She ground her teeth at the delightful waves radiating off Lumina's lips, the corners stretching high and bright. That smile could banish darkness. It could uplift life everywhere it went and remind people things weren't always so bad.

Blocks of tension piled inside Mina. Piled because of the smile, something she should've been able to also do. Smiling was a movement of muscles, similar to how the jaw clenched. Her body should've either been able to emote *everything*, or nothing at all, freeing her from a fractured life of confusion and desperation.

Lumina's brows rose. The painting Davian had of her hadn't captured her illustrious and grand, statuesque nature.

"Are you well?" she asked.

Mina's neck stiffened. She tried prying it loose and separating her teeth, but her muscles ground deeper. Straining. Tightening.

"May I see Davian?"

Magic sizzled inside Mina. It penetrated deep into her head, swallowing her rationality. She seized Lumina's wrist and tugged on her arm. Hard. She pulled her out of the courtyard, away from the crowd, the pair of women, and, most importantly, Davian.

Lumina twisted and stumbled along, cheeks turning red. "Stop touching me," she hissed.

Letting go, Mina took a step back from Lumina. They stood eye to eye, chests heaving. The noise of the party hadn't exactly faded but it sat far enough behind for Mina to think clearly.

"You're strange." Lumina straightened. "I mean that as a high compliment, of course. There's something familiar about you. Who are your parents?"

"I don't have any," Mina said quietly.

"Any at all?" Lumina asked, incredulous. She parted her lips and put her fingers by her mouth, as if mocking her shock.

"Any anymore," Mina rectified, trying to place a smile on her lips. One exactly like Lumina's. Her muscles screamed at the motion, a high-pitched tone ringing in her head, similar to an overheated teapot. She couldn't move them any further.

Mina stared deeply into Lumina's vibrant, violet eyes. An untouchable soul lived within her body. A free woman, aged and divine. In her chest lay a heart, pumping blood all throughout her serene body. If she stated she'd been born in the clouds, none would question it as a lie.

Lumina's regal quality made Mina squirm. She became aware of her awkward hanging arms, the bend in her knees, the hunch of her shoulders, the cut on her finger, and the black cracks around her right eye. For someone who was supposed to look like Lumina, Mina failed at truly capturing the grandeur of the real woman at every aspect.

"You appear," Lumina started and paused. She hummed. "Blank. Are you feeling fine?"

"Being human must be grand," Mina said. "Perfect."

Lumina blinked. "What is that you're saying?"

Mina shook her head. "I don't know. Nothing."

A tiny smirk formed on Lumina's lips. "I'm sure if you can't make sense of it, then it can't be important." The gift in her hands rustled. Her left index finger tapped the side of the tiny box. "Though I thought I heard the word perfect. What an astounding concept, is it not?"

"You're perfect."

"Me? Perfect? You don't know me."

"I do."

"Through Davian's words you do."

Mina opened her mouth. Then she closed it. She wanted to know exactly what Lumina knew about her and Davian. At the same time, though, she didn't.

"I don't think I'm perfect," Lumina said. "I'm far from it. In the past, I've hurt Davian and Irvin."

"But Davian says you're perfect, and he's never wrong."

"He can be, especially in the case of perfection. What does it matter anyway? Everything about life is pointless in the end. It's best to be happy with what imperfect remains you have." Her gaze swept over Mina. "Even if what remains *is* quite inferior."

Mina's fingers curled. "You need to go."

"I offended you." Lumina lifted her chin. "But I think you're the one who needs to leave. Poor thing, you should find something that makes you happy."

"I am happy."

"You don't feel like it."

"Look," Mina corrected. "I don't look it. That's because you're making me upset."

Lumina smirked. "I'm only saying what is true."

Mina turned, seeking out Davian from inside the courtyard, desperate for a glimpse of him to comfort her.

When she found him in the crowd, his back to her, warmth cradled her insides, and the frozen ball entered her chest. She'd experienced this combination late at night when she lay beside him in bed, putting her hand on his chest, knowing a heart beat underneath it. Occasionally she felt the organ push against her. In those moments, she sat content. Alone. Happy. Feeling the real heart of a real human, a twinge of sorrow striking her as she wondered who she'd be with a heart.

"Hello?"

Lumina's voice stroked the edge of a breeze.

"Poor thing, are you here with me?"

When Mina returned from the depths of her thoughts, she found Lumina somehow looking down at her.

Magic trembled within Mina. "You're leaving now, correct?"

"You want me gone?"

"You weren't invited. I don't know how you're here."

"I was invited in a way," Lumina said. "Someone from the village, I won't say who, may have written a note to me expressing excitement about seeing me here. Davian and I have been friends since childhood. It's natural to think I should be here."

"You left him," Mina stated.

Lumina's voice thickened. "I know. I didn't want to break his heart, but I had obligations. My brother, young and silly"—Davian was right, she did have a glorious way of calling people silly—"made a deal with a nasty spirit to become stronger, but the spirit tricked him. He managed to escape, saying he thought of us to pull him through. We found him alone in the woods, next to death. He said a young boy drained him of blood. Such a failure changed him, he hardly spoke or ate. Who he was had almost vanished. I worried if he wasn't looked after, he'd take a turn for the worse and never recover. At the same time, Davian offered for us to stay with him. I knew what he wanted but I wasn't ready. My brother needed me fully."

"Why didn't you use your one grand wish to have it all?" Mina asked.

Lumina hugged her gift to her torso. She studied Mina, something draining her face of any humor or kindness.

Within the courtyard, a separate world existed. The guests prattled on in their own bubbles, bursting out their funniest jokes about life itself and their weakest lies glorifying their accomplishments. Everyone shouted over everyone else, trying to be the loudest on the grass. The shiniest person there.

Swallowing, Lumina arched her brow, growing stern and taller than ever. "That's an odd thing to say."

Mina wanted to go to Davian and forget all about Lumina and the cruel, curious way she looked down at her copy.

"I'd rather live with truths than lies," Lumina said. "There was no room in my heart for Davian's love at the time. It wouldn't have been fair to him. My brother is grown and healthy now. He and I were able to mend our own relationship. We can part ways knowing our love is still there. He even encouraged me to come here when I got the invitation. He said I should do what I want of my own volition. It would fulfill me."

Each word pricked Mina's ears. She allowed them entrance, yet she struggled to process their meaning. Wishes helped people find happiness. The Wishmaker made it happen in a flash. Lumina was being silly. Why wouldn't she wish to have everything in one moment? Davian had done it. Mina had replaced a hole in his heart and did everything in her power to never let it form again.

"Rebuilding our pieces by ourselves is quite the challenge." Lumina cleared her throat. "Being here scares me. I don't know what they'll think of me. I want the best for everyone, so if you say I should turn around and go home, I will."

Mina gestured to the horizon beyond Virvin. "You have family out there?"

"I do."

"And you'd establish a new life if you can't stay here?"

Lumina nodded. "That's what people do."

Doing her best to give Lumina a hard stare, Mina took in a deep breath. She pulled back her shoulders, finally rising to the height of the real woman. Muscle spasms struck around her eyes, nearly toppling her over completely.

"Your journey doesn't extend here," Mina told her. "Davian won't like seeing you. He's moved on."

"But what if I told you something?"

"You're not going to," Mina said, "because I don't want to hear it."

"So quick to dismiss." Lumina lifted the gift. "Fine. Can I request you give this to Davian straight away? You can say a messenger brought it. That I wasn't here at all."

Mina took the gift, keeping her face and body firm for as long as possible.

Lumina clasped her hands together. "I wish we could have met in a better way." She smiled. "But who knows? There may still be a chance for us to speak again. That chance might be closer than we think."

Lumina turned, never looking back as she walked down the hill to Virvin. Smugness circled in her air. She acted like she'd won a prize. It didn't matter, though. She didn't and she was leaving. Wherever she planned to go, Mina did not know, nor care, so long as she did not go to Davian.

Pivoting, Mina went back into the courtyard, scanning faces and wondering who invited Lumina. She searched for the two gossiping women in particular, suspecting one of them, but they weren't nearby anymore.

The gift weighed heavily in Mina's hands. Her fingers flexed around the tiny box wrapped in plain red paper, neater than Irvin's. The box sat comfortably in one palm, though Lumina had cradled it in both hands, acting as if it were delicate. In Mina's grasp, her every impulse wanted to throw it into a pit of fire and bury the ashes in a deep, deep grave where they'd never be dug up again. The urge worsened when her thumb brushed the card on top, knowing what name was written on the inside.

Pushing through the guests, Mina held the gift at her hip, racing toward the card table. She could set it there and do as Lumina said by claiming it came from a messenger—

She staggered to a stop at the halfway point. What was she thinking? Davian could never know that Lumina was aware of the party. It was too big a risk at revealing Mina didn't invite her. Besides, the gift showed generosity. It showed that Lumina remembered to get one, while Mina hadn't. She could tear off the card and pretend it came from her, but that kind of lie made her sick. She wanted to bring Davian a gift conjured up from her own kindness, not Lumina's.

Right now, the main task was to wash away all traces of Lumina.

Wash away. Mina brightened inside.

A river flowed not far from Virvin. She'd heard enough about it to know where it approximately was. How could she bypass a river, anyway? She could go bury the gift with the rocks on the bottom. It'd take her no time at all. Nobody would notice her absence. They hadn't even noticed her presence.

Her feet carried her through the courtyard, desperate. She raced, knocking into people. Venomous, angry shouts chased her.

"Watch your elbow!"

"Hey, you could've spilled my drink on me!"

"Push me out of the way, why not?"

Nothing anyone said could've stopped Mina. Her mind stayed on one track, her body carrying her through on one task.

Except that wasn't true. There was one person who could stop her, and he made himself known as she took a few steps out of the courtyard.

"Mina, stop!" he barked.

She halted and spun toward Davian, stuffing the gift behind her back. The card on top rested against her wounded finger.

MISSING LIES

"*W*hat are you doing?" Davian asked, brows lowered. He crossed his arms.

Mina shifted. "I'm not doing much."

"You're causing mayhem," he told her.

"Am I?"

"Rushing through everyone?" he prompted. "It isn't polite. People want to relax, not get shoved to the side."

She glanced at everyone. Lots of the people she'd disrupted had already let go of their resentment. They were here for a party after all, anger had no place here.

"They'll forget it."

Davian waved a hand. "Fine. It's not important. What I'd like to know more is: what are you hiding behind your back?"

"I don't have anything I'm hiding," she said in staccato.

"Don't lie. I saw red before you turned around."

"I'm not lying. To the people behind me, the gift is clear as day."

His eyebrows flew up. "Gift?"

Oh, there, she'd done it. She gave away the truth.

Her shoulders fell forward. "It isn't important."

"Who is it from?" he asked, taking a step toward her.

She chewed on her bottom lip, glued in place. She didn't want a sudden move to draw more suspicion. "Nobody important."

He inched closer. "I don't believe that."

"Then it's from me. It's a gift from me, and I'm embarrassed by it, so I want to toss it away. I could give you a better gift later."

"I'm sure a gift from you isn't bad," he said. "If it truly is embarrassing, I'll toss it and forget it."

Mina leaned away as he lifted his palm to the sky, perfect to set the gift on.

"I don't like that idea," she told him. "It's too embarrassing to see."

"It's a good idea, though, you'll admit," he said.

"Yes, but I can't do that."

His face fell. "Mina, give me the gift."

She shook her head.

"You won't feel embarrassed. You don't feel anything."

"Please," she whispered. "Don't."

He lowered his hand and smiled at her, shrugging. "All right, if you're so worried, I'll leave it be. I don't want you to be upset."

Mina released all her tension. The perfection of Davian's face wrapped her in a trance. She stared at him, filled with love. She knew he understood her and the blemished feelings she had. He loved her back for what she was, his wish.

"Thank you," she whispered.

Davian nodded and then lunged at her.

She gasped as he grabbed her arm, tightening and struggling against him. He pulled her arm from behind her back, twisting it too far outward. He pulled her fingers one by one, prying the gift from her hand. His strength eclipsed hers and he got the gift free. It bounced onto the ground. As he picked it up, Mina stood, dumbfounded. She pushed up her blouse's sleeve. Bright red marks flared across her skin from where he had grasped her.

He gently took the card off the box and flipped it open. Tears brimmed in his eyes as he read the words. One pull of the string undid the wrapping, revealing a small chest underneath. He opened the top, his mouth falling open.

"What is it?" Mina pushed down her sleeve.

Davian ignored her. He plucked out a brooch of forget-me-not flowers. Each light blue petal resembled stained glass, attached to shiny gold circles on the inner parts. Five separate flowers glistened, intertwining into each other, sparks of silver and white twinkling at different spots, shifting where the light hit it.

Twisting the brooch, Davian admired every inch. Powerful love seeped out of him, layering dreamy distance upon him, a look that wore him whenever he spoke about Lumina.

Something stirred inside Mina, magic building up pressure, and making her skin feel too tight to wear. She pressed a hand into her stomach. Fire shot up into her throat. Vomit threatened to spill out of her for the first time in her existence.

"This didn't come from you," he said, still marveling at the brooch. "Who brought it?"

Speaking above the crowd became impossible. Every voice amplified into thunderous booms. Mina wanted to whirl and cry out for everyone to be quiet for a minute. She wanted to be sick in peace.

"Mina," Davian said. He lowered the brooch back into the chest and closed it. The snap of the lid struck harder than the hammer on the wreath. "Who brought this?"

Her posture shriveled under his scrutiny.

"Who brought the gift?"

Mina hated the faded love on his face, the impatience laced in his voice. She trailed her eyes down, landing on the card he held between the box and his palm. A heavy breath dove deep inside of her. She gave up trying to lie. The truth sat in his hand anyway.

"You already know who brought it."

"So, she *is* here," he said, breathless.

The terrible feeling in Mina's stomach rolled again, expanding outward.

"*Was* here." She glanced at Virvin and bit her tongue. "Well, actually," she started, backtracking to a lie, but it was far too late. Davian already hurried for the village.

CARRY THE PAST AWAY

*V*iolent breath rushed out of Mina as she hurried after Davian. He ran too fast while her gait slowed, drawing a larger distance between them. She choked out his name, her head swirling, hand clinging to her empty yet burning chest. It was hard to tell if he heard her or looked back at all with him gone from view. She had a feeling he didn't feel the need.

No, he simply can't hear me, she convinced herself.

Sharpness stretched diagonally through her, starting in the midst of her throat, wrapping around the length of her body, and jabbing into her hip. Another step shot sparks up her leg, electrifying the pain. She hated herself. Hated the magic twisting inside her. It knocked her down and kept her too far from Davian.

"Davian," she managed, weakly.

Virvin's wooden buildings turned into blobs of tall, dark goo clumped up in her peripheral vision. Her feet barely carried her, often sticking to the ground. Dizziness lashed her head, trying to knock her over. On one step, the toe of her boot dug into the dirt, kicking up a mound as she stumbled forward, fighting for balance. Part of her wished she'd fallen, just for some rest. However, she knew if she collapsed, she wouldn't get back up.

The clouds moved with her to the edge of the village, creeping over the faded blue sky, entangling in the rising night. Pinkish gold highlights of leftover sun rounded into the crevices of their fluffy white folds. The very ends, the wisps near the tops where the sun couldn't hit, grayed. Mina wondered if the clouds hated nighttime like a lot of humans did. She wondered if they ever wished to descend and wear flesh for a day.

At Virvin's edge, the road expanded far beyond the quiet village, going to places Mina would never discover. Places the clouds were allowed to go. They passed her by, laughing, able to go as far as they wanted, in whatever direction they chose. Even when they rained back into lakes and rivers, they'd still see more of the world than her. They didn't have someone holding them on a leash, keeping them confined in place.

The evening light sank lower at Mina's back. The remaining sunlight illuminated Davian against the dark horizon as he stood on the village's outskirts. His side faced Mina. The susurration of his voice drifted on a tiny breeze taking shape.

She wanted to linger on him but couldn't pretend he wasn't alone.

Lumina tipped her head toward Davian. Her eyes roamed his face, her lips slightly parted. She sparkled in the diminishing sunlight. Darkness couldn't take away an ounce of her beauty. Next to Davian, she fit well, the flame to his wax. Together they created the romance Mina imagined she'd been a part of with him.

The sharpness in Mina enhanced its cruel strength, squeezing the air out of her until the world muddled. Time became nothing of note, and space ceased to exist. She didn't know how long she stood and watched them for. It wasn't until footfalls neared her that she broke out of her haze.

"Mina," Lumina said, smirking. "See? We met again sooner than we thought."

Mouth closed, Mina brought herself into reality. She allowed the two faces before her to come into complete clarity.

"Mina?" Lumina asked.

Mind whistling, Mina needed three seconds to make sure she still existed.

Lumina lifted her chin. "Mina?"

One... Two... Three...

"Davian," Mina said, ignoring Lumina. "Davian?"

He avoided eye contact, keeping his face pointed at Lumina. He leaned in close to her ear. "Go ahead to the party. I'll meet you there shortly."

Nodding, Lumina gave Davian a kiss on the cheek. Red ignited his face. When she pulled away, he followed her a step, clearly wanting to pull her back into him. He refrained from doing so.

Lumina strolled in silence, passing by Mina, sparing her a glance. A glance that spoke of victory, a declaration that showed Mina who deserved happiness. She seemed even taller than before. She was a woman made to be seen. Unlike Mina, who was a shriveled, unwanted rodent.

Mina kept her fists in the folds of her skirt, glad to see Lumina go, glad the taps of her steps got farther away. Certain she and Davian were alone, Mina's fists loosened.

Tears lingered on Davian's cheeks. The dying light ignited them into little diamonds settled on the dark shadows puddled underneath his eyes. He finally lifted his gaze to her. Though she wished he hadn't. How he looked at her wasn't the way someone looked at the person they claimed they loved. His grim expression better suited a funeral.

The flesh on Mina's legs thinned out, taking away her strength and leaving her to wobble. The skin on her face grew heavy with lumpy magic. She imagined the scars around her eye extending, slicing over her entire face, digging deep beneath her and expanding in width to expose the dark violet light inside of her, showing the world her bloodless, imperfect nature.

"You were trying to hide Lumina from me?" Davian questioned, impatiently. He snapped his fingers in her face. "Mina. Stop ignoring me."

Lies tried to come to life. Excuses tried existing. No spark helped them take flight.

"I was," she admitted, her pathetic senses coming back to normal.

Davian's brows lowered. At his sides, his hands balled into fists. Ones much stronger than what she could make. She watched them, wondering if they'd find their way above the waist.

"How could you?" he asked, kindled with vexation.

Mina spoke a hint above a whisper, tone still flat, unfeeling. "Why are you asking me that?"

"Because I want to hear what's going on in your head," he told her. "What's your excuse for trying to send Lumina away? I thought you wanted to make my day special. Without her, that wouldn't be possible."

The lick of a distant flinch tried to reach Mina. Inwardly, her magic rocked against her flesh, wanting to escape with her concealed emotions, but outwardly she remained as still as a glassy pond.

Davian's gaze bore holes into her head, waiting for her answer.

"I wanted her gone," she finally said.

"Why?"

Running her tongue along her bottom teeth, Mina inhaled. "She wasn't invited."

"That's not the only reason," he said.

"What is another reason?"

"You're jealous."

She tensed. "I'm a vision crafted for the love you lost with her. You wanted me to love you. I do. I want you to love me, not run to her. Of course I feel jealous."

"You shouldn't have sent her away."

"She wasn't invited."

"She was." A glob of spit flew out of his mouth. It almost struck her. Had he been an inch or two closer, it would've.

Mina fidgeted with her muscles, trying to work out an expression. Confusion lay on her mind. Her bottom eyelids twitched, and her ears wiggled a little, producing a sharp ping in them. She couldn't find it in her to move them more, much less speak.

"I invited Lumina," he said, clasping his hands in front of him. The tightness of his muscles uncoiled, sliding his shoulders down and releasing the wild sheen in his eyes, matching the fluid way the golden sun sank. Where night grew larger and colder, Davian grew calmer and warmer at his confession. "I went through the invitations myself. I wanted to see if you loved me enough to include her. When I didn't find her card, I took it upon myself to write to her. I thought you may have been wise enough to catch on already."

Mina stepped away from him, studying the man she loved from head to toe. It wasn't often he provoked an emotion other than love out of her—or so one she chose to notice. That explanation coming from his mouth, however, washed away his glamour and the love she devoted her life to. Right now, betrayal slithered in her. She knew she had to get rid of it and break down the wall erecting between them. She had no clue how to do so but she urged herself to try something. To try anything.

Anything was better than giving up.

"You have me," she said. "What do you need her for?"

"Mina." He grabbed her shoulders and leaned in close, his face turning serious. More serious than he'd ever been. Dark clouds washed through his green irises. "You're not real."

She searched his face for the glimmer of a lie. That he didn't believe in what he said. That he loved her. That he was loyal to her. What she longed for didn't exist. He was right, she wasn't real.

"The mind I fell in love with all those years ago isn't in you," he said. "She and I share memories you don't have. I love her for things you can never be."

"I *am* her," Mina argued. "I am enough of her."

"You're a wish. Nothing more." His grip loosened from her shoulders. She already missed his full touch. "You're a piece of her from a time gone by, a frozen image of the past, and I'm getting older. I can't keep living this way. Looking at you still being twenty. *Her* twenty."

"But I need you." She paused. A crack rang out inside her. "So I can live."

He hung his head. "I'm sorry."

She searched him with more ferocity, digging for any hesitance. Any disbelief. To find a way to bring him back to her. It didn't help that he wouldn't bring his face to meet with hers.

"You swore to always love me," she reminded him. "All I can ever do is love you."

"A wish as beautiful as you deserves to rest now." He gave her a weak smile as his fingers slipped off of her completely. "I give you up. But I'll forever cherish the lesson you taught me."

Blurry. The world turned blurry. Blurry, blurry, blurry.

"What lesson?" she asked, her clogged ears hardly able to pick up her own pathetic sound.

He stepped past her, lifting his chin. The golden remains of the sunset soaked him in serenity.

"Letting go of a lie," he answered, his voice a soft kiss on the wind.

Sharpness twisted through Mina, constricting her in place. She peered at Davian. He hadn't left her yet, but his distant eyes told her he was already gone.

FIRST OF A MILLION STEPS

"It's a test," Mina told herself.

She stayed put at the edge of Virvin. Alone. Davian's distancing footsteps continued to trample in her mind even though he was now long gone.

Night blossomed. Mina's limbs hollowed out. Her arms dangling at her sides. Her legs somehow held her up. Ropes of dread curdled in her stomach. At first, she ignored them, but the more she replayed her conversation with Davian, the thicker they became, impossible to ignore.

You're not real.

Silence stood with her as she awaited the end of the world. When it didn't come, slivers of hope swirled into the dread. A wish given up meant it would go away forever. But Mina was still alive.

You're a wish. Nothing more.

Flickering images of Davian walking away chopped up her hope. Despair laughed its way into her inhalations. She was wrong to hope. He'd left her. Soon, she would be gone. Forever.

A wish as beautiful as you deserves to rest now.

She'd thought about spending her remaining time back in her bed at home. The scent of Davian lingering on his side, on the pillows, stopped her. She couldn't fade while smelling him. Thinking of him. Knowing Lumina would soon lay on the same spot she was.

Peace was her desired friend for her final moments. A quiet mind, a body free of tension, the shadows gently pulling over her vision. That was what she wanted. Replaying the conversation, being home with reminders of Davian, would only spin her into a whirlwind of chaos. She'd never be able to soothingly fall backwards into the clouds, mind shutting down forever.

But even if she avoided all which anguished her, the chaos would live. The simple fact that she wasn't ready to depart from the world was enough to stoke it wherever she stood.

That, and her mind crying out that—

"It's a test," she repeated, trying to believe herself. "Davian is testing you. A wish given up is a wish gone away."

Willpower wasn't enough to sustain her life. Only Davian had the power to decide what happened to her.

"It's a test." She clenched a fist. "When you see him again, he'll reveal he doesn't love Lumina. That he's testing your loyalty."

Her tongue stiffened as she spoke, and the ropes of dread in her guts didn't go away. She pushed those sensations aside. She had to prove herself correct. She had to go to Davian. With him, darkness would be no more. Life would be as bright as it was the night she came into existence. The night she'd awoken in the clouds, falling. She recalled most of it easily.

As she had tumbled through the air, a man, the Wishmaker, whispered to her, informing her of her nature and her purpose. While she remembered his voice, visualizing her descent to the forest floor evaded her. All she conjured up was a blurriness she couldn't fill in. One second, she'd been falling, listening to the Wishmaker, and in the next, she sat on lavish grass, watching Davian approach her through the trees to take her home.

In the depths of that night, fog laid heavy on the roads but it didn't block out Virvin, the village of log cabins that amazed her. The idea that people could lead such different lives in such similar looking homes continued to thrill her to this day. She'd always wanted to visit each family living here. To sit and see how they prepared, ate, and cleaned after their meals. To see what they did for fun, how they spoke to each other. She wanted to know who lived similarly to her and Davian, quiet and simple.

The dream of making friends in Virvin died long ago. She mostly stuck to the shadows, her head down. Davian hovered close by wherever she went. He made sure she never stayed with others in one place for too long for her existence made people scratch their heads. When they were preoccupied, like at the party, they didn't notice her. But upon closer study, Mina saw the wheels turn behind their heads. The inner workings of their own magic trying to figure her out—some even trying to understand why they recognized her face. Davian always whisked her away before anyone could work through their confusion. A confusion which the Wishmaker warned Mina of before she came to the living world. She used to think it wouldn't be a problem. That she didn't want anyone besides Davian.

And that was still true.

Being a constant stranger to her neighbors got easier over time. At first, Mina held her tongue in bitter resentment. Now she happily kept to herself. If there was one thing more important than her making friends, it was Davian's happiness, and his happiness meant doing all that he ordered.

Still, every now and again, Mina wondered if she would even be able to make a friend if given the chance. Perhaps her nature didn't allow her the ability.

As Mina made her way through Virvin, emptiness plagued its streets. She was only accompanied by lonely fog. Bellows of laughter boomed all the way across the village, coming from up the hill, at the courtyard. Following them were strums of instruments, placing a delightful melody into the air.

Mina nearly dropped to the ground. She hadn't arranged for music. Hearing it struck her with blatant obviousness as she went to the noises. Obviously, she should've arranged for music. People loved it. Davian must've gone behind her back to smooth over another one of her mistakes. He likely knew she hadn't gotten him a gift. Maybe that was why he disposed of her—no, he was only *testing* her.

Arriving at the courtyard, the brightness stung Mina's eyes. The warm, yellow glow of the lanterns ignited the streamers, showing off the dancing silver curling through the blue, yellow, pink, and particularly pretty red colors. When they moved, and the light hit them in the right way, the thin lines of silver lit up and rippled.

Standing in the middle of the courtyard entrance, Mina scanned the crowd for Davian. The constant movement of the guests made it difficult to find him. She couldn't decide what was brighter, the lanterns or the natural joy of the guests. Everybody danced, spinning into each other's places, linking hands together, and jumping to the upbeat melody from the guitar players all the way on the other side of the square space. They played near the card table, which still wasn't properly organized. Gifts were placed on top of the cards anyway.

Mina pushed up onto her toes, straining as she searched every face. She didn't think Davian would stay near the music. He hated loud noise. She didn't think he would be in the middle of the crowd, either.

Her eyes raked over the area, getting farther from the music, sifting through the many people. She made her way to a corner of the party with fewer bodies. A place easier to sort out.

She lowered onto her heels. There he was. But he wasn't alone. Of course.

Davian's gentle gaze pointed down at Lumina, whom he danced with. Peace encapsulated him. He held her around the waist with one arm and kept one of her hands firmly in his other. They swayed to a song different to the one being played. A song shared between their minds.

Mina waited for him to spot her, leave Lumina, come to her, and tell her of the test she desperately wanted to be true.

But he stayed with Lumina. He stayed. *Letting go of a lie.*

A breeze stirred. It knocked Mina's hair and skirt to the side, pushing her with unexpected, hefty strength. She pictured coldness sprouting on every inch of her. She lifted her left hand to embrace the air and see if she'd break out into a chill.

Nothing happened. Just as she'd thought.

When she went to lower her hand, however, the cut on her finger shifted. The flaps of skin around the red mark wiggled and stretched.

She brought the wound in front of her face, every inch of her insides twisting and turning in discomfort. A thread of her magic, black and skinny, snaked out of the folds of her skin, branching over the pad of her finger. It bubbled over her skin, stopping just before reaching the very top, near her nail.

Breath stuck in her throat, Mina shot her hand down by her side, turning it into a fist. She forced her wound tight against her palm. Her focus turned back to Davian.

She pardoned her way through the crowd, avoiding glares and loose, dancing arms. As she moved, she watched Davian and Lumina sway together, still absorbed in their own world. Mina made sure to walk up right beside them, so close they couldn't miss her. But she was mistaken by how taken in they were with each other.

Coldness struck Mina. It came from in her chest, sprouting down the lengths of her arms, and pooling in the pit of her stomach. It was the same cold she had when she saw Davian and told herself she loved him. Except, it didn't feel like love this time.

The world turned gray. Mina swayed alongside the pair. She kept herself aligned with Lumina. When Lumina twirled, so did Mina. When Lumina switched positions, Mina followed.

"I was wished upon to be you," Mina said to Lumina. "But I can *never* be you."

Lumina spun. So did Mina, continuing in invisibility.

"I was called upon to love him," she continued. "Yet he cannot love, unless it *is* you."

Lumina spun. Swayed. Mina spun. Swayed.

No test of love existed. No tricks. No jests. Mina stumbled on her own. She danced for a little longer, wishing she had the ability to cry. Without Davian, she had nothing else in the word. Without Davian, she had no purpose in her existence.

Still, a small slice of her was happy. Happy that he was happy. He got another chance at the life he wanted, really wanted, this time with the real Lumina, not a copy.

But that little piece of happiness laid deep under sorrow, hard to dig out, and was overshadowed by Mina's deep desire to be the one dancing with Davian. It *should* be her dancing with him.

"I'll never see you again," she said to Davian.

He didn't hear her. Even if he did, she suspected he wouldn't care.

She watched him a moment longer and then made her way out of the courtyard, allowing herself to glimpse back at him, letting in the hope that she'd find his head turned, sights set on her and an apology on his lips. Lumina kept his attention, however, infecting him with a real smile and a set of dimples indented on his cheeks. Mina turned away, leaving the courtyard. She'd forgotten Davian had dimples. It'd been a long time since he'd shown them.

Stars poked out onto the fresh night sky, accompanied by a crescent moon. Mina soaked in the view, noting how stars produced their own light, but the moon had the sun behind its luster. Still, painters didn't try replicating the moon because they knew the sun created the beauty behind it; they painted it because the beauty became uniquely defined through it.

Mina wished her nature transcended its origin. That when she sliced her finger, she didn't have to worry about magic pouring out. That when she looked in a mirror, despite the cracks around her eyes and gray on the ends of her hair, she wasn't reminded of Lumina. She wished she didn't have to fade and leave her life. If the Wishmaker suddenly appeared in front of her, she would've wished to become human and have emotion, thus extending her life, without any hesitation.

But he wasn't to be summoned. If she wanted to make a wish, she would have to go to him.

Mina stopped in the middle of the road. She uncurled her left fingers from her palm, glancing at the cut. "And who would stop me from going?"

She puffed out a breath and shook her head. "No, I can't go. That's too... No, I can't."

Being human.

If she were human, she'd never make a mistake again.

Being human.

If she were human, blood would flow through her, controlled by a beating heart.

Being human.

If Mina were human, Davian would love her. She would be more than just a wish. That would be *her* second chance. Her second chance at a life with Davian. He might have gone back to Lumina, and he might have been happy, but things might change if Mina showed him how much she cared. How she'd change for him, do anything to extend their time together. If he wanted a human, she'd give him one.

So long as she stood, she had life, and so long as she had life, she had the opportunity to better it. The Wishmaker could help her. Asking him, trying for more, was better than waiting around for death.

"I wish I was human," she said, her cold magic heating delightfully warm.

The cut on her finger wiggled again. More black magic, entwined with violet wisps, lurched out of the wound, attaching to the surface of her skin and spreading over the pad of her finger. It kept her finger's shape intact, acting as a second skin over her own. A second skin she couldn't peel off, not even as she tried digging her right finger nails underneath it. The magic stung instead, angry at her attempt to get rid of it.

Mina curled her left finger inward again, horrified. She needed to move. Now.

She walked through Virvin for what could've been her last time, taking it in. The drawl of the party sounded a world away. Everything outside of it sat empty. Very quiet. Very dark.

The dark and quiet hung heavier on the foggy road leaving Virvin. Mina knew where she was going. Davian told her the story of making his wish too many times to count. The Wishmaker lived in the glamorous city of Deamindis, a short walk from Virvin consisting of going through the forest, going up a hill, going past a farm, turning a right, turning a left, and curving by a stream. At the end lay Deamindis.

Davian never described Deamindis itself in vivid detail. He'd referred to the Wishmaker's house as a tall, tall building compared to other tall buildings, nothing more. Mina hoped that was enough to get her in the right place. Any tall, tall building could've fit that description.

Only one path led out of Virvin, and once Mina started down it, all she had to do was follow the story and make her own wish.

Her shoulders fell. "Sounds too easy."

Her teeth clamped on her tongue. Worry sprouted. What if a secret path out of Virvin existed? In fact, multiple secret paths could've existed. One might've hid on her left, or by her right, by the courtyard, underground. Maybe one hid in the sky. She could've already been messing up her journey.

"Calm down," she chided. "There's only this one road out. It's been that way forever."

Lifting her right foot, she went to plant it forward but turned it inward instead. She glanced at the sole of her boot, up to her ankle, her calf, her thigh, her leg as a whole. Davian may have called the walk short and easy, but that didn't mean the same thing to her. Compared to his strength, hers was diminished. He could've finished running two laps around Virvin before Mina finished walking half of one lap.

"Just take your time," she told herself. She lifted her left hand up, bending her magic-infested finger. The violet-black glow cut through the night. With more of it exposed, she noticed something peculiar. The magic appeared like a black cloud with violet lightning bolts constantly striking throughout. Having it on her entire body would make her a walking storm!

She lowered her hand. If she moved right now, she wouldn't have to see that happen.

The darkness outside of Virvin obscured the world ahead more than before. She swore the shadows stretched in unnatural, frightening ways on purpose. Now that she thought more about it, traveling at night was a terrible idea. She risked missing the correct turns because of the dark. Also, bandits loved striking where they couldn't be seen. Dangerous creatures themselves had an advantage, she'd read about them having night vision and sharp teeth, always hungry for a bite of anything. For safety, she'd have to leave in the morning.

She spun toward Virvin.

"No," she said. "You can't wait."

She spun away.

"But you won't be able to make it on your own."

She spun and spun again. The unknown night crawled with creepiness. She spun back toward home. To the safety of familiarity.

"Silly head," she said, pressing her knuckles into her temple. "Nothing bad is going to happen. If you wait until morning, well, you might not make it to morning." *You might not ever find the courage to leave.*

She pivoted back to the unknown. Fear sunk its claws into her. Going to the Wishmaker felt silly. Too far above her capabilities. Brave people went on journeys, not a wish who couldn't organize cards or run after one man without her body breaking down.

"Lumina wouldn't hesitate." Her own words made her want to slap herself.

She looked at her magic wiggling onto her, covering the entire pad of her finger. "You can't hesitate."

Her feet moved. Mina stepped farther out of Virvin, marching on the road at a steady pace, a touch faster than usual, though manageable on her muscles.

She went into the forest. Trees grew on either side of the path, blending into each other the further she tried looking through them. The shadows crawled up their trunks, angular and shaking.

Mina pulled on the muscles around her lips, occupying her mind with a smile before it made up tales of monsters stalking her in the trees. She grappled. Her lips twitched, tugging down against her efforts to keep the corners lifted. The increasing ache on her mouth overtook her strength to keep her smile alive and it settled into a flat line.

Misery rolled in the folds of her magic. Yet another attempt at smiling went astray.

"Lumina could smile all day," she said as she continued down the center of the path, crossing her arms. The mention of that name picked up her speed ever so slightly.

Wind disturbed Mina's hair and knocked through the trees. Up ahead, leaves tumbled onto the path, orange and sporadic like sparks from a bonfire. Fluttering crunches sounded as they crashed into each other and the ground. They spread over the dirt, the brightest part of the forest.

She put her head down, making her way to the end of the forest, where she immediately climbed the aforementioned hill.

On her way up, the stars shifted. They lowered, trying to touch her. Mina lifted a hand, extending her arm as far as she could. The magic on her finger reflected the white, starry light off of it. Her breath hitched. She snatched her hand out of the air, folding her arms so that her magic was hidden.

The stars snapped back into their regular places as she went down the other side of the hill. At the bottom, the farm Davian mentioned lived comfortably.

Mina's chest puffed out. Three parts of her journey were already checked off.

She admired the white fence on the perimeter of the vast, lush fields. The animals must've loved how much space they had. Must've adored how they had the sun to themselves during the day. They even had an enormous tree for shade if they wanted it and a crisp pond of water to drink out of. At night, they could rest snugly in their dens with delectable dreams, free from any rain and harsh winters.

Near the end of the road, the farmer's long, rectangular home sat quietly for the night. Mina wondered what they were like. She hoped to pass by here again when she was human and meet the farmer. Or if they hated visitors, she at least wanted to walk by in the daytime and see the animals. She had always wanted to see a cow grazing on a field.

The road split into a crossroad at the end of the farm. Mina took the right turn. The second crossroad came upon her shortly, and she hooked onto the left path. A stream ran alongside the road, curving with it. Water rushed in the same direction as her, hitting the tiny, rocky shore. The splashes echoed in the vast fields beyond, blades of grass bending in the occasional breeze.

Once the stream ended, she'd arrive at Deamindis.

She walked with her back straight. By the morning, she'd be human. The taste of it stung vibrantly. So she walked.

And walked.

And walked.

And walked.

No end came into sight.

"Did I miss it?" She stopped. Biting her bottom lip, she scanned the road behind her, noticing all the footprints she'd left. "I couldn't have. Davian said this was the way to go. But what if..." She shook her head. "No. Stop it. His story is right. He's always right."

She returned to her casual stride, eyes glued forward, though they itched to glance back. Her certainty on becoming human by morning waned, but she still wanted to beat the sunrise to Deamindis at the very least.

WISH'S WISH

*M*orning brought a warmth Mina could not sense. Sunlight stretched over her head, far and wide, hitting the horizon. Along its length, tall, rectangular, silver buildings twinkled. Every now and again, she spotted dots of blue shining off them.

Mina paused, taking in the scene of what was, no doubt, Deamindis. Even from afar, she could tell the tallest building of them all sat at the center of the city. That must've been what Davian meant by a tall, tall building compared to the rest. She chastised him. He could've just said the Wishmaker's home was the tallest building.

Picking up speed, Mina hurried to the city. With her energy spent walking, her excitement didn't reach the height she thought it would upon coming here. Later, perhaps, there'd be more of a thrill. Right now, all she wanted to do was make her wish.

At the threshold of the silver city, the dirt road changed. It transformed into evenly sized square pieces of cobblestone, further changing into a smooth, shiny surface of glimmering white a few feet into Deamindis. Stepping on it looped Mina with worry. The sheen of the road reminded her of ice. She partly expected to slip. Not doing so, however, brought a pleasant surprise.

Compared to the buildings, she was a tiny speck, alone in the early morning hours as she made her way to the city center. She hadn't beaten the sunrise to

Deamindis, rather, she tied with it. Not quite the perfect scenario she'd created, but a better outcome than never coming in second place.

Her cut long since spread over her skin. It reached around to the end of her fingernail, threads of thin black magic sitting over the surface as fog did over a lake in the early morning. She held her hand by her side, fending it off from even piercing her peripheral vision.

She arrived at what had to be the Wishmaker's home. Her magic thrummed in her chest as she approached the crystalline door. The magnificence of his presence already dawned on her. She hadn't formally met him before. She didn't actually know what he was like. Just that he granted all wishes and was about to grant hers. With that, he couldn't be less than marvelous.

Blue scales covered the diamond-shaped door, alternating in triangular and oval shapes. She knocked on one of them and waited. Nobody answered.

Knocking again, Mina made sure she hit harder.

Still, nothing.

She looked the door up and down. One of the oval scales was a little faded compared to the rest. Mina studied it. A jolt of magic swept through her arm. It bunched up in her hand, pushing.

On instinct, she raised her arm, magic boiling in her hand, dragging it to the scale. With her palm on it, her magic sizzled. The scale sunk into the door. She pulled away sharply. A click sounded and the door opened.

Mina's boots scraped the floor as she entered a cavernous room. The sound bounced off the walls, which were covered by a clean blue sheet of ice adorned with a crusty layer of frost on top. The grand space sat empty of any decoration or furniture, only having a staircase. If she didn't know better, she would've thought nobody lived here. How could they when there was nothing? It was odd that such a beautiful building in such a beautiful city held a void inside.

The floor darkened under her steps. Mina approached the stairs, dizzied by how high up they went. How much they resembled ice.

"Is there anybody up there?" she called out.

Her echo served as her response. Something told her to go up anyway, just in case.

Carefully, she placed a foot on the first step and it gave way. Her ankle tightened. She pressed her shoulder into the wall, desperately clutching the thin, gold railing. Stiffening her leg, she balanced on it while she placed her other foot one step up. She shifted all her weight onto her other leg, making her back foot follow and join the other. Her feet kept slipping and sliding, her energy diminishing next to nothing. At the halfway point, she regretted going up.

When she reached the top, and her feet hit a non-slippery, stone surface, she nearly crashed to the ground and kissed it.

Another spacious room domed around her. She would've called it as empty as the downstairs area if not for the throne made out of sharp icicles on the other end of the room. It made Mina want to scrunch up her nose in disgust. Who would want to sit on something with all those spikes?

She went to the center of the room. "Hello?"

Her voice echoed and disappointment flooded her. All that work just for nobody to really be up here.

However, a slam came from below. Mina spun around, intrigued by the harsh voices and rushed, clunky steps coming up her way.

Men and women in dark purple coats burrowed into the room and surrounded her, their elongated noses bouncing with each step. Tassels hung off their coats, gold and reflecting onto their frosty, blue skin, as crisp as snow. Icicles stretched out of their scalps, replacing regular hair.

Counting them silently, Mina got to ten. A nice, even number. That also meant there were ten swords extending from their hands with ten sharp tips pointed at her.

"How did you not slip?" she asked, incredulous.

"Intruder," one of the men said, disregarding her question. He had a scar on the bridge of his nose. "Come gently with us and we won't harm you."

"I am confused," Mina said. "Why would you hurt me?"

"You've intruded upon the Wishmaker's castle," a woman informed her. One of her icicles lowered in front of her eyes like a stray piece of hair would. None of the other guards had ice hanging in their face. Mina wanted to push the strand out of the way.

One of the men stretched his blue lips. They cracked and froze in place, stationing an eternal smile on his face. "You thought you were as sneaky as a ghostie, but you didn't know we have enchanted floors."

Mina shifted from foot to foot, peering at her boots on the dark blue floor.

"Be cooperative," the smiling man said. "We don't want you trying any funny ideas."

"The only funny ideas I have are jokes, and most of them aren't good anyway," Mina told him. "You're afraid of me. There's no need to be. I'm here to make a wish."

Sour faces and confused murmurs buzzed among the guards. One of them even started lowering their sword before noticing and jerking it back up.

"No one is scared of you," the guard with the scar said. "We're under a duty to protect our people from mischief. You broke into the Wishmaker's castle, so we're only doing what is right."

"If you have a wish, you need to wait for him to arrive here during the day, like everyone else," the smiling man informed her.

Mina shook her head. "But I need my wish as soon as possible."

"The Wishmaker isn't in," he stated. He moved toward Mina, sword drawn higher than the rest. He pushed it close to her chest. "Wait outside."

Mina stepped away from him. "No, it's urgent."

At the man's signal, two guards grabbed her arms, tugging her toward the stairs. Her fingers spread wide, the cut bare for everyone to see. The violet-black stood out in the pale room. Eyes drifted its way, growing wide.

Mina could've laughed. So they were afraid!

"Stop, stop!" she cried. "Or I'll use my magic and turn you all into spiders."

The guards gasped at her waving hand, her magic pulsing with violet bolts.

"Quick," the smiling man said. "Chop it off."

A subdued screech lingered in Mina's mouth. One of the pair of guards grabbed her arm while the other raised his sword. Her body twisted and struggled, the harsh movements blackening her vision. If only her magic could really turn them into spiders.

"You can't do this to me," she said, thrashing, unable to see a thing.

One of the snowflakes started to speak, saying something Mina couldn't make out, but a deep, wise voice floating from the stairs cut them off.

"And what is all of this?"

The room stopped. Mina stilled, the sword too close to her wrist for comfort. She made out a figure in her darkened vision ascending the stairs and entering the room. The new arrival stood taller than everybody else. Much more intimidating than any sword.

A sense of shame circled the room. The guards released Mina, and every one of them stepped away from the new figure.

More of her vision returned, and Mina made out the warm visage of the old man near the top of the stairs, finding him not actually intimidating at all. He wore a yellow robe, decorated with orange suns on the train. Cloudy white hair puffed out of his head and connected to the short beard on his chin. He was the embodiment of a peaceful summer's day. This icy domain should've pooled into a puddle at his arrival.

Her magic thumped. Knowledge of this man flooded her. His voice brought up old memories of falling through clouds.

After a few moments of studying Mina, the Wishmaker broke the silence. "Leave her alone."

"But she's an intruder," the smiling guard argued.

"Leave," the Wishmaker commanded. "Before you all make yet another grave mistake."

Without further protest, the guard signaled the others while grumbling something under his breath. He glared at Mina before huffing his way out of the room, fuming as he went down the stairs. One by one the guards filtered from the room, leaving her alone with the Wishmaker.

He approached her. A light smile touched his lips. Her magic swirled at the sight, delighted by his pleasant face.

"What can I do for you?" the Wishmaker asked.

The simple, warm question left Mina's throat dry. She opened her mouth to make a sound, but nothing came out.

"No need to be fearful here," he said, his tone close to matching Irvin's jolly one. "Speak out your purpose for visiting. Unless you can't speak?"

Mina's voice scratched against her dry mouth. "I am a wish."

"I know. The nature of your being weaves around you. It is your brightest thread, though it is a confusion to many." He circled her slowly. "As my creation, you have a home here. It is why you easily intruded."

"I didn't intrude," she protested. "The door opened when I tried it. If you want to keep someone out, you have to lock it."

"It was locked."

Mina tilted her head to the side.

He grinned. "My domain obeys my entrance and the entrance of any of my creations, even when locked."

"Then why didn't they know?" Mina asked, gesturing towards the stairs.

The Wishmaker sighed. "Protecting me gets in the way of their common sense sometimes. But I admire their dedication anyway."

"Oh."

His grin stretched. "Oh, how marvelous, correct?"

Mina gasped. If he smiled further, his skin would've ripped. At least, that was if he weren't human. But she knew he wasn't. Humans only had a little bit of magic in their blood. They went through their life never experiencing much power to their name. Nobody was as divine as the Wishmaker, and yet, he appeared as human as the rest of them.

"Are you more or less human?" Mina asked.

He blinked. Another trait she envied. "In a way, I am a lot, but also in a way, I'm not much. I have lived a long time. To recall my beginnings troubles me. I can't seem to do it. What I can do is continue on and make the best of the times right now."

"You must be human," she insisted. "You smile so easily."

He laughed. "A good observation, but a bad, bad conclusion."

She took great offense to that. "Why?"

"Because you miss a question: why wouldn't I be able to smile if I wasn't human? I have a mouth, and it operates the same as a normal person's. Therefore, I can smile, too."

"I've a mouth, but my smile doesn't hold for more than seven seconds." She tapped her chin. "You've probably practiced. You've had forever to do so, haven't you?"

"Pshhhhh, forever." He scoffed. "The word means nothing to me. A smile is born out of true happiness—no practice required."

"But I've been happy. I'm a wish you made for a boy named Davian. With him, I've had the best existence. I've been the happiest thing of all. My smile evades me because I'm not human."

"And what says you could smile if you were human?" The Wishmaker leaned closer to her. "Joy can be felt without a smile. Others will sense it. You will too. True happiness is more than an expression. Have you ever been happy for yourself?"

A tiny flutter burst through her stomach. She couldn't put a name to it. "I don't want to listen to this anymore. It makes no sense. There's something important I've come here for."

"Tell me, then."

Mina opened her mouth. She'd created a grand speech during her walk by the stream. The speech flowed with elegance and put together a lovely description about what she wanted and why she wanted it. She was proud of that speech and had grown more prideful as she repeated it over and over, committing it to memory. The Wishmaker would've been impressed by her, moved enough to grant her humanity the second it was over.

But the speech didn't leave her mouth. It eluded her completely.

"Well?" the Wishmaker prodded, lifting a brow.

"I want to make my one true wish," Mina blurted.

The amusement in his features bounced away faster than a lightning strike. He gawked. A reaction most baffling. He must've heard such a sentence so many times before that it should've bored him.

Uncomfortable silence lumped between them, forming a giant ball and expanding until it pressed against the walls, twisting angrily at being confined. Bubbles and hisses spewed from it, and it squeaked, unable to break through the ice.

"What?" the Wishmaker asked, popping the silence.

The room deflated. Mina's magic whimpered. He sounded less confused, and more like he genuinely didn't hear what she said.

"I want to make my one true wish," she repeated.

He patted the air. "I know what you said."

"Then why ask me to repeat?"

"Because I didn't understand what you said."

Something tapped Mina's eyebrows. She wanted to furrow them. To squish them into her eyes and stab him with her confusion. What movement she got out of them was small and swift, easy to miss.

"You are a wish," he said frankly.

"I know. I wouldn't have mentioned it if I didn't know."

Sympathy tugged his lips down. "A wish can't make a wish."

If blood existed in her rag of a body, Mina would've heard it rush into her ears, aided by a pounding heart. The pressure would've popped her head off her neck.

"You say this," she said, her tone a touch lower than usual, "like I should've already known. But there aren't any guides on being a wish. How should I have known?"

He tilted his head to the side, raised his eyebrows, and shrugged.

The light swimming in her head heated. Her voice returned to normal. "When I descended to this life, why didn't you tell me? Are there any other important things that I'm missing?"

"There's not a lot of wishes in the shape of a human, so there's no need for a guide," he said. "You don't know anything because you didn't seek the answers."

"All that's ever been important was Davian. *Is* Davian. I knew if he gave me up there would be a problem, but I didn't think I'd ever have to face that day." She looked at the magic on her hand. "Not ever"

"And that rule is the most important." The Wishmaker sighed. "I do apologize for the terrible news. It isn't ideal. I'm sure you were hopeful."

"More than hopeful. I'm a wish given up. That means I go away."

"This is why you've come here, then. You're attached to living."

"Davian deserves a woman who he can rest his head upon and whose blood he can feel rushing underneath her flesh. I want to be a human. Like Lumina."

"Lumina." He tasted the name on his tongue. Sweet. Sickening. "I'm sorry, but I cannot grant your wish. If I could, I would. It is my job, after all."

Mina's arms hung dead at her sides. "But everyone has one true wish."

"If I had the ability to change you, my child, I would. But what I create cannot be altered by my own hands."

If she were human, she would've sobbed on her knees.

"This is a fate I cannot accept," she whispered. "There is a life for me to live. A chance for my smile to grow. To last longer. For Davian to see it."

"I will provide as much solace as I can until your magic takes over your entire body and bursts you into a million particles."

"And when it does, I'm gone forever."

"Yes."

She dove deep into her head, ripping it apart for any solutions. There had to be something.

Someone. Something. Someone. Something. Someone.

There had to be something or someone that could help her.

"Child, how about we get you into a comfortable room, and I will provide you with anything you want," the Wishmaker offered. He put his arm around her shoulders. "There is still a little time left for you and you will be at peace during it."

That sounded good. But what sprung to Mina's mind sounded better.

She stepped away from him. "Wait."

His arm retreated off of her. "Yes?"

"You say you can't alter what has been created by your own hands, but you didn't say I can't be altered at all."

Pressing his lips together, the Wishmaker's gaze drifted to the floor.

"There is something that can help me," Mina said. "You know what it is."

He cleared his throat and shook his head, turning away from her.

"There is something." When he didn't say anything, she stepped into his line of view. "Please, I'll do anything."

The Wishmaker's shoulders fell with his sigh. "There is a being powerful enough to help you." His voice grew dry. "A spirit in the shadows. I try not to mention him often."

"Tell me," Mina insisted. "Tell me who he is."

The Wishmaker hesitated. "He's called the Blood King. The power he has is above my own. Caution must be adhered to when speaking with him. His soul is touched by a chilling darkness that things like him should not have."

"Would he help me?"

"Help is beneath him. He is a demand. A creature of bargain," he said, his voice breaking into a coldness matching his home. "Be careful. Many have tried playing his games before, but the results only end well for him. Dealing with him is an act of desperation I advise against. Please, child, don't call for him. Let yourself go easy."

Yes! Mina's mind screamed. *Go for easy.*

In the distance, she sensed a shiver. She waited for her skin to prickle, but the feeling remained too far for her to have. Always a feeling she chased but never caught up with. If the Wishmaker was afraid and distrustful of the Blood King, she should've been afraid as well.

Her fingers pressed against her palm. Her magic ate only a piece of her finger so far. If it needed to eat all of her then she had more time than she thought. With that time, there was hope. Something to do. A chance to change.

"Where do I find this spirit?" she asked.

A pitifully sad smile blew onto the Wishmaker's lips. "There is no finding the Blood King. He comes to you when you make a blood offering."

The corners of Mina's lips twitched downward. "I have no blood to offer."

"Reach inward."

Mina stared at him. "I don't see how that helps me have blood."

"You might be a wish come true, but I do not create the unfeeling. There is something about you that he might like if you get personal. Search inside and find what you can."

Before Mina began, she had to stop. Too many thoughts hurled toward her, jumbling into a giant mess. One she couldn't sort out. Not as more thoughts kept piling on.

"May I speak out loud?" she asked. "It helps me think better."

"If that will be best," the Wishmaker said, "please do it."

Steadying herself, Mina took her awareness inward. Seeking out the Blood King without blood was a silly notion. He probably already laughed at her for the mere act of trying.

The real Lumina would've taken on the impossible challenge with a sharp grin and won.

"But I'm not her," Mina said. "I could never be. I don't have her mind. I've never had a challenge. Ever." Her throat dried. She forced herself to continue. "Until now. I am challenged now. I am Davian's wish. A wish who wants life. Life would make an offering to the Blood King easier. He would appear quickly before me if I had blood."

She pressed her lips together for a second, putting a hand over her stomach, allowing the rhythm of her breath to push it up and down.

"What makes me real is magic. My blood is magic, yet it makes me inferior. It's kept me hidden. People don't know me. I want to know them. But Davian was embarrassed. Davian brought me here to breathe the same air as him. To give him endless love. I am a repeated person, unable to capture the mind of the face I resemble. It's impossible when I am as I am. Impossible. He's made it clear he will always love her. That's all he's ever done. I may have no heart, but he hurt me still. He tossed me away, no care, no kind goodbye. He never really thanked me for anything besides what he gained for himself. He went back to celebrate his birthday at a party I planned."

The Wishmaker stared at her, his expression unreadable.

"Why didn't he appreciate me?" she asked him. He gave no answer. "Did he always think that because I don't have expression, that I don't feel pain, that because my voice can't work out the correct emotions, that nothing about me can hurt?"

Sharpness stabbed the edges of her eyes. The invisible sensation of tears. Knowing they'd never be real burned the magic behind her face and stretched out the magic on more of her finger, trickling the storm thinly down the length.

"If a wish is able to hurt," she said, "then it deserves to become human."

Her neck craned. The ceiling sat so far from her, but from how hot her anger rolled within her, it didn't actually feel too far at all. She'd become bigger than anything she'd ever been before.

"If I were human, I would be perfect like him," she declared. "I would be perfect like the woman he loves. Like every human. Never again would I forget a gift, and never would I neglect to cherish my heart. It's the most beautiful thing in the world. Blood King, if you understand my pain, I plead for your help. Although my body now lacks what you take, when the magic in me turns red, I will gladly give you a taste of the substance you crave."

And nothing happened. Of course it wouldn't. Why should she succeed?

A luster of gold shone onto the Wishmaker. "Everlasting luck on your journey," he whispered to her.

"Thank you?" Mina asked, a rope of confusion tugging on her.

The Wishmaker smiled. Mina caught sight of the golden glow on her arm. She had no time to figure it out. Something crashed into her side. Tentacles wrapped around her, and a low, dangerous hiss crawled into her ear, unleashing her first ever blood-curdling scream.

DEAL WITH THE BLOOD KING

*S*hadows swung side to side over the thin scraps of sunlight creeping through the cracks in the ceiling. What light passed through shone onto chipped black roses carved on the walls. Dust piled in their crevices, spilling onto the floor in snowy piles. Elsewhere, out of sight, water dripped with drawn-out seconds between each splash.

Going from bright iciness to standing in pure darkness lashed Mina's balance on reality. Her head swam in spinning magic, twisting her vision. Maybe this was her first ever dream.

A first.

She touched her throat. A bonfire blazed inside. She rubbed her skin, making sure she hadn't torn a hole right through it. It was difficult to tell what happened on the surface so she pressed her fingers into her flesh. Magic knocked at her touch, contained within. She lowered her hand, satisfied her scream hadn't pierced a hole.

Her scream. Excitement bounced through her. Her first scream in all her existence. But nobody had heard it, and she'd never be able to make it again of her own volition. Her shoulders fell. Perhaps it wasn't even real. It could've been a trick of her mind, including the burning.

The tentacle slithered from around her waist and pushed her forward. She gasped.

Faces of utter terror—gray and bronze, broken and cracked—reached her through the darkness. Their mouths opened wide, holding back frozen screams that would've shattered the silence. Bodies contorted into different positions. Knees bent to different degrees, arms stretched out at all angles, and a few faces hid behind hands, eyes peeking through fingers.

Statues. They were statues. Ones facing their ultimate doom.

A ball formed in Mina's throat. It bobbed as she stepped backwards, knocking into what had to be a body. It darted from her.

Clicks pricked off the floor. They circled behind her from right to left, shoes scraping the ground after each click.

With her jaw tense, Mina turned to find who walked behind her.

A hand shot out and caught the side of her face. The palm pressed against her cheek, pushing her away. Fingers reached up high into her hair, slightly trembling. Though she wasn't too sure on that last part. Her brain might've made her think the tremble was there as it tried to figure out what the hand felt like against her.

"You can't see me yet," a man said, his voice hoarse. "I have not finished looking at you."

Flushed white skin burned in her peripheral vision. Embarrassment flooded Mina. Everything suddenly made sense. Her mind had warped her sense of touch yet again to make her think a tentacle had grabbed her. That hadn't been the case. A person took her from the Wishmaker's home. A man. Not some gruesome, snarling monster.

"I..." Her clogged throat made it hard to speak. Her blank mind made it hard to find something to say.

On her finger, more threads of magic wiggled down the length, curling around to the bends and making branching rivers to her palm. Stitches of jaundice skin glowed in the gaps between each stream. She flexed her hand, keeping her eyes away from it.

The man hummed as if he were assessing something. His hand pulled away, fingers dragged down the side of her face. They lingered on her jaw.

"Don't be so tense," he said.

Easy to say, Mina thought. But as his fingers left her, fingers she imagined were cold and rough, her jaw relaxed.

The dreadful clicks and scrapes rounded in front of her. Mina faltered slightly when her gaze landed upon the full length of the man, her arms rising to protect herself. Another scream would've barreled out of her had she the power.

Blood covered his every pale, hard feature, head to toe. The wetness seeped into his scalp. Only a few strands of his hair remained clean and blond. Red dripped off the soggy ends, trickling down his face, into his eyes, over his cheeks, and careening around his neck.

It stained his clothing—his ruffled shirt and long, straight-lined pants had both been white at some point. A mix of fresh crimson and dried burgundy replaced the color. Even his long black coat over top bore wet and dry stains. His shirtsleeves puffed out from under the coat's cuffs, the fabric drooping with red on every stitch.

And his hands... Oh, his hands!

Hardly an inch of pale skin peeked through. Mina didn't know how she thought they had any white before. Her mind must've latched onto something natural for comfort.

She touched the side of her face, wondering if he stained her.

"Pleading without bleeding is rare," he said. "Most people offer it to guarantee I arrive."

"But you came anyway," she pointed out, hardly hearing herself. More than talking, she wanted to throw him into a lake and scrub him down.

Keenness erupted in his eyes. Streams of gold circled through his amber irises. They shone off of him like a candle's flame on melting, white wax.

"Needles prick me in the shape of desperation. Each plea is another stab." His voice sounded ready to crack and break upon every word, trembling constantly in smoothness and hoarseness. High and low. "When I heard you in my head, I almost didn't come. Most will bleed and then plead, bleed as they plead, or bleed after they plead."

"I do not think I understand why you would ignore me," she said, knowing it was a lie. She knew there was a huge possibility he'd ignore her because she lacked blood. But still— "I promised you blood. Once I get it."

"Promises are *spit*—" At that, he spat. The blob smacked the ground. "I prefer assurance before I appear. I hate wasting my power on something trite."

"If triteness worries you, then your power must be weak."

His expression soured. Shadows whipped in the blood and then every patch glowed. Glowed with malevolence, a threat. Mina swallowed and took a step backwards.

"There is nothing my power cannot accomplish," he said. "It is all of me. Nothing is more important than my powers."

Mina spoke quickly. "I don't mean to be offensive." Her voice strained, throat aching. "I wanted to sound funny, but it's hard for me to. Please, I'm sorry. I don't know what I'm doing."

The Blood King met her dead in the eyes. "Are you afraid of me?"

Shifting, she studied him. A large part of her was afraid. He was a stranger, the Wishmaker hadn't said a kind word about him, and he was covered in blood. What more had she needed?

But then again, he was human, or appeared so, just like the Wishmaker, and he must've only been a few years older than herself, another point for comfort. Mina herself was the same age Lumina had been when she and Davian parted all those years ago, locking her into forever looking and being twenty years old. And apparently Davian didn't like that. Hadn't thought it through back when he made his wish. If he had, none of this would've been happening.

Mina lowered her head, wondering if things would've been different if she aged. Her mind had aged. She'd gained knowledge here and there. That should've been worth something. Oh, but of course, she almost forgot, hers wasn't the same mind as Lumina's. He'd made that clear.

Grinding her teeth, Mina heaved out of her drifting head. Now was not the time to dwell on the past. Not when a lovely future sat ahead. The Blood King couldn't be as bad as her own magic eating her alive. He was a man—spirit—who could help her, blood on him or not. She had nothing to fear, and therefore, wouldn't offend him by admitting she held a little reservation.

She soaked in his face, seeing just how much blood covered him.

"Yes, I am afraid." She sucked in a breath. That wasn't what she'd meant to say. "Because you're messy," she added. More than ever she wanted to melt and evaporate.

He peered down at himself. "I am. But it is only blood. Everyone has blood touching their insides, so why not wear it outside?"

She opened her mouth to disagree. She had no blood.

He waved a dismissive hand. "Yes, yes, you are not regular, and neither am I. Humans get diseased if they drink blood or let it get into an open wound. You and I wouldn't. Wear it, drink it—blood would never harm us."

"Drink it," Mina murmured. "Never."

"Maybe one day." He lightened up. "Now, now, onto you, dearest wish. You poured a lot of anger into your plea."

"I did?" She'd been so flat in her speech. So cold. So distant.

"It tasted divine." His hand rose and neared her face. She froze, awaiting the touch she wouldn't feel, but his fingers curled inward, and he pulled away. "You want to be a real person with my help."

"Yes."

His arm fell to his side. "This pure magic inside of you, I understand, is what keeps you alive. Unlike a person with a heart."

You're a wish. Nothing more. She clenched her fists, nodding.

"We are akin in nature on that matter," the Blood King said.

Mina wasn't sure if she heard him correctly. "Could you repeat yourself?"

"You and I are similar."

What a great joke. She wished she could laugh at it.

"You are divine, and I am a lowly wish," she said. "Here you live in a big castle, and I come from a small village. I don't even think Virvin is in the atlas." She shook her head. "We're not the same."

"You are not the lowness of people," he said, nostrils flaring. "As a wish, you *are* a grand being."

The phantom urge to scrunch her nose came. It wiggled. Burning ran up the bridge and into her sinuses, but no wiggle happened.

"I'm not a grand being," she said, trying to breathe evenly.

"But you're a wish, are you not?"

"Yes, I am."

"Made of pure magic, correct?"

"You already said I am."

His voice lowered. His head tilted. "But are you?"

"I am."

The Blood King's jaw worked. He pressed his lips together and eyed her. Slowly, slyness etched onto his features, bringing a smirk. He offered her his arm. "Take a walk with me?"

She hesitated, though she tried not to. What more important things did she have to do? She went to take his arm with her hand—the clean one, free of magic.

"Show me the other one," he said.

Mina bit her lip. Her fingers uncurled on her magic-infected hand. They splayed wide as she lifted it up. Violet dotted the black river running down her finger and over her palm, flickering and enhancing the storminess. The magic reached the top of her wrist. She noticed a faint mist of black swirling over her new skin.

She set her fingers on the crook of the Blood King's elbow.

He tapped her knuckles. "It is lovely. A wish has never come to me before. This is quite new."

"I'm glad to be the first," she said with a touch of playful sarcasm, shocked she managed to change her voice. She tried to get the change to stay, but her next words went back to being characteristically cold and flat. "The magic is eating me, you know."

He smiled. His boots clicked across the floor, Mina at his side. As he moved, he favored his left foot a little more, walking with the tiniest limp.

Fog lay thick on the floors outside of the room they were in, crawling up to their knees. Emptiness carved the place in a way sadder than the Wishmaker's home. There should've been more life here considering the rose carvings on the walls, the picture frames, the statues, the chairs sitting by the windows. But the dust all over everything, the pictures frames being empty, the fear on the statues, and the chairs being broken and worn beside the boarded up windows made the castle feel less than alive. There was next to no light anywhere, and the dripping remained distant. Mina regretted thinking less of the Wishmaker's home. She'd live there for a hundred years before she lived in this castle for one.

The Blood King guided her through his domain. Her feelings mixed between gladness for his guidance and disgust for the blood on him. While she couldn't conceptualize the surface of his bloody fabric, knowing she touched it crumpled up her insides in squeamishness.

The unsettling, drip-filled air between them came to a swift end as the Blood King took her down a short set of stairs. He opened a door at the bottom.

A hot sunset of red light and bright white fog spilled from the new room. The light emanated from its center, sprouting out of a brick well. Four people could've stood comfortably around its width. Five, if everyone were shoulder to shoulder.

The liquid in the well settled into a glassy sheet. A crimson one. Mina tensed.

"Don't worry," the Blood King said. "It's not as terrible as you think. There is some water mixed in it."

On the other side of the well, more statues were near the wall. Three stood much more broken than the others, especially on their faces. They had no eyes or mouths, and one had its nose snapped off.

Mina focused on the water, unnerved by the statues. But the deep red of the water also unnerved her. She lifted her gaze from it, not knowing where to look. The cracks on the walls and ceiling reminded her of the ones on her face, the fog was too lonely-feeling, and she didn't want to stare at the Blood King. He perturbed her too much and she didn't want to be rude by staring blankly at him. So, she settled on the well, knowing she couldn't avoid it forever. If she thought about it hard enough, she could pretend the red came from something other than blood. Like...like...*blood.*

Her shoulders slumped in defeat.

"A body of magic," the Blood King said. He broke away from her. "Everyone has a little bit of power in their blood, including humans. It isn't much for them, but it is something." He gestured to the well. "This is filled with previous offerings."

He approached the brick, setting his hands on top of it and peering into the magic.

Mina joined him. Its height reached the middle of her waist. If it were empty, she speculated how much of it her magic would fill. Maybe around the halfway point.

"Why do you want to become human?" the Blood King asked, a bump of real curiosity hitting his question.

She tilted her head. "Didn't I make that clear?"

"Tell me what you plan to do with humanity."

"The boy who wished for me no longer wants me," she said. "If I became human, I could go back home to Virvin, and we could love each other again."

The Blood King lowered his brows and frowned. "What a disgusting way to spend your time. You want to go back to this man who hurt you."

"He didn't."

He smirked. "You said he did. In your plea. Remember?"

She dropped her eyes to the fog. "I... It was a weak moment. Not true. I'd have said anything to bring you to me."

"Believe what you like, then." He shifted closer to her, eyes aglow. His bloodied fingers brushed the length of her arm, over her blouse, to her hand, where he found her magic breaking out of her. "Being human is a waste. You've seen how they only care about themselves. All they cry out about is how much they want something, and when they have it, they set their sights onto the next thing. That is how your lover was."

Mina ripped away from him, scurrying to the other side of the well. She clung to its edge, wanting to scowl.

The Blood King's hand retreated to his side, face tangled with amusement. "Why be foul? Why be human? In the end, you'll die anyway, so let the time come sooner. None of what you've done will have mattered either way."

Those words. She'd heard them back in Virvin. They came from Lumina, right outside the courtyard. "But..."

He pouted. "But what?" His head tipped to the side. "You're a wish. Even if you are human, that will always haunt you. The fact that you never would've existed naturally will haunt you. It will anger you until you become something unrecognizable to who you once were, because humans are angry. They can never be nice and selfless without hating others for making them that way, or be nice and selfish without hating themselves for being so. Save yourself from the regret of a foul future reflection."

"I came here for you to help me," Mina said. "Whatever you're doing now, I don't like it."

He softened. "I'm sorry. I'm only warning you."

"I won't change my mind."

"Very well. If you're so determined, I won't stand in the way. It isn't my life at stake. Once your magic is through with you, you will become nothing, but I can make you human before that happens, dearest wish, if that is what you want."

The words resounded through the room.

Mina stood firm, though a ribbon of impatience wound through her. She'd grown tired of constantly reaffirming her wish. She just wanted to hurry and be human. "I do."

He gave her a long, thoughtful look, and stuck his hand in the watery magic. "You beg for humanity." He glanced at her chest. "If you had a heart, you could be human. I can give you one. First, however, you must give me a heart of my own."

Stabs of terror, puzzlement, and fury hit her all at once. Her face blistered as she tried to move it, getting no emotion out onto the surface.

"Are you making fun of me?" she questioned.

"Not one bit." He pulled his hand from the magic and placed it atop his chest. "This is our similarity. I, too, am missing a heart. It was taken from me by trusted companions and stowed away in four pieces."

Cold dropped inside Mina. "Stealing a heart is awful. Why would anybody want to do that?"

"I don't know." He rubbed his fingers together, shrugging. "Our little clash over my heart got them stuck inside different mirrors."

"How did that happen?"

He readjusted his shoulders. "It's hard to feel without a working heart. It makes it harder to keep memories, too, as I feel no need to hold onto them, good or bad. My days are dead."

His face became blank and Mina finally understood what other people saw when they looked at her: a body of nothingness. Grief poured through her. She couldn't imagine what it'd been like to feel alive with friends one day and have it all ripped away the next.

Oh, but she could.

Davian. He'd been her entire world yesterday, morning, afternoon, and in one moment during the sunset, before he ended it all.

Pity melted Mina's fear. The Blood King stood such a lonely figure before her. She wanted to wrap her arms around him and take him out of his horrible place. That would do no good, however. If they left, they'd still have no hearts.

"My companions are behind the mirrors, always close to me," he said with distant fondness. He blinked, head shaking, face turning to stone. "Sometimes I miss them, but then I remember they have my heart."

"Can't you ask for it? Reason with them?" She searched the room, wondering where these mirrors he spoke of even were.

"They hate me too much." He shuddered. "We all make each other suffer. It is why I make these deals, so that one day, the right person could get the pieces, shape my heart, and give it back to me."

Sorrowful darkness washed over him, tugging the hardness off his features. His chin dragged down, gaze hitting the floor. "But everyone always fails. Some arrive here, hopeless causes already. I send them in, wanting to give them the benefit of the doubt, but they get stuck in the mirrors and won't try to get out. You might find those people." He lit up. "They might help you." He swallowed, hitting a fist against his chest. "I just hope you can make it and end this hollowness."

Sympathy tied a string around Mina. She extended it to the Blood King, allowing it to tug her spirit closer to his.

"Poor dear," she said. "Oh, the hurt you must be going through."

Glossiness pooled his eyes. A trickle of blood leaked out of the corners. "Would you like to feel my emptiness?"

Her mouth dried.

The Blood King squared his chest, peeling his coat open. Mina carefully made her way around the well, enticed by his bloodied chest. She should've been afraid of a potential lie. But that was just her mind trying to frighten her like usual. Her magic-infested fingers reached up.

The ruffles of his shirt grazed her hand, dipping blankness into her head. A heartbeat, however, was something she could feel when she focused deeply. She'd managed with Davian. The Blood King would be no exception. She gently pressed her palm down on the spot where his heart had once been.

She searched for the familiar beat she'd always felt within Davian. The beat she longed to have in her.

Steady, patient, she waited for a single pulse to hit her palm.

Nothing happened.

Familiarity settled in her.

She held her hand in place for a long time. The heartless wish with her hand on a heartless spirit. A human-shaped woman and man. He wasn't dead. Neither was she. He breathed as she did. He moved as she did. He spoke as she did. Both of them were human on the surface, yet empty underneath.

"Are you a wish?" she wondered out loud, wanting to snatch back the thought. She already knew the answer.

He laughed, the sound caressing her ears. "I am not, but where I come from doesn't matter. I live in the present and only the present. As anyone should."

"But you want your friends back," she said. "You want to feel again."

He leaned away from her. "Repairing what is damaged isn't so easy. I think it is best to leave people behind sometimes."

"When I go back home," she said, "I want to be with Davian again."

"Davian." The Blood King hurled that poisonous name from his mouth. "What a waste to dedicate your heart to him."

Mina pressed her hand deeper into his chest. "You know nothing at all. Davian is and always will be my greatest love."

"I can't wait for you to recover from these ill thoughts," he said. Grabbing her hand, he pried it off of him. "I would think a love so strong could've built a heart. As pitiful as it is, they say love is the greatest power. When felt true, it can make any heart beat again."

"Again," she repeated. "That doesn't happen when the heart doesn't exist. The Wishmaker would have mentioned something if love could fix me."

"Isn't the Wishmaker's lack of expertise the reason you're with me?"

Mina fell silent. She turned away from the Blood King. The fog swirled around her, lashing with cruel laughter. She entered a world so much bigger than she expected, lacking so much of the knowledge she needed.

"There have been others before you who could not give me my heart," he said, straightening. "If you fail me, your magic will overtake you and I will take it into my possession. Another drop in the well. Are you certain you want to continue?"

"I have to try," she said. "Even if I am overtaken while trying, at least my magic could be put to use in your hands."

The Blood King's face ignited in a blaze of flared nostrils and brightened eyes. "Our deal is set then: find my beating heart, and you will have one in return."

He raised his arms. The room rumbled.

Mina grasped the well's edge, legs stiffening. She let out a small squeak as the statues crumbled into dust and the ground broke at the edges of the room. Heavy white clag poured through the openings, and three mirrors rose from within them, each sitting against their own wall. They reached the ceiling, skinny and rhomboid in shape.

Mina spun around, shying away from her three reflections. Having met Lumina in the flesh, her reflection became more unbearable. Moldy gray hairs grew on her ends. The cracks around her eye looked more distorted than usual. The yellow hue of her skin thickened, mossy over what should've been a cool tone. Her purple irises were as faded as an overused wash cloth, nearly blending in with the whites.

"Pockets of memory hide behind the glass," the Blood King said. He placed a hand between her shoulder blades and guided her to one of the mirrors.

The dark magic on her hand exposed her nature as a wish so clearly in her reflection. Her nature's worst offense of all.

"Illusions from various minds lie within," he continued. "There is one piece of heart behind each mirror, each held by one of my old companions. You'll know them when you see them. When put together, the pieces will form one glass heart you could present to me as part of your end of the bargain."

"But you said to get a beating heart."

He smirked. "You listen very well, but you're forgetting how grand my power is. You seem to accept the fact that I can produce a heart for you out of nothing, yet it troubles you to think I can make a glass one beat for me. You should know, dearest wish, that anything can be changed."

That did make sense. The well of magic was proof enough of his power. Her being her should've stopped her questioning him, especially since it was her seeking his help. She knew so little about using magic.

"I see." She examined each mirror. "Didn't you say there were four heart pieces? I only see three mirrors."

"The last will be found," he said. "Don't trouble yourself about the future, when you should focus on what's about to happen right now." He found the magic on her hand, tapping it. Then he gestured to the glass, off to a place foreign to anything Mina had ventured into before.

"Could you come with me?" she asked.

He shook his head. "I won't enter of my own free will to help anybody. Only within, by speaking my title in desperation, can I be enticed inside. I advise you not to summon me there. My brain gets too veiled for good judgment. You'll hate me."

Mina didn't move. She hated that explanation. It meant she had to do this alone.

"Take your step," he urged. "You're already running on limited time."

Strings of her magic split and spread on her palm, reaching up onto other fingers, rounding to her knuckles and seeping onto more parts of her wrist.

"Stop dawdling. Just go," she said to herself.

The Blood King stepped back as Mina stepped forward. Her foot went through the glass. The world shifted, full of white clouds and uneven ground. When she went to take another step, however, her foot found nothing but air. Her body lurched forward and she soared downward.

RUNNING DOOR

*W*ith her limbs turned into ribbons and wobbling in the wind, Mina burst through pillows of white clouds, sparks snapping everywhere upon impact. They crackled and flashed close to her face. She twisted to avoid them, the wind hooking around her and crafting her into a thinly stuffed doll in its hands. Her head whipped forward, hips bending, face striking her knees. Tangles of gray and brown hair flung into her eyes and got caught in her mouth. The wind pulled her arms back every time she tried prying it out. They stuck over her head, waving side to side.

Sparks crackled as she plopped through another cloud. Her legs circled the air, going over her head. She tumbled in three full circles, the clouds blurring together.

"You can't be perfect," hissed a voice.

Within the white, hurled into existence by the sparks, a face appeared, smeared as if it were wet paint on a canvas. Purple, cracked, moldiness caked the skin around the lips and eyes. Cracks, like Mina's, formed on every inch of the face. *Her* face.

Gargled sounds erupted out of Mina. Her tongue hit the roof of her mouth.

"You can't be perfect," Lumina repeated. Her right eye swirled, dipping down onto her cheek.

Mina wiggled. She reached out with her left hand. It swiped through Lumina's face, leaving claw marks of violet-black magic.

Lumina screamed, *"You can't be perfect!"*

Those four words chased Mina. She twisted, a weak whimper emerging out of her. Everywhere she turned, Lumina's smeared face watched.

"Give up," Lumina urged. "You can't be anyone."

Mina turned her head, shoving her eyes into her arm, blocking out the world as best she could.

Gentle fingers took her by the wrist. Mina lifted her face and strained to see who grabbed her, but the cloud's brightness washed out the clarity of the human shape above her, leaving a shadow.

Stillness entered the clouds. Mina's hair fell out of her mouth, hanging by her shoulders, as she came to a stop. She hung in the air, swinging her legs. It was hard to make out the shadow's features. Only hints of red glinted here and there as they floated. She thought of the Blood King first, but he gave her reason to believe it wasn't him.

She and the mystery shadow descended. Her boots hit the ground. The clouds turned gray, pulling away into a dark sky. When Mina looked up, her savior vanished.

"Thank you," she murmured, hoping they heard her anyway. She lowered her arms to her sides.

A breeze tossed Mina's hair toward her left shoulder. She pivoted, facing it. A vast field of purple grass stretched far beyond, the blades arched in her direction. In the distance, the field pushed up into a hill. Atop the hill, a lonesome house sat. No, it was more than a house. A mansion. Grand. Complex. A dark mansion prettier than anything she'd ever seen. More so than the Wishmaker's home, though it wasn't as big.

Mina started for the mansion, pushing through the field and leaving behind a trail of crushed grass. Light blue stars sat hazed behind the thin clouds, the smears of light reaching closer to her as she made her way up the hill.

A black fence had been erected along the mansion's perimeter. Or rather, the remnants of a fence. The pickets bent like wilted flowers and were all too far apart, with no lattice or rails connecting them, to keep anything out. Mina waltzed right through one of the open spaces.

Worn-down bricks crafted the mansion itself. On top, four tall, sharp peaks of steep pitch curved inward on every corner as though they were flames licking the outside of a cauldron. The surface of the peaks resembled fabric, not brick, yet they were stiff in place despite the wind.

Mina's brows twitched. Throbbing aches penetrated her temples. She put a hand on her forehead and stepped toward the mansion's front door.

The sound of rubbing bricks rumbled off the house. In the blink of an eye—if Mina could blink—they rotated, flipping and taking the door away, leaving a plain brick wall in front of her, though the windows high above stayed in place. With the wall too flat to scale up to them, she had no choice but to use the door to get inside. But with it gone...

The bricks rotated again, so quick she couldn't distinguish what was within the house beyond the quickly exposed bright blur.

Mina approached the mansion. She peeked around the corner. Another wall of pure brick greeted her. She walked alongside it, arriving at the back of the house. Halfway down the wall, an orange glow passed through a square pane of glass. Glass embedded on the front door.

She lifted her foot. The bricks flipped. The door left.

Setting her teeth together, she stalked to the next corner. She took two steps toward the taunting orange glow before the bricks flipped, and darkness ensued.

Huffing, she made her way to the next corner. When she lifted her foot *again*, the bricks flipped *again*, taking the door away *again*.

"It's impossible to get inside," Mina said. She glanced out at the open fields of purple, setting her hands on her hips. "The heart piece must be out there."

Her stomach tumbled at the thought of navigating an endless, empty field. As the Blood King stated, she was running on limited time. She had to find a person to find his heart—well, only a piece of it. The only sign of life so far was the mansion. Even then, there was no guarantee anyone was inside.

Being turned from the house, however, made the wind hit her harder than usual, shoving her back toward the house.

She squared her shoulders and stared down the bricks. "All right. Be faster than the bricks." She mustered up the courage to bolt, but instead, she slouched. "I can't do this. I can't even run down a simple road."

Give up. She couldn't tell if the words came from her head or the wind.

"Maybe I should," she murmured.

Her magic fluttered over the back of her hand. It fully wrapped around each finger and spread over her knuckles, branches stretching farther than her wrist now. The ends touched the start of her forearm, going over her blouse's sleeve, consuming it.

And then it stopped.

She eyed the magic. The process of it eating her had not hurt. The after-effect, however, did. For once, the cold night air prickled her. Tingles splattered over the magical spots, making her hand turn numb. She flexed and relaxed her fingers. Her breathing turned ragged. Sharp bursts shot through her knuckles and when the wind directly struck the magic, her whole hand seized with an unbearable sting.

Mina shoved her hand into her skirt's folds, keeping it wrapped up in the emerald fabric. The touch still hurt, but it wasn't as bad as the wind hitting it.

The bricks rubbed together. Mina knew they'd take the door further away and if she waited any longer, more pain would come. With a deep breath, she picked up her feet and carried herself into a slow run, joints begging her to stop already.

Mina increased her speed little by little, her hair bouncing on her shoulders as she rounded the corner. The bricks rotated, stealing the door from her. She pressed on anyway, turning to the next wall. Pressure enveloped her chest. Tremendous aches settled in her muscles. Her feet were going to turn into puddles of goo and her knees were going to snap harder than twigs. Hot stitches sewed themselves across her abdomen, making it difficult to breathe.

But she ignored her body's pleas to stop, knowing if she did, she wouldn't move again.

Her toes pushed off the ground. Electric hope shocked her each time she got a little closer to the door, made her a little faster with a little less pain. The orange light glowed with the signal of victory. Underneath, the golden knob wanted her to turn it.

She rounded another corner, barreling toward the door, sights locked on the knob. Her arm outstretched toward it, uninfected fingers spread. She neared the bulbous knob.

As the bricks ground together, Mina leapt. Her fingers latched onto the doorknob. She used her whole body to twist it, shoving open the door. She burst through the threshold, tumbling onto the mansion floor.

Her knees banged into the ground hard enough to make her magic rumble around her joints. The door slammed shut behind her. She flipped onto her backside, watching it. The bricks flipped outside. Nothing inside changed.

Mina imagined a frown on her face. What a nasty sort of trick that was.

Two coffin-shaped windows framed the door. When she was outside, they hadn't been there. But there they were, and they brought a clear view of the front lawn. Tiny drops of rain started to pelt their surface.

For a while, Mina sat. She waited until she had gained control of her breathing before she climbed to her feet. She blacked out as she straightened, nearly falling back down. When she turned around, she immediately froze.

The floor changed from solid black, becoming a mixture of black and white dots. They spread apart until the white took over and spread out into one giant void. An unlit chandelier hung in it, being the only object in the void and dangling off of nothing.

"I've made a mistake," Mina mumbled. She swayed, floundering in place. The back of her hand hit her forehead. The chandelier turned double. She almost slipped as she turned to the door, reaching for the knob.

Her hand hit a person. A man yelped.

"Late-night traveler," the man said. He rubbed the back of his neck. Overtop his brown skin, it was like a red light shone onto him, blushy. "Oh, you're simply a girl. Sorry, I don't usually shout as a way of greeting someone."

"Sometimes I do," she said, knowing her intended joke didn't sound like one.

But something amazing happened. Underneath the man's thick, black, spider leg-shaped mustache, his lips stretched into a charming smile. A smile that could only be caused by a joke.

Mina stiffened. He couldn't have been laughing at her words. No, he must've smiled over something else. Maybe her haggard appearance.

"You know, I didn't think you'd make it inside," he said. "I've seen some people give up straight away. You wouldn't have stopped, though. I tried helping you by holding the door in place. Didn't work so well."

"What? Why didn't you open it?" she asked, eyeing his mustache. The right side hung lower than the left, more noticeably when he spoke. She wanted to grab both ends and straighten it out.

He shrugged. "I couldn't figure out how to do it."

A throttled sound tried to break free from the back of Mina's throat. "That isn't right. Everyone can open a door."

His legs crossed one over the other, carrying him to the door. "I can open a door. I mean, I can't open this door."

He grabbed the knob. It spun as it should. All of the clicks clicked in the right spots. He jiggled it, slamming his body into the door. Two tries, however, proved it wouldn't open.

"See?" He threw up his hands. "I can't get it."

The bricks shifted outside. Mina approached the door. "Here, why don't I help you?"

"Flub!" He jumped from the door. "Let us not. One day I can get it all on my own. As of right now, you have to meet the family because you have a mission."

"Mission," she repeated. "You know why I'm here?"

"Calin is my name, by the way." He bowed, taking the bowler hat off his head and extending his other hand.

"Mina." She took his hand and shook it.

"You're searching for the little red heart piece, aren't you?"

"If that's a piece of a bigger heart, then yes. Yes, I am."

"I knew it. You're like everyone else who walks through here." He dropped her hand and plopped his hat back onto his head. "So what is it that you wanted from the Bl—" He gagged on the word. Again, he tried to speak, but he got as far as a "Bl—" when his tongue stopped working. "I hate when I try to say it."

"You mean, the Blood—" Mina attempted to finish for him.

He snapped his fingers. "Yes, that one, and no, don't speak his name out loud. He's a distraction you don't want."

"He did mention something like that," Mina said. "But you were trying to say it—or you couldn't, or you were compelled not to." She tilted her head slightly to the side. "What exactly happens when—"

Calin straightened his spine. "What brought you here?"

Her head spun. "I need a heart. Anyway, about the—"

"Oh, you must be a ghostie then," Calin said. He hummed and rubbed his chin. "Those used to frighten me a lot as a child."

"I'm not a ghostie. I'm a wish."

"A wish? I've never seen a wish pass through these parts before. Usually, all the people going to the Bl—*get help* are just, well, regular people."

Wishing she could smile fully, Mina tried her best with the tiny movement she had. "And that's what I'm trying to be. A regular person. I need to give a heart to receive a heart."

"A little wish shouldn't have spoken to—" Calin grunted. "I warn you, that I—" He grunted again. "Things aren't—" He grunted *again.*

Mina's smile died. With it, her vision dipped black for a few seconds. "Please, don't fret. I have to find the heart quickly."

"Don't be so quick," he said. "It could be dangerous."

"I have to be." She lifted her hand. "If I have a heart, I save myself. If I save myself, I can be with Davian."

Calin frowned, his eyes soft. "I feel bad mistaking you for a ghostie now. You feel sad."

"It's all right. I know I'm unpleasant enough to look like a ghostie."

His eyes widened. "I never suggested that."

"Fine. Not unpleasant. I'm terrifying to look at."

Rosiness speckled his cheeks. "I don't think that either. Look, I'll help you find the heart piece. If it's your only chance to live, I'll help you."

"You would do that?" She tried to sound grateful. Her voice cracked. "Thank you." She faltered. "But you should only help if you want to. This is my duty after all. I should be able to do it on my own."

Calin waved away the notion. "People need help all the time. Except for myself, however. I haven't needed help since I was a baby."

Mina perked up. "Really?"

"*Really,* really." He flicked his head to the left. "The Herre family is over there. I think one of them had a red heart piece you might be interested in."

Mina looked. The room shifted.

Vines overtook the newly formed living space. They hung from the ceiling, cradling the floor and wrapping around table legs. Six people were in the room, all dressed finely in black—three younger people on a sofa, all hiding their faces behind their hands; a middle-aged man and woman, the man pacing the room and the woman swinging on a pair of hanging vines; and an old man sitting on top of the table, feet flat on the nearby chair. An open book sat on his lap. He puffed on a pipe as he flipped the pages.

Huge windows were on every single wall and small slices were on the ceiling, narrow beams of light filtered in from above. Clouds had long since covered the stars. Rain splattered against the windows, blurring the piece of the moon into a blue ripple on the dark gray sky.

"How should I introduce myself?" Mina asked.

Calin shrugged. "Hard to remember if I've ever met them before. We'll just have to see." He strolled into the living space.

PUPPETS OF THE FAMILY

*P*ain sliced up Mina's stomach, going past her chest and to her left wrist. Her magic wobbled and sloshed, crawling to her elbow, the airflow stoking it with electrical shocks.

She took one step and knew she would've fainted if she could. The running, the travel, it all turned her into a liquid mess struggling to keep upright. Tension ran thick through her muscles, tangy along her calves, and branding stitches in her stomach.

"Mina," Calin called. "Are you stuck?"

Flaring silver stars burst across her vision as she lifted her gaze. Calin split into a million copies of himself. All the eyes, glowing gray, stared at her. Millions of fingers twirling the end of his uneven mustache on his perplexed face.

She clenched her left hand. Tight strings pulled from within, plucked by her movement. She forced a step toward him. Tinges of electricity creaked in her joints. Her body craved rest. Even if it was for a minute.

"I'm fine," she said. The ache on her arm helped the words come out. Helped her stand. Despite it, however, she blacked out for a moment. When she came to, Calin moved beside her. He arched a brow, but otherwise didn't seem to notice the depths of her struggle.

"Positive?" he asked.

She nodded. A mistake. Moving her head almost sent her to the ground.

"I don't run much," she said.

"Ah." His brow lowered. "Me neither. A small pace above walking, and I have to heave on the floor."

"I don't believe that. That sounds too funny for a person."

"Believe it," he told her. "A lot of people dislike running. Some even faint. Me, if I fainted, that means a whole crowd, a scene, people climbing to help me. I'd never get over the embarrassment, so I never run."

"How did you get into the house then?" she asked.

He shrugged. "Pure luck."

"Luck." It sounded strange. "What brought you into all of this? I mean, you must've needed something, or why else would you be here?"

"Ironically, I'm just a person down on his luck," he said. "I never got to be a king, or a lord, or a knight, or anything. What I needed were riches for better clothes. Maybe a mustache comb."

"But you said you don't need help."

"Uh, well, I didn't end up getting much help." He smiled. "I'm stuck here."

"Why are you stuck?"

He cleared his throat. "Because I'm a failure. I wanted riches after I failed to be a big, rich person doing whatever it is that makes people rich. When I made my deal, to find a heart for riches, I spilled a bit of blood and was sent into the mirrors. As you can guess, I only got lost."

Lost. The idea congealed Mina's magic. Inside of her, the frozen lumps floated uncomfortably around. If she got lost, her life would be over.

"You had no limited time?" she questioned. "The Bloo—I mean, he gave no, say, before the stroke of midnight you must find the shards or anything like that?"

Calin stroked his chin, humming. "I don't recall. Supposing I did have a time limit, it would've been broken by now. I would've been collected and drained of all the little magic in me."

Seemed a little unfair that the Blood King gave Calin no limits as to when he could get the heart pieces. Then again, Calin wasn't in a life or death situation. If Mina had come, a normal girl who wasn't dying, then getting the heart pieces wouldn't have been so urgent. Or, well, they would've been, just in a different way.

"Let's not waste more time on me," Calin said, nudging her shoulder gently. He circled his gaze around the room. "Come and meet the family."

The vines twisted and groaned as Mina and Calin ventured deeper into the sitting room. Cracks ran over the green skins of each vine. A single tug would rip them right in half. The ones close to the windows crawled up the glass, tapping the glass as if begging for freedom.

Mina accidentally stepped on one. The vine squealed. A green puff of air blew out of it. She inhaled deeply, trying to discover if it had a smell strong enough for her to find. Flashes of mold dangling from the trees in a swamp ran through her mind. She'd seen the picture in a book once. The pungent smell in the picture had been described underneath. If such a smell could break through to her, she knew she'd adore it, so she inhaled a little deeper.

Calin plugged his nose. When he noticed what she was doing, terror struck him. "Don't breathe in this awful smell. "

"I can't smell anything," she said.

He twitched, narrowing his eyes at her, seemingly unsure of whether to let go of his terror or not. A moment later, however, he did let it go. "Be happy you can't smell it. This place reeks. Badly."

By the green tint over his face, Mina believed him. "Maybe the smell will get better. There could be a rose somewhere. I've heard they smell good."

"They do," he told her. "But you won't find any here, not alive. They'd be dead like Grandmother."

"Dead like Grandmother? What do you mean?" Mina asked, trying to inject horror into her tone. The sound sat all wrong.

"I mean the truth." He gestured to the man on the table. "Grandfather is a recent widower who doesn't care that he's a recent widower. Mourning someone you never loved is a waste of time, as he thinks."

"A waste of time? But she was his family."

Calin shifted between his feet. "What good is a family if you'll all be forgotten one day?"

Mina's shoulders fell. "Because it's nice to have it at the moment?" Though she wasn't sure. She'd never had a proper family before. The Wishmaker was the closest thing to her father, and Davian, well, she loved him like a husband, though he never did marry her. By becoming human, she could change that.

"Perhaps." Calin clasped his hands behind his back. "But..."

"You'll still be forgotten," she finished for him, turning toward the living space. The light from the moon sharpened with the flash of lightning.

"Take a moment and watch the play of this family," Calin said, becoming upbeat. "I've always loved plays. They pull you to new places."

Mina swallowed. Calin told her he couldn't remember meeting the family before. Now he contradicted that.

She opened her mouth.

Near the table, the middle-aged man paused his pacing and spoke before she had the chance for a syllable. "I, the Father, say that a dinner is in order." He spoke as though he were reading off a script.

Sitting across from him in the room, on the sofa, the three younger people perched shoulder to shoulder, shortest to tallest, hands falling from their faces. The boy in the middle lightly elbowed the tallest.

"For Grandmother?" the tallest boy piped up, shimmering with hope.

Mina touched her bottom lip. The tallest boy was different from everyone. His real face hid behind a blurry, blank mask. One matching his light skin tone, hazing his features underneath, a smeared, moving painting.

"The companion," she whispered.

The Blood King had been correct. She'd know the companion when she saw them. Except, she didn't think it was going to be as easy as it was. With his claim that others failed the task of getting the heart, Mina braced herself for challenge. For something to go terribly wrong. Things couldn't just be so easy.

Grandfather closed his book, startling the tallest boy. "Definitely not for her, Oldest Son."

"Indeed." Father clapped his hands together. "Grandmother has been dead for a day, and things have been nicer here. A dinner for her would be a waste, but a dinner for us in celebration of our newfound happiness would be beneficial."

"I agree," the woman hanging on the vines said. She pulled up on them. "Dinner for us is a wonderful idea. Although, how could I prepare anything grandiose? My fingers are dead."

"M-Mother, I would help," the tallest boy said. "As Oldest Son, y-you could teach me the value of a good meal."

"You would get skin flakes in all the food," said the boy in the middle. "You fed me, Middle Son, once. It tasted awful."

The shortest boy glared at the two. "Yes, Oldest Son, you're terrible at doing things. I, Youngest Son, handle my life much better than you."

Oldest Son grimaced. "It's because you whine so much."

"But I can whip a whistle and catch a bird all by myself."

Mother placed her feet on the floor. "It is admirable to accomplish everything on your own. Cowards are the needy, and the needy are the cowards."

"The strong," Father said, "make the indents on the world. You don't want to be like Grandmother, a helpless little beast."

"This is all awful," Mina whispered to Calin.

He shrugged. "They don't see it as awful."

"It is, though. You agree?"

His mouth twitched under his mustache. "I believe I've seen this play too many times to feel much."

Mina zoned in on him, eyelids twitching ever so gently. Pallor washed over him, shone by a sudden abundance of sweat. He gazed longingly, yet sadly, at the Herre family.

"You are right," Oldest Son said.

Mina turned to the boy. Something burned from inside him. An emotion. An array of them. Pride. Confidence. A sliver of anxiety. His blurry face pointed toward the ground right in front of his toes.

"Independence is our greatest strength," he continued evenly. "It is much more admirable to reach high status without another hand, such as those who came before me. I will become a great man one day as you all wish me to be. Perhaps a man of business. A lord. A prince. A king. I promise."

Mina stared long and hard at the boy, trying to imagine him in the same room as the Blood King. How did they speak to each other? What did they find in common? Both seemed dour about life yet battled for greatness in it. Stuff like that could not have made for great conversation, over and over and over. Like Davian talking about Lumina, over and over and over. Those were awful conversations.

She shook herself out. A pulse beat up her left arm, stopping at her elbow. She neglected to look.

"But nothing happens ever," Calin said.

"Are you—"

Mina cut herself off, gasping.

Calin's skin had turned green, decaying with wrinkles and moss. Drool hung out of his purple lips. His hat sunk into his head, welded to his flesh. In his eyes, he wasn't the same man, his gray irises had gone red and monstrous.

"Nothing happens ever," Calin—no, the creature said. "Give up."

Mina froze, her mouth hanging open.

"Give up," the creature urged. "Give up."

She pressed her lips together.

"Give up. It's easy."

It would have been easy to give up. One decision and she'd be back in Virvin, watching her magic eat her alive. Maybe Davian would come around and feel bad for her in the end, but the damage was done.

She needed to become human for him. To rid herself of her flaws for his love to return. But that was all easy to think about. So far she'd only been lucky. Lucky Davian told her the path to the Wishmaker. Lucky the Blood King and her had a common feature. Lucky that she found Calin. She'd been a leaf on the water, guided to all the right places. What would happen when her luck ran out?

"Give up."

She could. The Blood King could use her magic. It'd be better spent in his hands than in hers. And Davian would continue his happily ever after.

"Give up."

Davian's continued happily ever after. He found Lumina. He had a real girl. What use would another real girl be to him?

But he'd love me again, Mina told herself. *He needs me to be human.*

The spinning bodies of Davian and Lumina floated down from the vines, ghostly. They danced together, not having stopped since the party, where he was his happiest.

Watching them dance, Mina knew he'd made his choice before she existed. She existed out of his love for Lumina. Lumina, who was and would always be the center of his heart.

But Mina had loved him more. Lived with him longer. If she were human...

He would reject you still.

"Give up."

He and Lumina still shared more life together.

"I," she said, hesitating. "I think I should—"

A hand gripped her shoulder, shaking her.

"Mina, Mina," Calin said, voice back to normal. The green had melted off of his skin. "Is that you?"

She put her hand on his. "I should be asking if it's you."

"Me?" His chest rose and fell. "You just turned into a little monster. You cracked all over, and I saw an old woman pop out of you. You said I'm faux."

"Well," she gave him a little huff, "you said I should give up."

"I did not," he huffed. "Why would I say that? I'm trying to help you."

"Because..." There was no reason. "You didn't. It was the monster *you* turned into."

He put a palm against his forehead. "I can't remember."

She folded her arms over her chest. "You can't remember?"

"I can't remember if this has happened before. I feel like it did. With the others. Whatever the case is, I feel it is of little importance."

Pity sprouted in Mina. Calin's glossy eyes stopped her from poking him further. That, and the heavy pulse of magic beating on her arm, trying to spread further.

The Herre family had become a tableau. Their faces struck the same wave of horror as the statues sitting at the Blood King's castle.

"He has the heart piece," she said, pointing at Oldest Son. "How do we get it from him?"

"Steal," Calin said quickly.

"That's not an idea I like." Mina lowered her arm. "Is there anything better?"

Calin raised his brows. "You came to me for help, so let me take the lead."

Mina stared at him.

He broke out into a smile. "I'm only making a joke. We're not going to steal."

"Oh, thank goodness," she said, relaxing.

"My real idea isn't terrible. We just sit and have dinner with them, become their friends, and eventually Oldest Son will give us the heart piece as a token of our friendship."

"How long will that take?"

Calin shrugged. "I don't know. You have to trust me. I can get the job done."

"I'm sure you can, but look." She held up her arm. Strands of violet-black now crawled onto her bicep. "Will I have time to wait for dinner *and* find three more heart pieces?"

He shrugged. "Then we steal."

"That's not funny."

"It is either the joke plan or the serious plan," Calin said. "Don't worry about either one. I am perfectly capable of getting everything in order."

The corners of Mina's lips burned as they tried pulling into a frown. "You don't understand. I can't afford to waste too much time. What if we simply asked Oldest Son for the piece? He seems kind enough to understand."

Calin laughed. "That's not how that works. Relax and trust my judgment. You're panicking, Mina. The magic won't destroy you here. Believe that."

"I want to," she said. "I'm only worried about my time."

"I understand. Things won't be as bad as you think they will be, all right? If dinner seems too slow, I'll speed it up."

"All right." Though Mina couldn't stop chewing her lip and begging for the heart piece to drop into her hand.

Stepping forward, Calin cleared his throat. The Herre family broke free from their frozen states. They whipped their faces toward Calin, who took his hat off, clasping it in front of him. He smoothly fell into place as if he were about to make a grand speech.

"My friend and I would like to join you for dinner." He glanced back at Mina. "We will sit and enjoy your company for a bit and soon be your greatest friends."

"Guests," Mother said. "I wasn't expecting any. Dinner will take longer to make now."

Mina's stomach dropped. *Longer.* She tugged his arm. "Calin."

"That's fine," he said to Mother.

She tugged harder. "Calin, no."

He chuckled, patting her good hand on his sleeve. "It's all right."

Those three words were so easily said. She wanted to trust them, to believe it all, but her magic bit her. Ate her. If things took too long...she didn't want to think about that anymore. About never seeing Davian again.

Mother nodded. "I'll have to clean a few extra plates, and find extra chairs, and—"

Mina stepped in front of Calin. "A dinner would be lovely, but that's not why I'm here. I have a simple matter of business. It could be quickly done."

The three sons jumped off the couch, pushing up on their toes and leaning forward.

"Why are you here?" they asked in unison.

Young Son blistered with joy; Middle Son held an air of charm; Oldest Son devoured her with arrogant scrutiny despite his obscured face.

"I need to speak to you," she said to Oldest Son.

"And it can be spoken about at dinner," Calin declared, giving Mina a sharp look. "We're all going to become closely acquainted."

Father put his hands on his hips. "I quite enjoy making new acquaintances. It'll be an honor."

Grandfather raised his pipe. "I agree."

"No, no," Mina said.

"Mina, it won't take that long," Calin told her.

She ignored him. "Oldest Son, I need a piece of a heart from you."

Oldest Son perked up. "What piece of a heart?"

"From the—"

Calin jumped toward her. "Don't!"

"—Blood King," she finished.

The family's flesh expanded. They puffed up, throwing panicked yet excited glances at each other. Around them, the vines wiggled, screaming in various high-pitched tones.

"Blood King?" Father asked, eyeballs pushing out of their sockets.

Grandfather clutched his chest. "Blood King."

"Blood King," Mother whispered.

Youngest Son grew teary-eyed. "Blood King."

Middle Son choked. "Blood King?"

And Oldest Son hunched. The two smeared darker spots where his eyes should've been rolled around as if in search of a danger lurking in the shadows.

"Blood King."

Lightning smashed through the windows. The living space lit up into a mix of smoke and shattered glass.

Calin took Mina's shoulders, pulling her out of the way. "Are you all right?"

She nodded.

"Listen, things will be fine," he assured her. "I'll take care of everything. I mean, how warped can his head get?"

Mina choked on her own breath. The Blood King's old words floated to her mind. *You'll hate me.*

EVERLASTING DINNER

*B*oots crunched over glass. Smoke scurried from the bloody figure emerging into the room.

"Ah," the Blood King said, "I hear there's dinner."

The Herre family members glanced at each other, scrunching up their faces, except for Oldest Son—he hung his head.

Father scratched his scalp. He sought out Grandfather with panicked eyes but got nothing in return. Grandfather became too occupied emptying out his pipe. Father cleared his throat. "I..." He threw up his hands. "This isn't expected."

Mother jumped off the vines, joining Father at his side. "Yes," she said, shaky. "We don't have anything prepared. Neither to say nor to eat."

The Blood King grinned. "Allow me to help set up."

Mina opened her mouth, stepping toward him. Calin grabbed her wrist, pulling her back. He positioned himself in front of her and stuck out his chest.

"You haven't been invited," he said to the Blood King, lines of angry red crossing his face.

"You brought me up, so I have been. You would turn me away knowing so?" the Blood King asked, playfully pouting.

"Yes."

"But I could be hungry, too." He patted his stomach. "It'd be rude to rescind my invite."

"Go fill yourself with blood then," Calin spat, nostrils flared. "You're still not allowed here."

Yawning, the Blood King flicked his hand. Calin flinched. His lips stuck together, wiggling as he tried opening them. They wouldn't budge. His fingers flung to his mouth, eyes crossing, and he attempted to pry them apart. He floundered and hummed, unsuccessful.

"That's enough of that," the Blood King said. His gaze landed on Mina. In an instant, he softened, though there was a glint of mischief in his eyes. It made her hands clasp together, unsure of what to do. "Thank *you*, Mina, for inviting me here. No one is usually so eager to see me so soon."

Stinging sliced Mina's left knuckles while she rubbed her hands together, deep enough for her to almost double over. Her hands separated in an instant, the pain radiating as she stuck her left arm down at her side, avoiding touching it on anything, not even her clothes.

"Now that you're here," Mina said, "maybe you could help."

The Blood King cocked his head to the side. "How?"

She bit her lip. "Does it need explaining?"

He blinked. Then he glanced at Calin. "Did she tell you this plan?"

Calin glared. He placed his hands on his hips, tapping his foot.

The Blood King chuckled. "I forgot already, you can't speak. All the better." He rubbed his chin. "Now, let's see, help, help. Well, the Herre family needs a little help with their dinner. I wonder what I can do about that. Ah, I know."

He stuck up a finger.

Muffled noises broke against the sealed wall of Calin's mouth. He whirled toward each Herre, getting louder with each person he tried snaring the attention of. The noise changed into horrified, muffled, gurgles as the vines near him came to life, snaking around his legs and tugging him to the ground.

"Calin," Mina said, rushing to his side.

Vines moved all around the room. They wrapped around the waists and limbs of the bewildered Herre family members, picking them off the ground and bouncing them into the air. Indistinguishable shouts came from behind their now sealed mouths.

"No, stop," Mina said, turning to the Blood King. "Someone may get hurt."

"Not so hurt," he responded, eyes glittering. "Just fun."

A puff of air blew out of her. She was the only one not trapped. If she wanted, she could've ran away. The Blood King was too happy playing with the vines to likely notice. He lifted his hands up and down as though he were a puppet master, and in a strange way, she guessed he was.

Cracks deepened on the vine's surfaces. Green mist puffed from inside, glowing into the air. He kept them in his invisible grasp, bouncing his hand up and down, up and down. Each movement affected his newfound toys.

Mina glanced at her left arm. "Broken. The vines are breaking"

"They'll regrow," the Blood King murmured. His lips stretched into a strained smile. "They always do."

Air pressed around Mina, lifting her off the floor. She felt around herself, looking for a vine, but there was none.

A sharp wind twisted around and grabbed her. With a tug, it pulled off her and she spun in a rapid circle, the living space whizzing by in one giant blur filled with splatters of white and silver dots. She lowered as she spun back to her original position. A chair slid from far away, practically nowhere, loud across the floor. It met her backside as she came back to the ground.

The dots cleared. The blur left. Mina awoke at a long dinner table, her stomach pressing into the edge from how close she sat. She tried scooting the chair back, but the legs were stuck in place. Everybody sat tight against the table, too, the living space replaced by a dining hall full of rebuilt windows and vines.

At Mina's back was the void of white with black dots. The chandelier was the only light source and it only gave off a dim glow.

Youngest Son grinned from the other side of the table. "This is the best feast of feasts I've ever seen," he said, handing a bowl of stemmed vegetables to the right.

Middle Son took the bowl from him. "Perfect way to enjoy our family."

At the head of the table, Grandfather nodded. "It is all as it should be. Me, Father, Mother, Oldest Son, Middle Son, and lastly, dear Youngest Son."

"Don't forget," Oldest Son said. He sat on the other side of Middle Son, peering toward Mina and Calin. "Our brilliant friends."

"Always agree," said the Blood King, startling Mina. He sat at the opposite head, to her right.

Mina watched a spark of intensity blaze and expand within his amber eyes. He sifted through the faces, growing more calculated yet exuberant with each person he observed. But when his gaze landed upon Mina, the pebbles of callousness rolled off him.

Calin tapped her shoulder, trying to hand her a bowl of mashed potatoes. She took it. The bowl burned her left hand, cutting straight through the magic. She bit back her pain, mind blanking. So that was what fire felt like. Quickly, she plopped a scoop of potatoes on her plate, handing the bowl off to the Blood King. His fingers grazed hers, an electric feather on her magic, a missing sensation on her skin.

Another tap came from Calin. He slid a plate of sliced turkey into her hands. She placed a slab of the meat next to her potatoes. Hardly a second passed after it hit her plate before Calin nudged her with another bowl. Then another bowl. And another bowl. And another bowl.

She scooped more food onto her plate, trying not to spill any on the pristine tablecloth. Her efforts proved vain. Crumbs and stains were inevitable all around the table while everyone overfilled their plates. The serving dishes should've emptied at this point, but no, they didn't. There was no end. Each plate or bowl that came Mina's way looked as full as it was the last time it circled to her corner.

"Won't this stop?" she wondered.

"I don't know," Calin said. His face lit up. "I can speak!" He shot the Blood King a death stare. "You have a lot of nerve silencing me."

The Blood King smirked. "It was well enjoyed."

Calin huffed. "Muck, muck, you turn everything into muck."

The Blood King's hand fell over Mina's as she passed him a plate. Her face flung toward him. Although she imagined his hand as cold upon normal skin, she couldn't help but think it might have actually been warm from the way he sat, softly content.

He didn't take the plate. Instead holding his hand in place over hers.

The bustle around the table stopped. The Herre family froze, blurry veils covering their faces, matching Oldest Son's.

"No one seems to be enjoying this little dinner," the Blood King said. As disappointing as the statement should've been to him, he didn't truly sound disappointed at all. He passed the observation off too casually.

Calin's upper lip curled in disgust. His arm sat rigid, halfway through handing Mina the next bowl—brussels sprouts glazed in honey. His body angled toward her. Only his mouth moved, his eyes turning red the longer they stayed open.

"It is because you're cruel," Calin snarled. "Your company is not enjoyed by anyone."

Mina's lips twitched down for a split second. "Calin, that's mean."

He snorted. "He already knows it."

The Blood King licked his lips. "Yes, Mina, do not pity me. My skills at handling people are below what they used to be. Betrayal can impact that. At least I try harder at being cordial than some others."

"Cordial people," Calin said, "would let us go."

Mina tapped her chin. "Have you two spoken much before? I mean, seeing as Calin's been in here for a while, you seem well acquainted."

"No," Calin said. "Never."

At the same time, the Blood King said, "Not at all, though it is fun to watch him struggle in here. The way out is very near."

They gave each other stony, hateful glares, Calin's out of the corner of his eye, and the Blood King's head on. At least they mutually agreed on something.

Around the table, each Herre family member remained frozen. Oldest Son slanted toward Mina.

"Oldest Son is one of your old companions," she said to the Blood King. She couldn't imagine it. This boy on the cusp of becoming an adult had stolen a heart. Now he was trapped in a play of mourning. An endless dinner.

"Used to be. I don't keep betrayers as companions. I always advise against friendship." The Blood King gestured to Calin. "This one may knock you aside."

Betrayer. Mina's mind ticked. Suddenly, she wondered what Oldest Son's side of the story was. What he'd say about what he'd done. As much as she wanted to despise him for helping steal a heart, something about the situation didn't feel right. Too much melancholy broke through the Blood King's constant mask of bitterness. Perhaps there was a way to repair the heart and the old friendships.

No, Mina told herself. *Just focus on getting your heart. Your time is too valuable to waste on others.*

Still, she itched to help.

Calin grunted, struggling against his frozen state. "Don't you dare tell me who I am or what I'd do. I'm more helpful to everyone who comes through here than you."

A smirk danced on the Blood King's lips. "And once you help them through one mirror, you never follow them through another."

Mina perked up. "Calin's found the heart pieces before?" She peered at him. "You made it sound like you hadn't." Then again, he only said he got lost, not that he didn't find any heart pieces at all. That did beg the question then: if he had found a heart piece before, why wasn't it with him? Did he give it to someone else passing through the mirror? If so, what happened to them? To the piece?

An even bigger question formed over Mina's head: had *anyone* given the Blood King any piece of his heart before?

She swallowed. He didn't have a single piece with him.

Sinking into her chair, Mina clenched her jaw, wondering if she'd make it out of the first mirror at all.

Calin scratched his head, right under the brim of his hat. "It's all a little hazy. I only know that I don't ever make it past this table. Honestly, I know I don't."

"It's true." The Blood King tapped her knuckles. "Don't rely on him too much to help you on your journey. He's forgetful."

"I'm dependable," he declared. "I can help anyone get the heart pieces. That is, if I don't have sneaky interference."

The Blood King ignored the comment and turned sunny. "Isn't dinner so much fun?"

Mina grabbed the brussels sprouts from Calin. She couldn't overcome the hands of death creeping toward her as her magic made a home over her skin.

The Blood King went to take the brussels sprouts from her but his fingers curled into his palm when she set the dish beside her overflowing plate.

"This dinner is not fun," she said. The Blood King frowned. "While you two argue, I still have a mission to accomplish. Now, I would like to get up from this table—" She tried pushing away. The chair still didn't move. "And I would like to get going." She wiggled, trying to squeeze downward. The chair moved on its own, shoving her closer into the table's edge. "Quickly. Oldest Son has what I need." She tried squeezing through the narrow space anyway. One more push down. One more push and she'd pop out of her chair and underneath the table.

"Does he now?" The Blood King hummed, folding his hands together. "Or is it a distant part of him that holds it?"

She ground her teeth together, pausing her escape. "That is why I must speak with him."

"He's been silent."

"So has everyone else."

The Blood King lit up. "I could change that."

Calin groaned.

Voices erupted around the table, so loud that it swung the chandelier back and forth. All but Oldest Son's face shone back into clarity, bowls and plates resuming their path of going hand to hand. Forks and spoons clanked and screeched louder against the glass dishes. Movements quickened. Mina handed off the same dishes more times than she could count.

"This is ridiculous," Calin said, handing her another. "My arms burn."

Mina agreed. The magic on her arm flared. More streaks of violet lit up on the black. They flashed, stinging deep into her arm.

Calin's eyes widened as he peered around, swallowing as he looked behind at the white void. He set down his next bowl. "Mina, we need to try to get out of here."

On his left, Mother kept handing him more bowls. He stacked them up on the table, receiving violent glares from her, Father, and Grandfather.

Mina grasped the arms of her chair, using her body to thrust back and forth. The legs stayed stiffly in place. Her vision blacked out at the emptying of her energy.

Calin tried escaping, too, but didn't get any farther. He sunk in his seat. His chair scraped the floor, squeezing him tighter against the table. Groaning, his face turned purple.

"Adorable," the Blood King said, placing his cheek in his palm.

Grumbling, Calin sat back up. "Mina, you have to get through."

If she tried harder, she could sneak through the gap. She'd almost squeezed out already. One more push. She just needed that one last push.

"Hey, son," Father snapped at Calin. "Hand out the dishes."

"Yes," Youngest Son cried across the table. "I'm hungry."

Deafening chatter raged on, much like it had during Davian's birthday celebration. Mina's magic heated behind her cheeks upon recalling the party.

Voices, old and new, bounced through her head. Mina pressed her back against the chair, straightening. She stared into a mess of cloudy blackness. Her hands sat in her lap, the glowing violet the only thing cutting through her murky vision.

Calin tapped her. "Mina, you have to get out of here."

"Pass the food," Middle Son urged.

"Be a good man and do it," Grandfather said.

Sickness waved through Mina. There was too much happening. Inside and outside. She couldn't move.

"What have you done?" Calin growled, his words thrown over her head to the Blood King. "Why must you be awful? This poor girl is dying. Have a heart."

"It doesn't work," the Blood King replied, distantly.

"She can help if you let her out!"

The Herres shouted louder and louder, their fists banging the tabletop. It shook the plates, knocked over the forks.

"It is time we go forever," Calin said. "This has gone on for long enough."

The Blood King snapped. "Silence."

Noise dropped out of Mina's ears. The back of her head rested against the chair. She breathed in. An invisible soothing cloth wiped the pain from her. With each breath, she regathered her vision. Her strength. Her senses, what little there were.

Everyone turned back into statues, Calin included. Blurriness entered every face.

"They'll return to normal shortly," the Blood King said. He leaned his face into his palm, blankly staring at the table with a little frown. "They all will."

He snapped his fingers. The blank faces remained, but everyone's arms moved again. The bowls and plates slipped from hand to hand, more food piling on the covered plates.

Only this time, Calin didn't hand Mina a dish. He reached across the table, avoiding her and the Blood King, passing the food to Youngest Son, who proceeded to keep the pattern going.

"Please," Mina begged the Blood King. "This has to stop."

He didn't look up. "But this is fun," he told her, devoid of any humor. "You could just leave."

The Herre family set down the dishes and began gorging on their food. Even Calin stuffed himself too full to chew.

"Stop," Mina told him. "You'll choke."

He grunted.

"Go on, Mina," the Blood King said. Her chair backed an inch away from the table. "Leave."

The chewing and slurping noises trapped Mina in a case of disgust. She wished more than ever she could travel back in time and tell herself to just listen to Calin. To trust his judgment.

The magic spread over her elbow, climbing up half of her bicep. She hissed at the exposure of pain.

"I can't let them stay here this way," she said. "It's cruel. Please, let them stop first and then I'll go."

"I've been thinking." The Blood King shifted. "A heart is no use to a decrepit creature like me. Maybe this is a waste of time."

Panic flashed through Mina. "You can't change your mind. What you're feeling inside must be terrible, but once you have your heart, you can get better."

"Nothing can stay fixed forever," he said.

Peering at him, she couldn't help but wonder about his pessimism. If he gave her a heart, after she gave his, things would all be fine after. There couldn't be more he was hoping to gain, was there?

His face rose. "Simple solutions aren't always the trick. Like a wish."

Her teeth clamped together. She stared at the Blood King, magic turning thick inside. The expression on his face, gloriously conceited, itched her right hand. It wanted to slap him. Slap him out of changing his mind. Out of being a nuisance.

But the feeling faded as she stared at him, noticing that the coldness he tried baking onto himself wasn't true. Beneath it, hints of pity lingered. Blue spots colored the pale parts of his skin. He referred to his old friends as betrayers and now he was alone. Maybe he didn't think he was good enough to have his heart back. Mina could understand his wavering mind. The vacillating on what was deserved. What was possible.

"What is your name?" she asked softly.

The question cushioned the hard edge of his face. "What's the need to know?"

"I want to use it when I scold you on how awful you are," she said.

He cracked a smile, snorting. "That alone makes me want to give it to you. Just to hear that."

"So what is it?"

The smile faded. "I can't... I don't know. I know you hate that answer, but it's true. I don't know." He sat upright, leaning toward her. "When you're not human, it's hard to cling to certain human traits, like names."

Magic lashed around her chest, warped with pity. Mina wanted to pull him closer and embrace him tightly. She wanted to be there when the glossiness in his eyes evaporated.

"There's so much I should say," he continued. "So much I shouldn't do, but it's so..." He flicked his temple and touched his chest. "Desolate."

"If you do recall your name, ever," she said, "you could tell me. If no one has said it in a long time, then I'd like to help you hear it. That is, if I make it out of here."

"I guarantee, my name can't be recalled." He sat back, studying her face. "I think you might be tricking me by saying you have no heart."

She curled her fingers. "I am not."

He held up a hand. "Please, no excitement. I know you aren't lying. I'm fumbling a jest."

"So why do any of this?" She gestured around the table. "Why prevent us from success? You said you aren't the same here, but you do feel the same."

He became sullen. "Not true—to you perhaps not, but I can't comprehend much thought."

She wasn't sure what to make of that. "You know, out of all people, Davian has been the most upfront person I've ever met. At least had the decency to tell me why he cast me aside."

"That man," the Blood King sneered. "You compare me to that fool, but remember, he has no magic. Not even as much as a lowly magician. He shouldn't hold your hand again. He doesn't have the right."

"He—"

"Mina," a familiar voice said. "Mina, I miss you."

"He's here," she said.

"He is," the Blood King said. "So long as you keep letting him back, he'll stay."

"I love him," she said, hollow.

"Even though he sentenced you to a gruesome fate." He chuckled. "It really is commendable of you to be so forgiving."

Mina broke the chair out of place, sliding it back. Her toes wiggled in her boots as she got up, hunting for the sound of her love.

"And what about them?" the Blood King asked, gesturing around the table.

Mina went to sit back down.

"Mina," Davian called out. "Where did you go?"

She stood back up.

"Be careful, dearest wish," the Blood King cooed. His words fell on deaf ears as Davian called out to her again.

Bit by bit, Mina turned toward Davian's voice. Worry washed away in a river of invisible tears. Nothing mattered beyond Davian, and when she saw his face, resolve came over her. He came for her. He loved her. She did everything for him.

He stood inside the opening of a corridor which wasn't there before. While he stood a little ways away, Mina knew it was him. She could just feel it. The loving cold struck her chest and she fell into a glorious trance once he beckoned her to him with his finger. All she wanted to do was follow him.

So she did.

TAKE THE HAND OF HOME

*V*ines whined under a majority of Mina's steps as the heels of her boots stepped on them, ripping their skin and releasing more tufts of green air.

"Sorry," she whispered to each victim. She tried her best to land on the clear spaces of the marble floor, but they were few and far between.

She made her way to the corridor where Davian stood. He darted deeper into the gloomy hall. Its iron walls arched overhead in a square coffin-like shape. Blue moonlight broke through the distorted holes on the left side, the twinkling shapes resembling diamonds stuck to the surface.

Davian's rich head of dark hair caught the light, a firefly guiding her from ahead. Billowing behind him was a pristine, navy cape. An elegant choice which turned him into a prince. It made Mina think of the Blood King, making her wonder if he ever wore something similar. Of course, his would've been covered in blood.

The way Davian clobbered down the hall was different from the Blood King's stride, who, despite favoring one foot over the other, moved gracefully. But while Davian walked messier, he spoke cleaner. His sturdy voice could run for days on end. The Blood King, he cracked and scratched his way through a sentence, his timbre a bit higher, stretching thin, but when he lowered his voice, it rumbled a thick intimidation Davian could never produce, finally finding strength for a moment.

The vines lessened their presence in the hall. A stab of guilt knocked the back of Mina's head and she looked back. She'd left Calin behind.

Oh, she wanted to rip off a fingernail—if it didn't mean exposing more magic. She should've stayed with Calin. She pictured his gray eyes narrowing at her being alone here, afraid, his lopsided mustache wiggling as his lips turned into a frown. "I could've helped you," his voice drifted. "I promised I would."

More and more, following Davian felt...surprisingly wrong.

"Mina," Davian said. She whipped toward him, his voice stoking the familiar loving cold in her chest. He stood ahead at the center of the hall. Silver ignited half of his face. His one lit green eye bore a darker shade than what seemed right. "Aren't you coming home with me?"

"Home," Mina repeated. "Virvin?"

"Of course. I miss you."

"But I have to become human for you."

He slowly blinked. "I made a mistake."

Lifting onto her toes, Mina angled his way. "You really want me home?"

"Forget all of this nonsense. You're enough for me. Always have been."

Mina pushed her clean hand into her hair, scrunching it up. "But you hurt me."

"I'd never do it again." He smiled, lifting a hand.

That was it. Mina's cure. She'd go to him, take his hand, and they'd return to Virvin, living happily forever.

She inched toward him.

Then she halted.

"I made a promise, though," she said. Her arm and feet lowered. "I have to find a heart first. It would be awful of me not to."

"You won't need a heart if you come with me."

She shook her head. "It isn't for me. It's for someone else. I have to help him."

Davian sneered. "Come with me now, or you'll never see me again."

The harshness of his tone would've made her flinch if possible. "Don't say that. Come with me instead. We can help these people together, and then go home."

Gray branches seeped onto his face from the edges, reaching over his forehead and cheekbones. "Why waste so much time on people you might never see again? You won't get anything from them."

She thought of Calin sitting at the dinner table. Calin, who'd been so prepared to help her. Calin, who she already discarded. He had a deal to fulfill, too. If they helped each other, they'd both get what they wanted.

Davian pushed his hand closer to her. "Mina, just come home. I want you back. Being with Lumina is not the same as being with you."

The magic in Mina halted its flow. The lancing pain in her arm ceased. She stared at the man who wished her into existence. The man who she once declared she'd love forever. He hid her. He lied to her. He betrayed her. None of that mattered, however. Not anymore. He spoke the words she'd longed to hear from him. That she was the better companion against Lumina. The superior being in his heart.

He wanted her. He wanted her back. Lumina would leave and they'd live in bliss.

"I want you," he said, tilting his chin down. Something dark entered his face.

"I..." Mina could hardly get the words out. "I want you, too."

"So come home with me."

Her feet carried her closer to him, her arm rising. A loving look carved on his face. It was the look she always wanted him to stare at her with. The one she'd seen him use on Lumina.

The palm of her hand hovered over his. She froze. The man she'd left behind hadn't wanted her. She remembered the party. His words. How he didn't notice her beside him.

Calin's lost nature and the Blood King's hollow chest both floated through her mind.

"I still want to fulfill my promise," she insisted.

"You won't have to work for humanity anymore if you come with me."

Her hand lowered an inch.

But being human. The idea made her too happy.

"There wouldn't be any risk to your existence," Davian went on.

Another inch.

But she could be human.

"You and I would go back to the way things were."

She stopped.

But she could be human for Davian.

"Mina?"

She wanted to return to him with blood in her veins, a heart in her chest, to ensure she'd never have to experience this pain again. She could be human so he'd love her properly and let her out into the world.

"I have to find a heart," she told him. "It will make everything better than it was."

"I don't want better," he snapped. "I want the past."

Her jaw shifted. "Davian, Davian, always so in love with the past. I'm not, though. I want us to be different. It'll surprise you when I'm human and you see how much I care."

The light faded from his face. "I don't like surprises."

Mina stepped back, pulling her hand away from him. His shoulders hunched forward, sweat covering his face. It sizzled against his skin until it turned to liquid. Slowly, his legs shrunk, melting into the ground. His body pooled into a growing puddle of gray, which would've hit her boots had she not stepped back.

Davian looked at her from under his brows. His green eyes sunk downward, darkening.

Terror flourished. Magic pulsed in and around Mina's left arm. The violet-black climbed a great distance up to her shoulder, consuming clothing and flesh.

Mina sucked a sharp breath through her teeth. She reached for Davian, his head melting into the ground. Bubbles popped up to the surface of the puddle. He let out an agonized shout as his chin melted, the sound choking out as his mouth disappeared. Hateful eyes kept their hold on her, even as they melted. Then, all that was left was the top of his head. It swirled in the liquid, hair shining, and sizzling into the gray, disappearing forever.

Falling to her knees, shame came over Mina. Davian was gone. Her chance to go home with him melted into a murky puddle. Her magic stung. It was all wrong. She'd rejected him. *Rejected* him, Davian of all people. The one person she circled her life around.

"What have I done?" she whispered to the puddle and tried to convince herself that she truly longed for him to come back.

FIRESIDE STORY

*"H*ello."

Buzzing rang through Mina's head. The gray liquid long since evaporated. She stared at the remaining steam.

"Dear."

She breathed deeply, trying to sort things out. Davian had been here. He'd offered to take her home. She'd turned him down to become human. But that was for him, she reminded herself. *Convinced* herself. Everything she did was for him.

Magic consumed Mina's entire left arm. It twinged with the air pushing on it. Sharpness snapped on every violet electrical burst atop the black.

She wondered if she should've just gone with Davian. If she should've just been his wish again. That could've repaired her.

It would've been easy. But another word popped up under the surface of that thought. *Dissatisfying.* Then some more. *Was he even here?*

She swallowed, gaze trailing the steam upward. *Not anymore.*

"Hello, dear."

"What?" Mina whipped her head to the side.

An old woman stood over her, wrinkled yet beautiful. Wisps of white hair framed her face, unable to join the rest in the twisted bun on the back of her head. Kindness exuded from her brown eyes.

"You're lost?"

Mina halted on answering immediately. She was and she wasn't. "Well," she said, taking a pause, "sort of."

"Let me tell you a story, then." The woman folded her hands together. "It'll brighten your mood."

"I'd like to, but I shouldn't. I have to get back." She glanced down the long hall, back toward where she came from. "Calin. I need to return to Calin."

"But you have to listen," the woman insisted. She gave a grim smile, a yellow line of teeth poking through her lips.

Mina climbed to her feet. "Perhaps I could another time? I'm in a rush."

"Listen to her." A rush of air blew from behind the woman, carrying her voice, mixed with Calin's, right into Mina's face.

She touched her lips. "Calin?"

The old woman's eyes changed. Gray swirled in the brown. Further inspection pointed out their similarly shaped chins, pointy. The wider distance between their eyes. The little curve on the bridges of their noses.

"Listen to me, Mina," the woman—Calin—the woman—Calin—the woman said. "I have everything under control. Trust me."

The last two words were all him.

"I don't get it," she said. "Calin, how are you an old woman?"

"My spirit is in the old woman," he explained.

"Then you have to get out."

The old woman folded inward, placing a hand on her chest—the movement likely fully in Calin's control. "She's very loud."

Mina grabbed the woman's shoulders. Her left hand blistered. "Calin, I don't know what to do."

"She's tormenting me, reminding me I failed to get the heart piece because I neglected her." He used the old woman's hands to cover her eyes. "I could've been rich if I'd not been so stubborn."

"Be stubborn again," Mina told him, "and get out of that body. I need your help—I can't do this alone."

"Alone."

The woman hung her head. A long groan fell out of her, a fighting mixture between hers and Calin's voice.

At the end of it, she won. She held up an elbow, fully in control of her body and mind. "Could you help me walk a little as I lead? My bones hurt."

The sad warmth on the woman's face made Mina take hold of her elbow, careful not to squeeze the fragile bones in her grasp. The woman pressed against her, balancing as she walked.

"Turn left, dear," the woman said. "It'll take us a few seconds for me to sit in my storytelling chair."

Mina hesitated, but ultimately helped her turn left. The way the woman clung to her arm, as though desperate for company—eyes glittering, mouth bursting at the seams to talk—made Mina want to stay and give the woman a bit of her limited time, for everyone was limited on such a thing. Some more than others, but the small moments of a simple conversation could make that time feel longer. Fuller. Happier.

Wind tore through the corridor. It whipped around Mina, a tornado pushing her hair into her eyes, blocking out the world. When it stopped, her hair fell, and she parted her lips at the world's change.

They stood inside a room with warm yellow walls and a black carpet with orange lines running across it, making overlaid squares. A fire blazed bright from a brick hearth. In front, the old woman sat in a rocking chair, gently pushing herself back and forth, a blue blanket draped over her lap.

Mina's hand was still settled on an elbow. Inside, she jolted. When she turned, however, and found Calin, hat and mustache intact, she relaxed.

He wobbled. "How unsettling."

"You're here," Mina said, so very relieved.

"Unnaturally so. I was sitting at the table, right? I felt a tap, right? And then I was whisked away, right?" He blew out a breath. "At least I found you again." He peered at the old woman. "Through her. We need her."

"She'll help?"

He nodded, turning to the rocking chair.

The woman gestured to the floor. "Sit and listen."

Calin went first, crossing his legs as he sat on the carpet, very childlike. Mina approached, eyes stuck on the fire. She put out a palm, unable to feel the heat on her actual skin, though her magic flared, twisting on her arm in an attempt to jump off and run away. It blazed deep below the surface.

"Can the warmth be good?" she asked.

"It can," Calin said. "This fire's more than warm. It's the sun dripping into the room, hugging away your pain."

Mina's palms retreated from the fire. If only she could've really understood what Calin was saying. "Are we going to find the heart piece soon?"

"We are. Trust me."

And she did this time. Her lips drew together as she awaited what came next.

He looked at the old woman. "Please, tell us your story."

Feet flat on the ground, the woman stopped rocking the chair. She smiled, taking in a breath. "I'll jump straight to say that a naive girl once fell deeply in love with a boy who already crafted the image of his perfect lover in his head. This imaginary woman, to him, was stronger than anyone he ever knew, never dependent upon others, and she would never cry.

"The girl knew this boy's strange demands, and since she was in love with him, she carved herself into the woman he wanted. She got him to fall in love with her since he saw her as the perfect girl from his dreams. They rushed to get married and started a family together. All the while, the girl kept up her facade, but over time it faded, and he saw it. She let herself slip, as she believed he loved her no matter what. But he declared she was everything he hated in a person and not at all who he wanted for a wife. He encouraged everyone in his family to hate her, as they all shared his views about what a person should be.

"She was then banished to being mostly a maid. It was a lonely, cold life. One that made her cry a lot, but soon a crack of light slipped into her dark hours, giving her strength. Her oldest grandson was the only kind person to her. He'd sneak away and stick to her side, helping her bake the goodies and weed the gardens. In return, she read him stories every night in this very room, that being the thing she looked forward to most each day. She captured those happy moments for as long as she could, knowing good things don't last forever.

"And she was right to know that, for the boy's family ridiculed him for helping his needy grandmother. They beat him out of loving and being like her, and one day, he stopped visiting her. While the abandonment hurt, she knew his act hurt him far less. So she lived on, clinging to the memories of their happy days, longing for one last chance to tell him one last story."

The woman fell silent for a moment, wiping the corner of her eye with her knuckle. Her feet rocked the chair again.

"My death was a celebration," she said. "Not for the life I had, but for the life they got rid of. Even my eldest grandson celebrated. I like to think he mourned me in secret, but as my spirit watched him grow, I knew he did worse than simply hate me—he forgot me completely. No one in the family remembers me. I should've left Grandfather when I realized he'd never like me. I should've known that someone who loves ideals can't love a real person."

Tears streaked down Grandmother's face, dripping off the point of her chin.

Mina launched forward onto her knees. "Please, don't cry." She touched Grandmother's hands. "You're lovely."

"Thank you."

Grandmother pulled her hands away. Slime stretched between them.

"I should be angry at how my life went," Grandmother said. She got up and stalked toward the hearth. The slime stuck to Mina's good palm, beginning to break the further it expanded. "But I'm glad I got to meet my eldest grandson. I hope—" She choked, wiping her eye again, pulling a chunk of skin off the corner. "I hope one day he'll have a fond thought about me."

Mina stood and backed up, holding her gooey hand away from her clothing. In a matter of seconds, the goo loosened, turning watery, and dripped onto the floor. Calin got to his feet, watching with wide eyes.

Grandmother turned toward the fire and crouched. She inched into the flames. They licked up her legs, searing her body.

"No," Mina said, lurching.

Calin placed a hand on her shoulder. He shook his head.

"Thank you for your ears," Grandmother said. "They're very kind."

Mina's insides quivered.

In a matter of seconds, Grandmother turned into a mound of flames, fading away. "One more thing," she said, ghostly in the heat. "Oldest Son liked to keep precious items hidden under the ashes."

The flames exploded. Golden dust glittered in them, settling onto the wood. Grandmother became nothing but ash. The fire returned to normal, and the room settled.

Calin unbuttoned the top of his coat. Sweat glazed his face, thick beads on his temples, and thicker near his mustache. "She's gone. Forever."

"But we'll remember, right?" Mina asked.

"It's hard to say. We can hold on as long as we can, but there's only so long before we're gone, too." He licked his bottom lip. "While we're alive, we can remember."

"Do you think Oldest Son ever remembers her fondly?"

"I don't know." Calin sighed. "He seemed to be spiraling far from himself. For as long as I've been here, I've never seen a sign of him admitting such care."

Mina recalled how Oldest Son had piped up with hope that his family would honor a dinner for Grandmother. "I believe he loves her deep down. If he got away from his family, he would embrace that memory."

Calin's lips quirked up. "You think?"

"I know."

"You must've been quite wise back at home. Quite level headed."

"I wish," she told him. "That's the sort of thing Lumina would be."

"Yes, the woman Davian left you for, right?"

Those words so plainly spoken turned Mina's insides cold. She didn't remember telling Calin that much detail about her situation.

"How did you know that?" she questioned.

He shrugged. "Lucky guess, good hearing, magic all around. I'm shocked you speak about her."

"I don't hate her." A pang struck Mina's chest. She couldn't identify what the feeling was or what her magic was even doing there. "She's brave. I should be more like her."

"Well, I bet she wouldn't have made it through that dinner," he said, crossing to the hearth. "Nor would she get this heart piece." He knelt down, blowing on the fire.

Mina placed a hand on her hip. "I think it'll take more air than that to put it out."

He paid no attention to her, continuing to blow. His breath penetrated giant holes in the flames, swirling them, weakening them.

Mystified, Mina crouched. How wrong she'd been. She began helping, using all her might to blow, unable to get out as much air as he did.

The fire dwindled. Mina's head spun, and her breaths thinned. Calin tapped her shoulder.

"Take a break," he told her. "I can take care of the rest."

Mina rubbed her forehead. "No, I can help you."

"Thank you for trying," he said, strained, but Mina didn't miss the way the tightness in his shoulders came apart. "I can do this."

Sitting back on her heels, Mina let Calin finish blowing out the fire. Smoke billowed from the ashes. He waved it away, dusting aside the ash. Underneath, something red glimmered.

Mina perked up. "The heart."

"A piece of it," Calin said. He plucked it from its spot, cradling it in his fingers.

Red ignited the room. Its own kind of fire. The rounded bottom of the heart piece came to a small point in the middle. The top had a jagged edge, showcasing that it indeed was part of something larger. A whole heart.

"Here." Calin placed the heart piece on her good palm, pushing her fingers over it. "Keep it safe with you on your way back."

Mina observed the red glass within her magic. The piece covered the horizontal length of her palm, jutting out on both ends by a few inches. "Thank you."

Calin smiled and gestured into the hearth. "You can leave through here." He chuckled. "You can leave through here," he repeated softly, more so to himself.

With the smoke now cleared from the fireplace, a mirror revealed itself on the inside. Beneath their reflections, the shadowy outline of a man sat on what must've been the other side.

"I'm happy to have met you," Calin said, extending his hand. "Good luck on becoming a human."

Mina refrained from shaking his hand. "Come with me."

He blinked. "What?"

"You heard me right. Come with me."

"To find the heart pieces?" He shook his head. "You're capable of doing that on your own."

She looked him right in the eye. "But it's not for me."

"What?"

"The heart," she said. "The heart isn't just for me. Calin, you said you had no time limit to fulfill your deal. You can still complete your end."

"What about you?"

"I wasn't told that I couldn't share my end of the bargain with someone else. If we present the heart together, then I'll be human and you can get your riches."

He blinked, taken aback. "There's no way that would work—*he'd* never be so kind."

"As far as I'm concerned, you gave him your blood, and your defeat was never declared, therefore you could still present the heart." She gestured to the mirror. "This is where you can find your way out. You don't really want to stay here forever, do you?"

"I don't." He ran his tongue over his teeth, mustache shifting. "But Mina, things aren't always so easy."

"I know. So we'll fight a little harder."

"My presence could put your life in danger."

She shook her head. "You helped me."

"I didn't really do that," he told her, face falling.

Mina offered her magic-filled hand to him, forcing her lips into a crooked, weak smile. Even though it hurt, she kept it on. "I want you to come with me, Calin."

His expression held a warmth that could rival any fire in any world. He searched her face for a few seconds, a wrinkle forming between his brows.

"All right," he said softly, linking his fingers with Mina's, stinging them.

Together, they crouched. Mina kept the heart piece close to her chest, in her good hand, as she crawled through the mirror first. The glass turned into a cloudy space which cleared as she entered a gray tunnel. Calin's shoes shuffled, scraping the floor, and for a second, he paused, fingers loosening from hers. Mina gasped, ready to turn around and see what was wrong, but then he reaffirmed his grip and moved with her again.

RETURNING PART OF A HEART

*T*hey crawled through the small tunnel behind the mirror, arriving back at the Blood King's castle. The man himself rested against the edge of his magical well. He smiled and straightened as he watched Mina get onto her feet, dusting off her skirt.

"You're back." A tremor rumbled in his upbeat voice. Hastily, he added, "I'm glad."

Mina ventured to return his smile. As always, it didn't go as planned. Her muscles strained at the stretch, immediately falling back into their dullness, making her a void of emotions once again.

Swallowing, the Blood King stepped away from the well, placing his hands behind his back. His lips parted, but huffing and grumbling coming out of the mirror stopped him from what he was about to say. He cocked his head to the side, searching the space.

"You brought a friend," he said, frowning.

"He's going to help me," Mina said.

"That he is, I bet."

Calin shot up to his feet. He immediately eyed the Blood King. "Doubt me all you like, but I am going to help her." He fixed his posture. "I already gave a drop of my blood, and I was given no time limits on when to give you your heart." He patted his chest. "I've come right back into the deal. Ready to win!"

"Good for me," the Blood King mumbled dryly.

"You'd think for a straight path," Calin said to Mina, craning to look behind, "that would have been an easy trip. At some points I believed we'd never get anywhere." He readjusted his hat.

Mina agreed. The tunnel had been long.

Calin gasped lightly. "Mina, your hand."

He picked her normal fist up from her side. Carefully, he unwrapped her fingers from around the heart piece, plucking it out of her palm. Dots of violet-black poured out of a fresh wound caused by the piece's jagged edge.

"Oh," Mina said. She swiped her hand out of Calin's grasp, curling her fingers over the dark light. The glow crept through the cracks of her fingers. Already the magic wiggled, breaking free from inside of her, attaching over her skin.

"Oh," Calin repeated. "Such a funny way to react to bodily mutilation. You could have cut off your hand."

"More so sliced it in half," the Blood King said.

Mina observed Calin for a few seconds. "I have no blood. Don't you think that's strange? Frightening?"

Brows lowering, Calin scrunched his nose. "Why would I be frightened? Does your magic cause any threat to me? Broken bones? Poisoning?"

"No," she said.

The Blood King folded his arms, humming. "Poison by pure magic, no spell to it, would be rather intriguing."

Calin shook himself out. "I'd hope never to find out if it's possible."

Mina took the heart piece from Calin. "Here," she said, holding it out to the Blood King.

He turned his nose away. "I don't want that."

Mouth working, Mina flexed all over. "This is part of what you asked for."

Calin stepped forward, jabbing a finger at the Blood King. "Don't you dare snuff her out. You made a deal to help her."

The way Calin defended her bloated Mina with joy. They were becoming a team. A perfect duo. He could be her first true friend.

Being in the real world changed him for the better. His skin glowed, healthy and full of life, and his eyes brightened. He stood sturdier and breathed easier. For the first time since they met, he looked, well, alive.

The Blood King moved from the well, gently taking Mina's right wrist into his hand. He stroked her skin, running his fingers over her freshly exposed magic, avoiding the heart piece.

"What are you doing?" Calin asked, stepping forward, hands in fists.

"We'll get back to the heart piece in a minute," the Blood King said. "I want to observe this first."

"Are you going to fix it?" Mina regretted the question as soon as it left. Of course he wasn't going to fix it. That meant jumping ahead on their deal.

"I can't," he said.

She dug the toe of her boot into the floor. "I know."

"As always," Calin said, "you create nuisances wherever you go. Coming into mirrors to bother the deal makers, refusing to help first, and...I don't know. My brain is cloudy."

"If I bother you, I don't mean to," the Blood King said. "I get a little different in the mirrors from all the magic twisting me up. My head gets fuzzy, and my thinking isn't completely clear, though I did warn you about that."

"But you remember everything that happened," Mina said.

"Exactly." Calin wiped the sweat beading under his hat. "It seems like you want to make us fools for a twisted agenda."

"Quite the contrary." Joy entangled the Blood King, lifting his spine. "I want Mina to succeed. Having a heart means no more twisted heads."

"If you had a heart," Calin said, "you wouldn't know how to use it."

"Calin," Mina chided. "That's rude."

"It would stop beating in your cold chest," he continued. "You let others fail, I feel it. This is a game to you."

"Calin, stop."

The Blood King ground his teeth. "Others fail because they are too wrapped up in their own selves to notice where they should be looking." His eyes swept over Calin. "You couldn't let go of your pride in your case."

Mina pushed closer into the Blood King's space. He froze.

"You stop, too," she told him. "Not everyone is so vain."

Circles drifted along Mina's skin, spun by the Blood King's fingers. He stared down at her, a slant of confusion on his face. "A lot holds people back. Their own heart is usually the problem. Desperate people are willing to stomp over what they can to get what they want, blinding them from what they are actually doing. It's disgraceful." He continued making the circles around her magic, his lips twitching up. "This magic is beauty."

Mina wasn't sure she agreed. To an outside eye, perhaps it was. To her, with the pain, not so much.

"Does this magic differ from others you have seen?" Mina wondered.

The Blood King's fingers danced on the magic. "This is more interesting than what human blood holds. A smear of human blood on the skin can be beneficial, but it's nothing compared to this." He grinned. "I would know."

Calin gagged. "Sickening. That's what you are. Sickening for covering yourself in blood."

"I think," Mina said, "everyone can do what they please so long as there's no harm to anyone else."

The Blood King brightened some more. "Yes, I agree."

Calin folded his arms. "It's still unpleasant."

The Blood King took the heart piece and dropped her hand, gesturing to the wall adjacent from the only one that didn't have a mirror. "I say no more of this talk should be had. There awaits the next heart piece."

Mina turned, though still a little perplexed by the Blood King's behavior. He seemed to want the heart piece now. Whatever the case, that was good for her.

The next mirror, the one sitting where the statues once were, glowed. A bright sheen illuminated the room, cutting out the red light of the well and turning everything white.

The Blood King set the heart piece on the watery surface inside the well. "Be careful about your shoes," he warned Mina as she inched toward the mirror. "They might stick to the ground."

BUZZING FOREST

*T*he dark brown branches, sticking out everywhere and all tangled together, caught Mina's clothes and curls. They scraped her magic, flourishing an abundance of pain down her left arm. Her right fist turned into a ball and she focused on the tension there as the new growth of pulsing magic didn't hurt as badly.

The bright orange leaves covering the ground broke under her boots. They mixed with thin yellow blades of grass and loose twigs, which were a lighter shade of brown compared to the ones on the trees. When they cracked, the sound took off in a thunderous boom. With that and the shadowed distance, Mina's heart would've raced if she had one. Instead, her magic rumbled around her chest in fear.

A twig snapped under her. The boom rocketed through the forest, rumbling the ground. Mina pulled Calin close to her.

"What is this happening?"

Calin cleared his throat. "Loud...twigs, simply. How about we try not to step on many of those so we don't attract any danger?"

Mina agreed, but when she quickly scanned the area she noticed that the twigs covered so much of the ground she began to think they'd be more unavoidable than the vines.

"This place is endless," she said.

He trembled. "You're saying so to me, but I need to say so to you: there's no end to this place. I don't know it at all. It's so different from home."

"This is all my fault."

"Why? Did you invent this place?"

"No."

"Then why blame yourself? All we have to do is find someone, or hope they come along, and get the next heart piece." His teeth chattered. "We just can't be afraid."

"Easy to say?"

He hung his head. "Too easy to say."

Thin beams of sunlight streamed in veils through the trees, smooth as watercolor on a canvas. The light was so scarce, as it was in the Blood King's castle, that it made it impossible to see up ahead. The dark, however, made the magical dots rippling over Mina's skin more noticeable. Soon she'd have two sleeves of magic. No blouse. No skin.

She twisted her upper body, searching for a sign of where to go. Beehives stuck to the high branches, withered and gray. Fortunately, no bees actively flew about. Not that a sting would hurt her on her normal skin, but they could hurt Calin.

"The only sign of life," she murmured.

Calin sharply laughed. "Bees are too shrill, vain, selfish, obnoxious, nasty, unpleasant, unkind, too...more words along those lines. They wouldn't help us."

"You're being too quick to assume."

He stuck up a finger. "I'm speaking from experience. Of dealing with bees."

Propping to one side, Mina gently placed her knuckles on her hips. A light sting flourished. "And which experience is this? One you can't remember?"

He flushed. "Never mind that. I'm only using gut instinct. You know, I did have a life before all of this. Have you ever met a bee?"

"I've met a butterfly. Mrs. Degree. She and her husband baked Davian a cherry pie once. He really liked it."

"Butterflies are much kinder." Calin swished his lips back and forth. "Perhaps we should change direction. The one we're going in has proved it has nothing of value. Change could help."

Mina lowered her hands to her sides. "I guess that's better than nothing." She glanced back at the beehive. "Still, last time I went to the first sign of life, I found you and a heart piece. What if this is the same?"

"And how would we get up there? In there?"

Swallowing, Mina closed her mouth. They could always try to climb the tree and shout into the beehive. But then what? The hives looked so degraded that it was possible no bee actually lived inside.

"Look, I'm trying to help you," Calin said. "This is the best way I know how." His voice wavered. "Do you think I'm wrong?"

"I don't know what to think."

"Welcome to my shoes." He puffed. "Fine, we'll keep going in the same direction."

Mina's lips twitched up for a second, and at the same time as him, she said, "Let's switch directions."

Simultaneously, he went left, she went right, and they walked in opposite directions. Mina took five steps before she realized what was happening.

When she turned, Calin already faced her, shaking his head with a smile. Mina tried smiling again, too. Not a second twitch on her mouth came.

"We'll go your way," they said in unison, crossing past each other.

Calin laughed. Mina attempted to laugh.

"All right." He stuck a thumb to the right. "We'll go your way."

Mina bit her lip. "Or maybe we should go your way. I think you're right about change."

Extending his elbow, Calin didn't look at Mina as she took his arm. Together they walked his way through the trees, getting snagged on branches and accidentally igniting the thunderous twigs at their feet, her doing so more than him since she tried hurrying more. Racing for anything to help them.

"Be careful," he kept warning her. "These sounds could attract danger."

After a while, Mina got used to the touch and stepped more carefully to create less sound. More important things began to occupy her mind, like whether they'd find someone, if leaving the bees was a good idea, and if the magic creeping onto the back of her right hand was real or not. She at least knew the answer to the last problem—it was real. The cold stab of air brushing it let her know.

"Listen, I..." Calin started after a long pause. "Well, you know me. I want to help, but I don't know anything about this place." He kicked a pile of leaves. "Even in my own mirror I wasn't much help. You could've done all that on your own."

She shrugged. "Maybe. Maybe not. I think good people can come out of what they try to do along with what they are able to do. You did help me, Calin."

The red on his face spread quicker than Mina's magic. He waved a hand. "You're too kind, but I have my faults. Everyone does."

"No, everyone is perfect."

He patted her right shoulder. "I wish. Everyone has flaws. It's part of being human. One of the worst parts, but it's there."

Calin didn't know then that Davian was perfect. Lumina was perfect. The only bad thing they did was cast Mina aside to die.

Her insides froze. That was quite the flaw. But to them, it was necessary for their love. Selfish love.

Maybe everyone was selfish in a way. They had to be in order to get what they wanted. She was selfish for using Calin to help her get a heart. But she also wanted to help him in return by getting his riches. So what did that really make her? Selfishly selfless? Her heart would also bring the Blood King his heart. He was selfishly selfless, receiving and giving. A trade-off. Did that make them both horrible? Both good? He demanded he get his heart first, so it could've made him more selfish compared to her. Still though, he had been betrayed. Maybe he asked for the heart first because he was worried Mina would betray him once she got what she wanted. She would never, but she couldn't blame him for his caution.

Oh, she didn't know what she was thinking anymore. Everything wove into a complexity she didn't like. People were supposed to be perfect. That was it. Not flawed and picked apart because of it.

"Mina?"

"People *are* perfect. Once I'm human, I'll change."

"Why would you want to change? You're perfectly fine as you are."

"I'm not."

He chuckled. "Relax. There's been some real creatures I've met through these mirrors. I'll give the Blo—one thing. Some people *are* held back by their own hearts. But yours is good."

Mina stared at him.

He flushed. "I mean, it feels like you have one. Say, I bet you could turn yourself human. You're already made of magic. Maybe it can do something."

"It doesn't work like that."

"Maybe it could."

Disagreement died on her tongue. The Wishmaker never told her she could use her power for anything other than living. He stated, as she fell to the Virvin forest, that her magic would keep her alive. That was all.

The Blood King, however, must've thought there was more to her. If she failed, he'd collect her magic, spilling it with the rest. He used the other magic for power, so hers would be no exception. Except, how? As a wish, she never did any tricks, not like the Blood King had. His power must've been strong enough to make her magic alive, too. He'd told her he could turn a glass heart real, that the Wishmaker's lack of answers brought her here. There was plenty Mina didn't know about herself or the Blood King.

No matter the possibilities, Mina didn't plan on letting anyone find out what her magic could be used for.

She let go of Calin, pausing. She stared at him, harsh in her mind, but knowingly blank on the outside. "You're confusing me. I know what I know, and that's it."

"All right."

There. Talk of her magic ended. Just like that. However, the conversation stayed silently with her. What if Calin was right to think she had power? No, he couldn't have been right. It'd been twenty years; if she had any power to her magic, it would've been exposed by now.

Her shoulders fell. "I'm sorry. I've never been on my own before. All I had back at home was Davian to tell me what to do. Life was so easy. I had to listen to him, let everyone else look through me, and never let them know what I was."

"I'm sorry you lived that way," Calin said, glancing down at her.

She hugged herself, magic flaring, warming. "Don't be. I want to live that way again."

"Why?" he asked, brows furrowing in genuine concern.

"That's all I know. All I want."

"You know, Grandmother did that. She accepted her fate, no attempt to fix it."

"Fate can't be fixed."

"Can't it?" At Mina's blankness, he waved a hand. "What am I saying? I stayed stuck in the mirror because it's all I knew." He jabbed his fingers under his hat to scratch his scalp. "Being here feels a bit funny."

Mina hummed in agreement. She didn't think Calin heard it from how low it was.

His fingers moved to his temples. He rubbed them in small circles. "Grandmother thanked you for all the wonderful moments before getting up to leave."

"I don't remember that," Mina said.

"She kissed my cheek and hoped I'd find a way out soon. Then the fire died, and we left."

Though she didn't have an itch, never had one in fact, Mina scratched her head. "That's not what happened. We listened to her story and blew out the fire."

"Funny how that works." He gave her a lopsided grin.

"It's like before," she said. "When we went through a different moment at the same time. We were lucky we had a good outcome, but what will happen if things go badly?"

"Keep walking," Calin suggested. "If I fall behind, or you fall behind, keep walking. What's important is your heart. It would do you no favors wasting time over me, and I want no argument against that. My life is tethered to these mirrors, but you need to get out and live the one you want."

She placed her hand on his arm. Despite the magic spreading on her right palm, and the pain it caused when she touched something, she endured it, wishing she could pour as much love as she could into her newfound friend.

"Your life isn't tethered to a single thing," she said. "Oh, I wish I could smile for you so you'd be reassured properly."

He tapped the tip of her nose. "I think you're smiling just fine."

Lightning struck Mina's head. Her fingers flung to her mouth. She felt around, doing her best to decipher a smile. All she could make out, though, was a flat line.

"That wasn't funny," she said, dropping her hand. She huffed by him, stepping on a twig. Inside the thunderous snap, she thought she heard something buzzing nearby. A little voice calling out for attention.

"Not smiling for real," Calin cut in with a shaky chuckle. "You give the sense of it in your air. You twitch and flick quite a lot."

Quite a lot. She knew she did that sometimes but this was news to her.

She put a hand on her cheek. "When do I do that?"

"Always. It's easy to feel your every emotion. You have a lot of them, very genuine, too."

"It can't be possible," she said. "Davian would have told me."

"Well..." Calin whistled. "I'm sure he's told you a lot of *other* things. But what I'm saying is true."

No. It couldn't be. If Davian could sense her happiness, he would've said it. He wouldn't have gone along knowingly upsetting her each time he talked about

Lumina. He would've seen how happy she was with him, with living. All this time she thought she was a pitiful ball of nothingness, but Calin said otherwise.

"It's too easy," Mina argued. "The real Lumina—real people—they... I'm not close to being like them."

"But who is like everyone else?" Calin questioned. He stuck his index finger into the air. "No one, that's who."

Confusion swirled. Calin made a lot of sense and no sense at the same time. In fact, everything that ever existed both made sense and no sense. People sensing her emotions made sense. The Wishmaker and the Blood King treated her like a normal person, responding to her as though she showed her feelings externally. It also made no sense: Davian never said anything. Never changed.

He told her she didn't feel, but he must've secretly known otherwise. Perhaps he didn't want her to think he sensed anything so he could say or do whatever he wanted and feign ignorance if she spoke up.

"Maybe we should switch directions," Mina said, distancing herself from thinking about Davian, magic shaking inside. "Let's go back to the bees. They can help us find the heart piece."

Pivoting, Mina marched in the direction of the beehive. She kept her head down, arms close to her sides. Davian—his face circled her head.

Calin chased after her. "Mina!" He let out a shuddering breath. "Slow down."

The magic in her chest thickened. She could hardly breathe. She hardly heard him. Hardly hear that she stepped on more twigs than before. Hardly heard the little buzzing voice cry out for her to stop, to come for help.

"I'm trying to help you," he said, wincing at each booming crack. "Now would you slow down? We don't know if the bees are nice. I could be wrong, they may help us, but I could also be right that they won't."

Branches tried slicing Mina's shawl. She kept going.

"Once we're out in the real world," she said, "I'll find something to give you for your help. More than riches. A personal gift from me."

"Mina," he said, panting, "I can't leave the mirrors."

"But you can. You already did."

"I can't leave the—" His words died altogether. He pushed branches out of the way. As he struggled to get them to break through, his cheeks puffed. No matter how hard he tried, whatever it was he wanted to say, he couldn't.

A blast of air escaped his mouth. He cursed softly. "I can't leave *his* castle. I never have, and I never will. I simply can't."

"You don't know that. This is the first time you've been out of your mirror since you went in. You never said your deal prevented you from leaving the castle. You only needed the heart to become rich, that was it."

"Maybe if the—if he—the—if he shows kindness, I could go. But I don't think he'd let me go far. I know too much."

"If we find the other heart pieces, then we could ask about you joining the real world again."

Calin's forehead wrinkled with doubt. "None so mean would dare to be so kind."

"He has been kind to me," she said, stomping the ground.

A branch cracked against her boot. Hard. The sound echoed far. It circled the endless forest, jostling the trees. The distant buzzing grew louder, more abundant. A low note on a horn sounded in the unknown.

"I don't think that was a good sound," Calin said, freezing.

"Somebody could find us."

"Right, but let's hide away and watch before we meet anyone we don't know. Better to assess them before jumping into things too quickly."

"We don't have time to waste trampling through the forest on our own. A sign of people is a sign of the help we need."

Calin opened his mouth.

Buzzing stampeded toward them, interrupting any further argument. The trees rustled in the amplified sounds. It entered Mina's head, mixing it up. The vibrations crushed her to the ground, her insides ready to burst. She crawled toward a tree trunk, under an abundance of branches, resting against it as she covered her ears.

"Mina!" Calin shouted.

She needed to get up. They couldn't be separated.

The buzzing circled the area. Mina focused on the leaves by her ankles. She drew her knees into her chest. The magic pulsated on her right side, etching its way onto her fingers and wrist.

"Mina!" Calin called again.

She needed to get up. They *couldn't* be separated.

Voices slashed through the air, but they did nothing to cut out the buzzing. Whatever words were being said, Mina did not know. She was too busy keeping herself together.

The buzzing drew far away, closer to silence. She sat for a few long moments, listening as they eventually went away. She calmed herself down, affirming she wouldn't explode before sitting up on her knees, uncovering her ears.

"Calin?" She stood up, fixing her shawl. "Calin, where are you hiding?"

Mina spun in place, one slow, tiny step at a time. She steadily observed every inch of the forest, trying to make out any sign of Calin. As she looked harder, the tips of the branches changed. Faces popped out of the wood. Faces all the same. One that was dear to her.

"Davian?" She pulled a branch closer to her. Her other hand rose, grazing the side of his face, curving along its edge. "You're a tree."

"That I am." He cleared his throat. "I came back to offer you my hand again. This forest is huge and unsuitable to you. I could keep you safe."

By his face, her magic ate her entire left hand alive. At her side, it consumed her right one.

"Safe," she muttered, letting go of the branch. It flung away, bouncing in the air. "I just need a heart."

She turned. "Calin," she whispered, wringing her hands. The motion engulfed her magic with a dull ache.

"Calin, Calin, Calin," she said as loud as she could. It wasn't quite a shout, but close enough for her. The repetition already dried out her throat.

"Calin! Calin! Calin!"

Mina turned into a statue. The echo wasn't hers. It had a shrill voice. One mixing girlish excitement with regal quality. An older, wiser voice. The voice of a woman. A Queen.

She pushed aside a few branches. The empty spaces between the trees pinpointed how alone she was. The darkness strengthened.

"Who is there?" she asked.

No one answered. She knew it. The voice was too good to be true.

Mina thought of the Blood King. She could ask him for help. All she had to do was call out and he'd come to her. He'd help her find the second heart piece and get Calin back. First, she'd have to stop him from causing any trouble. It'd be a lot of work, but she'd be willing to do it so long as she wasn't alone.

"Blood—"

A buzzing sounded to her right.

Mina jumped away from it. A bee stalked toward her. Except, it wasn't only a bee. It was a human, too. An older woman. She had a human head, neck, arms, and legs. The rest of her was made up of bee parts. Bee at the torso, with the short, fuzzy black and yellow hairs on her skin. And bee especially with her wings and stinger protruding from her back. The yellow dress she wore, summery and loose, flowed down to her shins and draped over her stinger, the spiraling fabric longer on the right side. It bounced as she moved.

A cracked, gold crown sat on her fluffy head of hair. Gray streaks ran through the wavy brown strands. Age crinkled the skin on her face, contrasted by the youthful bright red of her full lips.

"If you need royalty," she said, voice cheerful. She held up a golden scepter, the red, round jewel on the end pointing at Mina. "Then I might do as the trick for you."

THE ONCE QUEEN OF THE BEES

*T*he bee–woman propped her scepter on her shoulder, sharp blue eyes surveying Mina. "A picky tricky, but a tricky indeed," she said. "Though I'm not so sure. You seem to stand enough."

Mina's toes curled inside her boots. She tried uncorking the woman's words to release the meaning behind them. It didn't take her long to give up.

"Sorry?" she asked.

Her lips curled like she tasted something sour. "Why be sorry? You haven't done anything," the woman said. The quick cadence in which she spoke was faster than Calin's.

"Sorry, I didn't understand what you said," Mina corrected.

"Simple." The woman flung her scepter across her body and slapped it hard against her palm. "You are standing in a forest."

"That's not—"

"You are standing in a forest," the woman continued. "Standing from having summoned the armada. Summoned the armada from having walked. Having walked with a friend. Away from me, back to me. I tried calling to you. You've come from the Blo—a place." She tapped her temple. "I hate dead words."

Mina's head whirled. All sense jumped into an ocean of violent waves, leaving her stranded in confusion.

"You're looking for a little red jewel," the woman said. "I, Queen Amberly Bee, know that because others have come here before, from Nore."

"Where's Nore?"

Queen Amberly Bee shrugged. "No clue. I know you're not from it. Neither is our friend—Calin? Yes. I watched the pair of you. He's silly for being mean to a bee. He must've been cheated by one before." She gasped, hand going to her cheek. "What if it was me?"

Mina bounced up on her toes. "You know Calin? What do you know about him? This place? The people? Have you ever left this mirror before?"

Stepping toward her, Queen Amberly Bee picked up a bundle of Mina's hair. She twisted the curls, brown and gray twirling into each other. "You have such lovely hair. The mixture of two colors delights me, though I would prefer lines over splattered tips." She tapped her own head with her scepter. "See, here are my way grays, all firm lines. When I was younger, the whole hive copied my stripes, even the ones on my stinger. They did so out of admiration, out of compliance." She sighed, dropping Mina's hair. "Those years, so young and nimble, I ruled greatly. Every day I did something great. Now the most exciting thing to me is a stranger's hair."

"Queen Amberly Bee—"

"No, no, just Amberly," she interrupted. "I should've introduced myself as Amberly Bee. I'm not a Queen anymore, and bee, well, I am a bee, but Amberly Bee is a syllable longer, and what a long syllable that is, so call me Amberly. We have no time to waste on extra, unnecessary syllables. Not when you have a task, and I have a task to help you with your task."

Mina couldn't believe it. "You already want to help me?"

"It'll keep me busy. My life has been wasted already, but maybe I could finally help one of you get what you need. For you it's a heart?"

"Yes." Mina's gaze lingered on the crown sitting on Amberly's head. "But if you're a Queen, it doesn't sound like you wasted any life."

Amberly's chin raised. *"Was* a Queen. Was, and what a good one I was. Or so others say each day, and each day they say, 'Amberly, you were once Queen.' On those days, I say, 'I know, but where did those years go? Did I do anything? Did I deserve what I had? Did I make good of what I had? Now that I am not what I was, can I even say I had what I had? That what I had made me much of anything at all?'"

Throughout her little speech, Amberly bounced on her toes, matching the fast speed at which she spoke, and while the flow connected, her tone did not. Where her body seemed to float on clouds, unable to keep still, underlying bitterness seeped into her voice. It thickened, becoming more apparent by her final few words. She faintly sniffled.

"You're still in the middle of your life," Mina observed. "You've done a lot already. What if you relaxed? After being Queen, it'd be nice to do so, wouldn't it?"

Speaking of relaxation, Mina's magic drooped inside of her. She could've used a huge amount of rest. Of course, she'd need her heart first so that she'd have the time for it. Once she was human, she planned to lie in a field, perhaps the one near the farm on the way to Deamindis, and relax. She could see the cows, too. Afterwards, she'd venture into the world, discover all the things she'd only read in books, like oceans and mountains, lions and dolphins. To live as herself. To simply exist, no matter what time she had left.

"But Mina," Davian's voice echoed in the sudden breeze. "You miss me."

She searched the black branches, waiting for his face to appear again, waiting for his shape to come. He wasn't anywhere.

A deep sigh seeped out of her. *Thankfully.*

Mina stiffened. *Thankfully?* she questioned herself. "That's all wrong. I have to go back to him. I'm doing this for...him."

"Whoever 'him' is," Amberly said, her face turning into a blank slate, "don't. Some people aren't worth the time."

"What?"

Amberly shook herself, features coming back to life. Her face contorted in disgust. "I what? Relax? Are you saying I'm good for nothing more than relaxing? For the rest of my life? I've always been older than most friends I've made, and all my siblings, but that doesn't mean I should sit around while everyone else gets some fun."

"Relaxing can be fun," Mina said.

"No time," Amberly responded curtly, flicking her wrist.

"You have lots of time. I don't right now."

"You're only a young woman. You do, indeed weed, have lots of time to make your greatest achievements to hold onto forever. Hard work is everywhere, and it is the only way forward."

Mina's jaw tensed. She let the sensation guide her words in a place she hadn't discovered before. A resentful place. "I am dying," she said, low and tight. "Not as in a slow eventual death, but a soon death. Sooner than you."

Amberly gasped, eyes going wide. "I think I missed that part."

Lifting her hands, Mina showed off her magic. Her entire left and right hands glowed with violet-black encasing them. The magic nibbled at the right cuff of her blouse. Violet flickers weaved pain around her knuckles and fingers, a constriction of barbed wire.

"As a tossed wish, the magic is expanding," Mina said. "I have a heart to collect for someone else in order to stop the magic."

Pinching her brows together, Amberly pursed her lips. "That is why you're wilting."

Mina's arms fell. She hadn't thought of her condition like that. Hearing herself get referred to as wilting felt worse than simply saying she was dying. Wilting meant decay, ugliness, a sweet flower past its prime.

"Sweet young woman," Amberly said, softer now, "what a sad and bad, and bad and sad thing to go through. I am so sorry."

Mina lifted her shoulders. "Are you here because you made a deal with a spirit?"

"Oh, yes, yes, and since you shared your predicament so nicely nice, I'll say this, I was outcast from my hive once my reign as Queen was over, so I came to beg for another chance in another hive. A hive where I'd never get too old for my role. I already showed you my way grays. See how shiny they are?"

Mina observed them once again. They were pretty shiny.

"Coming into the mirror felt out-of-body, but I recall already being distracted by the mirrors on the outside. The spirit must've noticed, because he spoke a lot about how I probably won't make it out on my own." She giggled. "So now I'm here, but it's finely fine. The mirrors have twisted so much that there's a great beehive here, much like the one I used to live in."

"So you're lost?"

Amberly nodded.

"Then you could still find the heart and be a Queen."

Amberly appeared deep in thought for a moment. She cleared her throat. "Say, I think I know where your friend is. What was his name? Calin?"

Mina inhaled sharply. "Yes. You mentioned him already. Do you know him?"

"I can't remember how. It was so long ago. Must be my age decaying my mind."

He lied then. Calin *had* been out of his mirror. He'd met Amberly here. Or maybe it was the other way around. Maybe she went to him.

"Did you visit him in the other mirror?"

Amberly ran her tongue along her bottom teeth. "Likely not. Nobody usually takes me along on their journey. Something about me, they say, is too, too, too talky and walky."

Mina sighed. Answers were a lost cause from both Amberly and Calin. She couldn't hold any animosity against them, though. Their hazy brains weren't a conscious effort.

Unless...

She shook her head. No. She wouldn't accuse them—the people *helping* her—of a heavy thing like lying.

Amberly spun on her toes like a perfect ballerina. "What I do know is who took Calin, and I have an idea where we can find a little heart piece."

Mina leaned forward. "You do and you do?"

"I do and I do," Amberly said with a nod.

"Can you please show me?"

"I will." Clearing her throat, Amberly made circles through the air with her scepter. "You're going to have to get comfortable becoming small. Unseen."

That wouldn't be hard. Nobody in Virvin ever saw Mina. And Davian never let her do much that made her feel big.

"Lately, there are worse things I've gotten comfortable with," Mina said, her second sleeve beginning to disappear under her magic. "I'll do whatever you ask of me."

Amberly's breath shuddered through her mouth. She pressed the back of her hand against her forehead, feigning faintness. "Wheeze if you need, but please do not hint of death."

"Sorry."

"Ack, back, no it's nothing to apologize for, but if it happens again, your body will stay shrunken forever." Amberly laughed. "A jest of course, but please, no death."

Inside, Mina laughed along. Though she held onto the possibility of the jest not actually being one, mentally noting not to mention death, an easy promise to keep.

Amberly pushed her scepter directly above her head, her arm stiff. The red sphere on the end pointed at the sky, or rather, the higher branches blocking the sky.

Holding out her other hand, Amberly beckoned Mina to take it. Little hairs poked out of the yellow and black stripes running around her skin. Upon the link of their hands, Mina didn't register any texture to her stripes. They appeared soft, however, with their fuzzy shine akin to a freshly cleaned blanket.

"Make sure to hold on tight," Amberly said. "Oh, and do you like your shoes?"

"Yes. They protect my feet."

"But do you enjoy how stylish your shoes are?"

Mina twisted a foot, digging the toe of her boot into the ground. Coming up to the ankle, age beat her black boots into a wrinkled and worn-out state. Silver buckles once decorated their outsides, but they had since fallen off, leaving behind the square pattern of dirtied white stitching underneath.

For as old as her boots were, Mina couldn't hate them. At least she had shoes. She couldn't imagine going on her adventure without them. Rocks and sticks would've slashed her feet, making her navigate on razor-sharp magic. What ate her arms hurt enough already. She didn't want to ponder how much worse things would've been had the magic started on her feet.

"They are pretty enough," she said.

"So pretty that you can't ruin them?" Amberly questioned.

"They're quite used already. I don't know how much more they could be ruined."

She half shrugged. "If you say, then you say. I'll warn you, they're going to get a little sticky."

Mina lit up. "The Bloo—he said something similar."

Amberly's scepter sliced in front of them, splitting the air in two.

Wind tangled around them. Mina's skirt blew into Amberly's legs, and her hair pulled in every direction, wrapping in front of her face, sealing her vision behind it.

Stabbing dug into Mina's flesh, claws pricked at every joint, every muscle. It stretched and deepened. She whimpered, clinging to Amberly's hand, desperate to kick the pain away. As she moved her legs, the invisible claws sunk and twisted. Her body warped, becoming putty and getting misshapen by the claws.

When the wind died, and the pain faded. Mina swallowed. Her feet dangled off the ground. She stretched her toes downward, trying to find something solid. She fought in vain.

Amberly's wings fluttered. She kept her scepter above her head. Mina turned into a rag doll hanging from her hand. The branches had grown bigger around them, and they flew in the empty spaces, going higher and higher, a pair of bugs in the fray.

Magic dropped into the pit of Mina's stomach. Bugs. They were as small as bugs.

"Oh," she said, looking down. The ground sat so far away. It dizzied her.

"Just a second more," Amberly announced. "Until..."

Mina turned her head up. "Until what?"

The answer to her question came in the form of darkness, which immediately brightened into a sea of orange clouds. They broke through, going up and then down.

Mina's feet plopped onto something solid, a squelching noise ringing upon impact. When she tried moving, her feet remained stuck. She looked down. *Honey.*

STUCK AND STUCK

*M*ina bent, straightened, strained left and right, her teeth clenched, and her feet wiggled in her boots. The honey encased her in place. It lay thick across the entire floor, pooled in a room of honeycomb walls, the hexagonal pockets filled with dark liquid—likely honey, though she wasn't too sure; honey wasn't supposed to be near black. Whatever the case, the fluid bulged against the clear coating of each pocket.

She worked a foot back and forth, squishing and squelching. Her body at least pointed at the narrow opening ahead, the only way out of this room. As soon as she broke her foot out of the stickiness, she plopped it straight ahead. But alas, that only landed her in another blotch of honey and she was stuck once again.

The hem of her skirt hovered close to the honey's surface. She'd stepped too far ahead, splitting her legs too far apart. Mina's arms windmilled frantically as she wobbled.

A little buzz floated from behind. "Oh, fret me," Amberly said, flying over the floor, startling Mina, for she swore the former bee Queen wasn't there a moment ago. "This is a lot better than I imagined."

Amberly's wings blurred together from how quickly they fluttered. The tips of her curly-toed shoes hung mere inches from the honey.

Mina tossed some hair out of her face, wishing she had wings. "Better? Amberly, I'm stuck."

"Yes, picture it"—Amberly clicked her tongue against her teeth—"we could've come to a honey layer built up to the shoulders. Your pretty hair would've been caught and ruined in it. A tragedy." She flew close to the wall and tapped her scepter against one of the honeycomb pockets. It jiggled. "At least these aren't ready to burst."

"Burst?" Mina faintly squeaked. "When might that be?"

"Hard to tell. Perhaps five minutes."

"Amberly!"

"Perhaps longer." She flew to Mina, shaking her scepter. "Yes, yes, you are stucky stuck, but the man in the castle said you'd get sticky. Right, you told me that right after I told you that, right?"

Mina nodded but when she did, she nearly fell onto her back. She steadied her legs, arms out at her sides.

"Such a man he is." Blushing, Amberly crossed her arms. "Sending people here and here, and there and there, all for what? Jewels?"

"His heart."

"He's with us, you know."

Flexing all over, Mina glanced around. She straightened her spine and popped out her chest. "Wait. That's impossible. He can't come here without us summoning him."

"But our worlds sit side-by-side. Give it," Amberly said, gesturing to the wall, "a closely close, looky look."

Mina turned her face to the wall. She studied it for a prolonged length of time, eyes feeling around the blackened honey. A tug of magic guided her toward a darker shape within. She fixated on it, finding a slight movement. She traced the shadow, outlining a man. He wore a long coat over his tall stature and filled-out form, and he leaned ever so slightly to the left. No decoration of blood was needed for her to know who that figure was.

Mina waved. She pressed the tiniest smile onto her face, counting its lifespan. *One... Two... Three...*

Four... He shifted. *Five...*

She almost lost sight of him.

Six...

Lowering her arm, Mina wondered if she looked as shadowy to him as he did to her. Part of her doubted it. If he couldn't see her clearly, then why would he waste time trying to find her?

Seven...

Her smile broke at her usual, pathetic seven seconds. Hardly worth anything. Yet, that wasn't quite right. Seven seconds of smiling or not, people could feel her emotions. That was worth something.

"What are your thoughts on calling him here?" Mina asked Amberly.

She hummed. "Minds get so twisty here. He'd show off his grand power to a distracting, endless end. A nice power." She crossed her arms. "But what a show-off."

Letting go of the Blood King's visage, Mina cut loose any ideas of mentioning him directly. He *was* a distraction, and even though she found the heart piece last time, it didn't mean she'd find the same success here. Digging up the dinner party jolted a sickly feeling.

"We have to find the heart piece and Calin, too," Mina said.

"Easy, and easy, both easy." Amberly spun. "I know where they keep prisoners. I, too, know how to take prisoners out of their cells. And I, too, too, know where jewels are. Don't worry, I have a plan."

Mina beamed as best she could, which wasn't much. "I will listen to your plan."

"After we get Calin, we get the heart piece and run." Amberly lifted a finger. "In the whole of the wholes, there's only one army of bees that would take a prisoner, and only one army of bees that would have a heart piece. Lucky for you, there's only one army of bees that fit both those descriptions, and there's only one army of bees in the forest."

All the words spun Mina's head. Considering they were inside a beehive, she hoped the right army of bees lived here.

"The young Queen of the Bees here is the ruler of the only army of bees in this part of the world. She has prisoners, and she has the heart piece. I know where she keeps it."

"That means the young Queen of the Bees is the old companion," Mina said.

"Yes, yes, yes."

"Is the Queen of the Bees friendly? Is she anything like you?"

Amberly scoffed. "Not at all." She flew toward the room's opening. "Follow me."

"Wait," Mina called after her, but it was too late. Amberly disappeared around the corner.

Adjusting her foot, Mina dug deep to find as much force as she could to break the honey. She mashed her back boot around, loosening it. Aches rippled through her, turning her limbs into an equally gooey mess, but she managed to take another step, making sure not to step too far this time.

She worked her other foot out of the honey and into another step. Her entire body vibrated, ready to collapse. If the thickness of the honey stretched beyond this room, a nightmare lay before her. She'd hardly gotten a quarter through the room, and her energy depleted next to nothing. Navigating this way through the entire hive was out of the question. She'd never survive.

Amberly peeked around the corner, pink tinging her cheeks. "Poorly, poor me. I left you stuck behind." She flew to Mina, impressed. "Though it appears you made great distance."

Mina looked back. Four footprints imprinted the honey. She thought she'd made it so much farther.

"Nicely nice." Amberly wrapped one arm around Mina, pulling her up. The honey stretched from the floor, stuck to the bottoms of her boots. She bent her knees, staying far from the ground. The stretching honey broke.

Amberly carried her out of the room and set her down in the corridor outside, where the ground squeaked with stickiness, but more importantly it could be walked on normally.

"Thank you," Mina said. She shifted her feet, double-checking that she could move. "You're extremely strong."

Waving off the notion with her scepter, Amberly cleared her throat. "Don't thank me." She lowered to her feet. "I needed the exercise. These useless bones must grow stronger."

"They're already strong, though. They carried me. Impressively so with one arm."

"If I had strengthened myself more as a young Queen, I could lift you, and five other yous." Amberly flipped back her hair, shifting her crown. "I can't believe I wasted so much of my time being so weak."

"You are strong," Mina reassured her.

Amberly looked both ways. The corridor curved out in both directions, the same black honey walls joining them.

"Have you any ideas on where the Queen is hiding the heart piece?" Mina asked.

"Why would I know?"

"You said you know."

"Oh, I did, right," Amberly said. She smiled. "I know the sneaky sneakiest way possible to get that heart piece."

"Perfect." Things were already getting better and better.

Starting to the right, Amberly sprinted across the floor, not looking back to see if Mina followed. Mina, however, did follow. She really had no other choice.

"What is your plan?" Mina asked, panting and biting back the flames licking up her sore, tired muscles and magic.

Amberly frowned. "You ask so much."

"I need to know. For assurance."

"You'll see it all in a few little seconds."

A few little seconds came quicker than anticipated. Mina and Amberly rounded another corner and were faced with what had to be hundreds upon hundreds of humanoid bees.

Stark white skull masks covered their faces. Over their black and yellow stripes, they wore navy coats. The men and women buzzed in place, their wings stuck together as they all faced one thing: the young Queen of the Bees, the only one without a mask. Instead, her face was a cream-colored slate of blankness with red smeared over the spot where her lips should've been.

Mina thought of Oldest Son and his blurred face. It further affirmed the Queen as an old companion alongside another piece of damning evidence: the heart piece sitting in a nest of fluffed-up brown hair, shining red beside her tiny, gold crown.

While her hair reached high above her head, her dress hung far below her feet. Yellow with uneven, black stripes, her skirt extended out in front of her, barreling over the numerous steps below her throne. A slit at the side allowed her stinger a little freedom.

"There she is," Amberly said through her teeth. "The young Queen of the Bees."

The Queen stood in front of her orange throne. She kept her chin held high. If she had eyes, they'd likely be narrowed as she scanned her subjects. Eyes, Mina pictured, radiant and blue. Much like Amberly's.

How odd it was that the Blood King's old companion was similar to the one person standing beside her. Both women appeared to have the same height and body shape.

"Honey," the Queen said, as shrill as how Amberly sounded. "It is always the season for abundant honey."

The bees stomped. "It is always the season for abundant honey," they repeated in unison.

Amberly watched the bees with a twinkle in her eye. Mina couldn't help but turn the gears in her head, going over the coincidence between the pair. If someone said Amberly and the Queen were related, she'd believe them. If someone said they were the same person, she'd doubly believe them. But that meant Amberly would've stolen part of the Blood King's heart, and she did say she had come here to make a deal.

Just like Calin had. Just like herself.

Besides, how could the same person be in two different places at once? And also, the blurry face—how could Mina make an assumption without seeing an entire face?

Illusions from various minds lie within.

A million questions rang in Mina's mind, and she turned to Amberly, ready to probe her, but stopped. Amberly wasn't who she wanted answers from. Not just yet.

"Isn't there more honey when it's warm, though?" Mina asked instead. "Back home, that's what Davian said."

Amberly furrowed her brows. "Who is Davian again?"

Humanity would've made Mina blush. "He's the one who wished for me."

"Ah, and he gave you away?"

And the blush would've faded. She nodded.

"What a terrible man," Amberly said. "You don't need to impress him. As for your inquiry, back home, indeed, you are right. Here, though, in these walls, we never stop the honey."

Falling back into silence, pity sprung up for Amberly. Great sadness haunted her voice more so now than before. In a way, it reminded Mina of how she felt when she first saw Lumina. How she wanted to shrink into the dirt and never face her again. How she knew deep down that if Davian saw her, he'd choose the real girl every chance he got.

"When I watched you and Calin come through the mirror," Amberly continued, "my chest stirred. Little Mina, I think you have a great chance at getting all the heart pieces."

"What are we going to do?" They couldn't walk up to the Queen and pluck the heart piece from her head. With all her subjects around, they were bound to get caught and punished, likely imprisoned forever, and Mina would be eaten by her magic.

Amberly patted Mina's good arm, though the good part wasn't going to last long. Her magic climbed over her sleeve, devouring its way to her elbow.

"I have a wonderful plan," Amberly announced, unable to suppress her smile.

"What is it?"

Clearing her throat, Amberly raised her scepter, waving it above her head. Her voice boomed, "Here, here, everyone."

The bees turned from the Queen, perplexity beaming from behind their masks as they fell silent.

The Queen curled her fingers. "What is this?"

Amberly went on, "Mina, the company, and me, Amberly, have a secret to share. We are thieves. Great, great thieves, and we are trying to steal the red heart piece from the Queen's head."

Mina gasped and jumped. She grabbed Amberly's waving arm and tried pulling it down.

"What are you doing?" she hissed.

Amberly ignored her. "We have come to steal. As thieves, we should be imprisoned."

The Queen pointed at them without any hesitation. "Seize those thieves, and throw them away until we hold a proper trial."

Mina dropped her attempt to silence Amberly. She stood at the older woman's side, helpless, angry, and confused. "What did you do?"

The nearest bees marched, hands lifted. They approached, their shadows growing larger. Mina backed away. She turned on her heels, ready to run, but a few bees flew over her, blocking the way out. In a matter of seconds, they surrounded her, leaving her with nowhere else to go.

Amberly went easy with the bees, smiling as they held her by the shoulders, tying her hands behind her back. "This is fun, being on the other side. I've never been a bad one before."

"We're not bad ones," Mina protested. "We're innocent."

"Silence," one of the bees commanded, grabbing her arms. His hands seared against her magic. Her knees buckled and her vision turned black.

Mina struggled, kicking and wiggling, trying anything to break free, but it was no use. The hands tightened on her skin and on her magic, shooting bolts of electricity through her, numbing her. It made it easier for the bees to pick her up and carry her away from the second heart piece.

BREAKING CELL BARS

*T*he buzzing of wings beat into Mina's ears, reverberating deep into her head. Swirls of light flashed before her eyes. In them, skull faces stared at her. Hands tossed her limp body onto the hard floor inside a cell and she landed on top of her left arm. Squeezing aches lanced through her, the exposed magic squealing. The entire side of her body lit up with thin, shooting stabs. Tingles pinched her hips, wrists, and feet. She stopped breathing for a moment as she writhed.

Sliding bars slammed shut behind her.

She wanted to close her eyes and escape into an imagined world of yellow flowers growing in a vast, green field, mountains standing along the horizon. There, peace thickened in the air. There, she breathed an easy flow, in and out. There, no magic chewed on her skin, destroying her clothes, and turning her into a featureless, human shape of violet-blackness.

All she had, however, was the blurry cell stuck in front of her open eyes and heavy buzzing endlessly wrestling with her thoughts.

Calm down, she told herself, pushing the words to the top of her mind. *Calm down.*

A few deep breaths cleared the buzzing from her head, allowing the emergence of squelching noises from outside her cell. She sat up, scooting to the bars. Through them, lumps of brown covered the outside walls, sticky and shiny. Tiny, long bodies slithered together. Worms.

Mina bolted from the bars, stomach twisting.

"Mina?" Amberly called out. "Did you make it in there fine? I sure did."

"I'm fine," Mina responded, though a bit agitated that they were in this predicament at all. She wanted to place her anger on Amberly, but she sighed. Arguing wouldn't solve anything. "Are you okay?"

"Finer, fine." She sounded so proud. "Wasn't that funny fun?"

A peculiar urge fell over Mina, one she'd never had before. She wanted to rub her forehead in exhaustion. "We're stuck in here. That's not, I'm sorry, very fun."

"So I don't need to clean my ears and wash my eyes," a third voice joined in, high-pitched with shock. "I did see you pass by, Mina, and I *am* hearing you."

"Calin," Mina realized. "You're here, too."

"No," he grumbled. He cleared his throat. "It's better to say *you're* here, too. Which, by the way, you shouldn't be."

"Are you fine?" she asked him.

"I am," he answered. "Now tell me, what are you doing here?"

"We came to free you."

"No," he said, exasperated, "that shouldn't be how it is."

"Be thankful," Amberly said. "Without us, you'd be stuck forever."

He groaned. "Amberly. I was trying to believe you weren't here."

She clicked her tongue. "Not a possibility. Poor Calin, still the same, always speaking about yourself, yourself."

"You speak of yourself, yourself, too," he sneered. "Besides, I could have freed myself all by myself."

"Myself, myself," she mocked. "That is no way to thank your heroes."

Their conversation rocked Mina's head back and forth. The pair spoke how old friends would—old *companions*.

No, that couldn't be possible. Calin wasn't similar to Oldest Son. Though, to face the facts, she hardly knew either. As much as she believed he and Amberly were her friends already, it was too quick of her to assume so. She knew that friendships blossomed over time. That they grew with knowledge. Connection. Davian had described it all. He said he knew Irvin and Lumina since he could remember and ever since then, they held their love for each other no matter the distance.

Mina could have that, too. Yes, Calin and Amberly hardly knew her, and she them, but why should that stop her from pursuing friendship? They seemed to like her well enough. They even helped her.

Helped her find the stolen heart. Stolen by the old companions. When Mina pictured the young Queen, she overlapped Amberly's face onto hers. They clicked. Perfectly.

A ball formed in Mina's stomach, pushing outward. She placed a hand over her stomach. It must've been the worms making her so sick. At least she couldn't vomit.

"It appears you're in as much need of saving as I am," Calin huffed. "What do you plan to do now? Charm your way out of here? Good luck. That Young Queen of the Bees wouldn't budge."

Heels clicked from down the hallway, far from Mina's cell.

"Perhaps I shall try anyway," Amberly declared.

The clicks drew closer. Buzzing followed them. The noise leveled higher the closer they got. Mina pressed into the bars, craning to see down the hall.

The young Queen of the Bees strode with five soldier bees behind her, all with straight posture and raised chins. She wore a different skirt, one hanging to the length of her knees, and held a golden scepter with a red sphere end by her chest like a bouquet. The scepter matched Amberly's exactly. Her blurry face angled forward, smudgy red lips swishing. Her upper body kept still, not a twitch in her wings, arms, or head.

She pivoted to face the cells. The guards remained at her back, positioned with their legs spread apart and stingers lifted slightly. They looked ready to protect her at any minute, a fruitless effort. With the iron bars so close together, no prisoner would be getting to the Queen.

"Two thieves and a trespasser," the Queen said. The heart piece on her head taunted Mina with a blinding twinkle. "I came to look at you."

Mina tried to find her voice, but the spellbinding woman before her turned words to mush on her tongue. She stuttered a few syllables, nothing coherent.

"Grand Queen," Amberly spoke up, scoffing. "Your presence is unwanted."

That definitely wasn't what Mina tried to say.

Calin joined in. "It takes a lot of time getting down here. Coming to initiate our trials?"

The Queen tipped her head to the side for a second, the red on the bottom half of her face thinning out.

Mina perked up. If the trial happened soon, they could get out of here, get the heart piece, somehow, and be on their way to the third.

"No," the Queen said.

Mina slouched.

"You've come down here," Amberly said, "so why not?"

"Because it is a task I don't want to do," the Queen explained.

"It is a quick task," argued Amberly. "Innocent or guilty—and I say, we are innocent."

The Queen looked to her right. "The rest of the prisoners are awaiting their trials. If I start here, it is unfairly unfair. They were here first. If I start over there, then I'd have to give everyone a trial as that is fair, too. But that is far too much work. We have accumulated"—she sucked in a big breath—"*a lot* of prisoners."

"Bratty brat," Amberly spat. "Horrible bratty brat. There could be so many innocents here wasting away."

The Queen huffed. "Because of your sharp tongue, old bee, you will not have any trial, nor will your accomplice."

Mina hit her head against the bars from how fast she lurched forward. "No. Please, no."

"Let them free," Calin said quickly. "I can take all of their wrongdoings and put them into my trial."

The Queen tilted her chin in the direction of his voice.

"No," Mina whimpered. "Calin, you can't."

"You would bear all of their wrongs in your own trial?" the Queen asked.

"I would," he said, no hesitation.

"It would put more scrutiny onto you."

"My answer will not change."

"Pitiful, pitiful fool," Amberly said. "No."

The Queen tapped her scepter. "Very well. More guilt is added to the trespasser's case. He will be deeply analyzed if his trial comes."

The soldiers buzzed.

"Does that mean you will let Amberly and Mina go?" Calin asked. The streak of hopefulness in his voice made the magic in Mina's chest ache.

A flash, like lightning in a thunderstorm, struck the Queen's face. "I..." She shook her head. "They are still guilty of their crimes, and you are guilty of your own *and* theirs."

"That is nonsensical!" Calin cried.

"I told you," Amberly whispered. "Pitiful, pitiful fool."

"Please," Mina said, pressing into the bars. The iron sent fire through her magic. "I can't wait for long. I will repay you with whatever I can if you let us free."

The Queen turned. "No," she threw over her shoulder, spiteful. She clicked away, taking her soldiers with her. The buzzing drowned out Calin and Amberly's protesting and washed away Mina's will to even try.

The bees vanished all the way at the other end of the hallway. Only the worms remained to squelch in the ensuing silence.

After a moment, Clain's shoes scraped the floor back and forth in his cell. "This isn't how things should go. Amberly, you and Mina shouldn't even be in here. Now she won't get the heart piece."

"Don't go blaming me, or her," Amberly responded, hotly. "Helping you wasn't a question. We would do it no matter what."

"Well, the way you went about it wasn't even efficient. I could've gotten out of here myself."

Amberly sucked in a sharp breath. She sounded ready to spit back some venom, but a drawn-out pause drained it away. When she made a sound again, it came as a whimper. A soft sniffle she partially concealed behind her hand, or arm, or whatever she stifled it into.

"This is my fault," she said, nose stuffy. "I'll be the downfall of you, Mina."

The magic bundled in Mina's chest started bleeding out in anguish. She wanted to break down the brick wall between them and go to Amberly to embrace her. It didn't matter who she might've been or what she might've done, she needed comfort right now.

"You won't be," Mina told her, a hair above a whisper.

Calin let out a harsh grunt. "There's no possible way to break down these bars. Not without an extra dose of strength."

"They can't be squeezed through either," Amberly added, strained.

He sighed. "If I met the Wishmaker right now, I would wish for all these mirrors, deals, and heart pieces to go away."

Mina slumped. "Me too," she said, even though he couldn't actually help her.

"If we have to stay here," Amberly said, "I will find a way to convince the Queen to let us go."

"No, you won't," Calin bit out.

"I will," she retorted. "I've had more time than you to accumulate a certain level of wisdom, so listen to me. I..." She puffed. "Or have I? Maybe you're right, Calin. I don't know anything. How could I? My younger days were so fit with trivial beauty, sloth, and such. I should have developed my mind better."

"Relax—"

She cut him off. "Never, ever, ever."

Mina held her head in her blistering hands. "Stop arguing, please. It does nothing. What we need to do is come up with a plan. Amberly, you must have had some idea about what to do after this point."

"Yes," Calin added, sour. "I'm sure you have something brewing."

Amberly took forever to answer. She choked up when she spoke. "I thought the best way to get you, Calin, out of being imprisoned was by becoming imprisoned."

"Then what?" questioned Calin.

"Then we would..." she hiccuped. "I didn't think too far ahead, though there is a plan, one I hate, one I should've spoken about with everyone, but it is goody good. It could help us."

The magic on Mina's hands thumped. "What is it?"

"I don't know if I want to share. But oh, the young Queen might come back and rip us in half if we do nothing, then we'll all be uselessly dead."

Calin cleared his throat. He spoke through his teeth. "Tell us this plan you have."

"I'm sorry," Amberly said instead. "This is all my fault. If I didn't have a buzzing brain, I could've been a master of everything."

"No," Mina said. "None of this is your fault. You two wouldn't have to help me and be in this predicament if I wasn't a useless wish."

"You have nothing to fault yourself for," Calin said. "Nobody can control everything about their life."

"You don't understand," Mina said, setting her head against the bars. "I'm not even human. I'm much, much further from being anything at all. Mistakes, that's all I can make."

Amberly laughed dryly. "Look at what happened to us. I do that, too."

"You made it farther than others have," Calin said, "so what does it matter if you made a mistake or two?"

Mina sat frustrated with herself. With Calin. With Amberly. They could have argued all they wanted about who was right or wrong, but the fact still remained: she was a wish, different from the rest of the world. Nothing but a real heart could change her.

Fingers thrummed against the wall of her cell, opposite from the one she shared with Amberly's cell. But there wasn't anybody on the other side. From what she'd been able to tell, she was in the very last cell on the row.

She skittered. The sound must've been her imagination. Or the worms outside grew hands and used them.

"Amberly?" Calin called out.

"Yes?" she responded.

A ball of air popped out of him before he spoke. "What is your plan?"

"I hate it as much as you will," she said.

"But I'm listening."

"Please don't hate me, too."

"I won't."

She inhaled, exhaled, inhaled again, then spoke on the next exhale. "We get help from the Bloo—"

Calin gurgled. "From the—"

"Yes."

"Amberly," he said darkly.

"You said you'd listen."

"But I didn't say anything about not being angry about it."

Mina swallowed. Summoning the Blood King was better than nothing, but it also came with its own risks. The young Queen of the Bees, however, would never get to their trial if her word was anything to go by.

"I like it," Mina said.

Calin groaned. "Of course you do. You're the only person who likes him as he is now."

"You've any better suggestions?" Amberly demanded. "He's in the walls. He's watching in his mirrors. I've used his help before, and it has gone both upways and downways."

"Before?" Calin sounded like he was reeling from a broken bone. "You've done this before? How many times?"

Amberly buzzed, happily. "I always recommend using his help. As much as he can be a painful wart, he can also be a useful one."

"I've never heard of a useful wart," Calin said.

"If Mina wants to bring him into the fray, I say we follow her," Amberly stated. "This is *her* life to save."

Calin fell silent.

"This is for all of our lives," Mina said. "We're all going to bring his heart to him. That means we should all agree on what to do."

"But Mina—" Calin started.

"I want us to be in this together. Now think, there's got to be another way out of here that we can all agree on." She rummaged for any other idea on how to escape. She wouldn't fit through the bars, but perhaps... "Amberly, you used magic to shrink yourself. Maybe you can shrink some more."

"Magic is a wonderful idea," Amberly said. "My scepter can help me do loads of tricks with confidence."

Mina bloomed. "Great, then you—"

"I practiced magic on and on and on when I was younger," she continued, full of pride. "But I never got good at it, so I quit."

"But you turned us into bugs."

"Because I am a bug." She hit her scepter on the bars of her cell. "The size we are is as small as I can be. I can turn to bug size and human size with anyone or anything in my hand. That's all I can do. It's probably why the soldiers didn't take my scepter away."

"Oh," Mina said.

"Mina," Calin said. Her name came out louder than usual. Unsure. "We're wasting time arguing. You have to summon him."

"If you don't like the plan..."

"This isn't about what I like; it's about what we need to do. Summon him."

Mina turned her face to the wall where she thought she heard fingers tapping. She studied the cracks deeply, plucking a shape out of the darkness.

Another round of tapping came from the other side.

Getting on her feet, she inched closer to the wall, pinning down the wiggling fingers. Slowly, they became more visible. Her hand hovered over the wall. When certainty that the fingers were real settled over her, she pressed her hand over them.

The tapping ceased.

One side of her lips briefly pulled upward.

"Blood King," she said. "Please, help us."

The wall trembled under her touch, reaching to the ground. Waves filtered the air, thick enough to push Mina a step back.

Swiveling, the world changed. Mina rocketed to the floor, rolling into the wall as the room turned and the wall she laid on became the new floor.

Calin and Amberly shouted from their cells. Clanks and scuffs rang as the world changed again, now turning the ceiling into the floor.

Mina crawled to the bars, peering through them down the hallway. The wind howled and metal screeched at the other end of the hall. Bars ripped out of place one by one and slashed the worms. Not one prisoner in any of the many cells flew out into the river of wind barreling into the bright, hazy blue light at the far end of the hall.

Making a fist, Mina clenched her jaw. More bars flew out of place, getting closer to her.

Then, three bars tore out of place, their long lengths dancing into the light. Calin shouted. His body flung into the hall, his limbs flailing as he went to the light.

"Calin!" Mina cried out, a scream bubbling into her throat.

Amberly called his name as well. The wind, however, cut her short of the second syllable, grabbing her bars, reaching into her cell, and plucking her out of place. She flew down the same path, wings fluttering but not strong enough to overcome the wind.

Mina braced herself for the inevitable as her cell's bars shook.

The first bar went immediately. The rest ripped out of place in rapid succession.

Wind lashed at her, scooping her up and dragging her across the ground. She whorled out into the hallway, sailing weightlessly with a bunch of worms and iron into the unknown brightness.

FABRIC RAIN

*S*leek curls, an eye without scars around it, and a perfect smile stared at Mina. All belonging to a face disembodied in a thick void of violet and black.

Davian loved that face. The human one.

"So why don't you say you wish you were me?" asked the floating face.

A sound question. Mina parted her lips. "I wish…"

"Mina, Mina." Hands shook her all over. "Mina, Mina."

Someone tore the palm she'd placed over her eyes. Mina gasped. She wasn't trapped elsewhere with Lumina. Thank goodness. She was in a domed room with Amberly shaking her. Red light ignited the place, yet she couldn't decipher where it came from. This place had no windows, nor were there any lanterns or candles. Only masked bees lay on the floor and they definitely didn't emit the glow.

"Mina, Mina," Amberly said.

Wet stains dotted Amberly's cheeks. The whites of her eyes turned pink, enhancing the glow of her irises. Distinct waves of lighter blue rippled through them.

"You're fine, dearie dear?" Amberly asked.

Mina nodded.

"Not a sweat to drop then."

Calin groaned. Mina turned. He sat up from a cradled position, gripping his knees. His hat sat by his feet, leaving behind a mess of hair stuck up in all directions. The fluffiness on his head complemented his bushy mustache.

He rocked back and forth, his teeth clamped on his bottom lip. Eyes squeezed shut, he sucked back a huge breath.

Mina inched toward him. "Calin?"

His eyes snapped open. When he spotted her, he let go of his knees and grabbed his hat, acting as if nothing was wrong. "You're all right, right? That wind was strong."

The concern lit a beautiful fire in her chest. "We're fine. It's you I'm worried about. There's a scrape on your cheek." She reached out to the red mark.

"Everything is fine." He backed away from her and cleared his throat. "We're back together. Free, too." He jerked a thumb toward the bees. "Let's get out of here before they wake up."

As if on cue, the bees lifted their heads. They buzzed menacingly as though they were starving wolves. They climbed to their feet, skull faces turning toward them, the expressions somehow changed. The bony textures contorted, wrinkled and pinched as if they held grimaces. There were a lot more bees than before. A lot—a lot more. The entire room was nearly filled with them, hardly leaving any open spaces on the floor.

Calin frowned. "Well, freedom was nice for the moment."

"Criminals!" shrilled the young Queen of the Bees. She burst through her subjects, her blurry face turning red. Redder that the jagged heart piece in her hair. "You are not only trespassers and thieves, but you are now escaped criminals." Her chest rose and fell. "Your punishments will now be much more severe. You'll wish you never tried to escape!"

"Listen here, little Queen," Amberly growled, getting to her feet, "you won't punish us because, well, we're leaving."

"I am the Queen. Everything I want, I get."

Amberly shook her head. "No, that won't happen."

"Be silent," the Queen demanded. Her words bounced off her scepter, lighting it up, and an icy wind blew in from the reddened walls, freezing everyone in place. She swept her scepter horizontally in front of her, lingering it on Amberly, Mina, and Calin each for a second. "Fighting is useless. A trial shall never come your way, as there is no question of your guilt. My beautiful bees, take these rapscallions back to their cells, where they will await their punishment."

The bees started to move, eager to take them away. Mina backed up. Her jaw tensed as she looked around and found no escape. She huddled closer to Calin and Amberly. Both held stronger stances, Calin making fists and Amberly gearing her scepter up by her shoulders, ready to strike.

Mina made her own weak fists. She knew, however, they couldn't fight off the bees. The magic in her chest sank. She'd called for the Blood King. Where was he?

Bees swarmed them. They swiped at Mina and went for her arms. This time when they grabbed her the pain shocked her so badly that she blacked out and went limp. Any fight she had in her fled in an instant. She wanted to cry at her lack of strength, especially when she witnessed the harder time the bees had in grabbing Calin and Amberly. They fought back. They had strength.

Whimpering, Mina accepted defeat. She found the young Queen's blurred face and said, "I'm sorry you have such a bitter heart. Whatever soured it, I'm sorry that happened to you."

The Queen's shoulders fell along with her scepter. She tilted her head to the side. "What?"

"You have a terrible heart," Mina said simply. "But you're so beautiful, it makes no sense."

"Bees," the Queen said, "stop for a moment."

They did, though very slowly. Beside Mina, Calin and Amberly looked at her with raised brows and open mouths.

The Queen approached Mina, the red of her lips swirling. "I am not cruel."

"You are," Mina insisted.

"The bees, they adore me."

"From behind masks, how can you see that?"

The Queen fell silent. She angled her face, peering around the room. Her bees kept to themselves, avoiding looking at her through the eye holes on their masks.

"I..." Her voice came out hoarse. "My mother told me they must wear masks. She made me wear one. I adored her anyway."

"One day you will not be the ruler of anything," Mina said. "You will see that your cruelty has separated you from others, and you will regret not making more out of yourself." She shifted, feeling lighter. "But you will be able to make friends. You will be able to warm your heart and do everything you thought had passed you by."

The Queen drifted a hand to the red piece on her head. The lightness in Mina dropped. Out of the corner of her eye she saw Amberly gazing at her, tearful. If they were the same person, then Mina hoped her words pierced her heart and made her recall herself. Recall what had happened.

And if not, she hoped anyway that Amberly knew she had greatness in her.

Taking the heart piece out of her hair, the Queen displayed it on her palm. "I have this feeling," she whispered, her blank face turning to Amberly, even though she kept speaking to Mina, "that I need to give this to you."

The magic leapt to Mina's chest, pulsing as if she had her own elated heart. She took a step toward the Queen.

Hammers hit the outsides of the hive, ringing like a bell and shaking the ground. Shouts erupted out of the bees and the Queen shrieked. A splash of darkness encased the room for a moment. Then the red light returned.

Bees gasped. They backed away to reveal the figure at the center of the room.

Mina's lips twitched up.

The blood on him glowed. The grim expression on the Blood King's face and the ferocity of his stare made Mina's insides thump in fear and excitement.

But then he spotted her, and his harshness diminished, leaving her empty of any fear.

"Of course he had to show up," Calin grumbled.

Amberly sprinted to the Queen, reaching out for the heart piece.

The room tilted, throwing everyone but the Blood King off-balance. Bodies flung to the floor, rolling into each other. The young Queen cracked her head against one of the skull masked bees near her.

Mina hurried forward and reached her arm out toward Amberly. Amberly reached back. Their fingers grazed before they both lost their footing, falling away from each other.

Calin stumbled past Mina, hissing through his teeth. He banged his knee on his way down, shouting in agony.

Mina called after him. She took two steps and hit the ground as the floor lifted some more. Bees rolled into the wall, piling onto each other. Wings clashed against Mina, and an edge hit her in the eye. She rolled, hair in her face, sensing arms and feet colliding into her. When she hit the wall, her magic lunged as if it was going to splash off of her body. Instead, it climbed further up her right forearm, strands beginning to wrap around her elbow.

The Queen screeched, blood leaking down the side of her face. "Off of me, off of me! Everyone get off."

As the bees climbed off their Queen, the floor swung the other way, evening out again, followed by a series of thuds. One bee fell too close to Mina, their elbow striking her jaw. Her head whipped to the side, her nose getting crushed into the floor. She lay face down with her hands flat at her sides, ready to push up.

But all she could do was allow her hands to go numb while she flipped onto her back, indulging in stillness.

Fabric fell gently from the ceiling. The silky shine of each color radiated in the red light. It piled onto the floor, one beautiful mess.

"Wonderfull," marveled the Queen.

The bees buzzed with her, showering in the rolls of fabric. Their loudness rushed heat into Mina's head. She gripped her face, allowing the fabric to cover her. Her body, which cried for rest since the start of her journey, finally relaxed. It never wanted to get up again.

"Aren't these shades delightful?" Amberly gushed. She raised her arms, joining the dancing bees.

"They are," Calin said. His voice wavered, distant from himself and a little slurred. "Mina?"

Opening her mouth, Mina couldn't find it in her to speak. Words would've required too much effort. She stayed in place, arms folded over her stomach. Her legs settled, toes pointing outward. Fabric landed on her, hiding her as well as Davian had. Keeping her nature and origin a secret. A wish in the dark.

Fabric shifted from her face. A hand passed over her cheek.

"Mina," the Blood King cooed. "What are you doing under here?"

"Sleeping," she murmured, eyes wide open.

He rested onto an elbow by her side, picking at her hair. "I would like to sleep, too, if I could."

She readjusted her head.

"I thought you weren't coming."

He blinked. "But you asked me to."

"You were late. I almost had the heart piece."

A puff of air escaped him. "No, no, no," he said. "I ruined everything."

She hummed, unable to find it in her to be angry. It was an accident after all.

They gazed at each other, heartless being to heartless being. A peaceful slice in a world of ensuing chaos. This was the kind of moment Mina wanted with Davian at his party. Had Lumina never showed up, it might've been possible, though part of her knew he wouldn't have slipped away with her. It made her want to laugh. For a man who fought to hide her when he could, he had quickly abandoned her in a crowd the moment the opportunity arose.

Mina didn't think the Blood King would leave her, even though neither swore attachment to the other, and they were only working together on a deal. He seemed the type, however, to hold decency in high regard, deal or not.

When he gazed at her in earnest, she liked him. When he flicked away from her in stubbornness, she liked him. It was a strange sort of feeling, one she couldn't exactly make out. From how the Wishmaker trembled, she'd expected a more calculated man.

But he wasn't quite that. He spoke plainly, truthfully. For that, Mina appreciated him.

Something ticked in his head as his face worked. He stared at her, melancholy blanketing his amber eyes. The flick of his gaze going up and down her face made her think of the feeling she had when Davian first let her go. When she knew he didn't want her, when she knew she needed to start letting him go. It was an intense battle of truthful need against false wanting.

She sat up. "What is happening?"

Their faces were close, noses inches apart. Magic flourished in Mina's chest and stomach, pattering about in an absurd manner. They hung in a plane of their own existence, bees long since buzzed away from consciousness. Mina hoped he felt as deeply entrenched in this new world as she did.

So strange, she thought.

"Everything," he answered.

"What's wrong?"

"Any idea as to what I'm feeling escapes me." His jaw shifted. "I think I want you to win our game."

A game. The haze cleared from her head. *Why would you say it like that? Why is a heart a game?*

"Amberly is your old companion," she blurted out. "She's the young Queen of the Bees, but she doesn't know."

The Blood King grunted, angling away from her, a seemingly disgruntled answer. One good enough for her to go on.

"You thought I was stupid enough to not notice?" she prodded. "Look where we're at! A beehive. The Queen had your heart piece, and Amberly sounds just like her. Are Calin and Oldest Son the same, too?"

Lifting a brow, the Blood King shifted his jaw, meeting her face. "I don't think you're stupid. I think you're brave. Part of the fun in all of this is letting others find out your secrets." He frowned. "Though I do warn you, they are bad people, Mina. They stole my heart. They could prevent your success. See, their heads are warped from all the magic around them. They can't remember much, but they were once terrible."

Crossing her arms, Mina felt one of her brows twitch, trying to go up. "But you're terrible, too. You lied to me about them."

"It's wrong for me to have done that," the Blood King acknowledged. "I guess you could say I'm a little heartless."

Now Mina's lips twitched. "Of course," she said, her hand finding his chest. Such an empty thing it was. Like hers. "Finding it would help you feel better again."

"That's a nice thought," he said, falling into a deep stare.

"And what if, when you feel better, you and your companions reconcile?" *Is that why you want me to have a heart? To help you?* But she wouldn't ask those two questions. He was already too aloof about his companions. She had to take this situation one small step at a time. "Then you won't be so alone."

"Would you want to reconcile with Davian? He wronged you." He snorted. "Oh, I forgot, you do."

She tried to find a way to say why she was right and he was wrong, but nothing came. Mina simply shrugged. "It...you seemed sad that you don't have your companions anymore," she said. "I don't want you to be unhappy. Even if it can't work in the end, won't you want to at least try? Tell me what happened."

A blink brought the Blood King out of the distance he'd stumbled into. He put his hand on top of hers. "Isn't this place marvelous? Everyone is dancing so splendidly, including your strange friends."

Bees waltzed over the fabric still pouring from the ceiling. Calin spun Amberly around, both laughing and showing off their friendly compatibility again. Even the Queen floated her arms gracefully. The red blotch over her mouth widened. If she were put together properly, she could've been a ballerina.

The Blood King stroked Mina's wrist. "Do you think we should join them?"

Seeing how careless the world could be, the conversation melted from mind and Mina jumped upon her answer. "Yes."

"Then it is sealed." The Blood King grabbed her hand gently, caressing the magic so it wouldn't hurt. He helped her to her feet.

Mina sighed. This was the closest thing she'd have to a dream.

The Blood King turned his face from her for a second. "I'm not sure," he said as if in response to someone. Someone who wasn't there.

"I didn't say anything," Mina told him.

He glanced around the room. "Isn't this place marvelous?"

Arms flailed about. One of the bees fell. They laughed.

"Everyone is dancing splendidly," Mina said, vision hazy. "I've never seen better."

"Even your friends."

She admired Calin and Amberly. They waved at her, full of delight. It was so unlike the last time she weaved in the space of dancing people. The heartbreak of that day was the opposite of the fullness she felt now. Here, people saw her. Lauded her for who she was. This was how her life was supposed to be. Happy all around. The pain surging in her magic had no place here, not even as the Blood

King's shaking hand secured hers, holding it as though it was the most precious jewel in the world.

It was wonderful. All of it. At that moment, Mina was determined to help them all. To unearth what made the heart get stolen, to see if its return could repair their companionship.

"Where is your head?" Mina asked the Blood King.

"In a trial of my own."

She studied him. Unlike his appearance at the Herre house, he seemed further from conscious thought. His eyes constantly darted from her, and he jittered.

"How so?" she prompted.

"I lied to you like I have in other deals, but now I regret doing that. I hate treating you as I have others. Those I didn't believe in. Mina, I think I want you to find your heart."

"And for what reason do you phrase it like that?"

"I simply want to grant you your wish."

"You will." She turned away from him. "The heart piece rests again on the Queen's head. She's distracted right now. I could take it easily."

When she strayed too far, he pulled her into him, holding her with her back pressed against his chest.

"We must enjoy what time is left," he told her.

"There can't be much if we waste it. We can dance as much as we want after I become human."

"Not a second will be lost," he assured her.

He kept her firm in his grasp, swaying over the mountains of fabric.

Mina rested against him, feeling his lack of a heartbeat. Perhaps she could spare a few seconds. His arms around her told her so. She wouldn't experience this again if she ran off and failed. At least she'd have the knowledge of how his arms fit around her before that happened.

Very strange, she kept thinking, sliced up with guilt. These thoughts shouldn't have come. Not when she lived for Davian.

"Do you enjoy being alone?" she asked the Blood King, pressing her head deeper into his chest.

He remained silent.

"You told me you wanted your heart back because it belongs to you," she said. "I wonder if you truly feel pitiful without it, just as I do. Do you want to be with your friends again? To fix those bonds?"

"Never. My work is easy being alone. It is only I who suffers," he told her. "Yet I find myself clinging to you. When you made your plea, I wanted to know more. A human-feeling wish, that was what I thought of you. A warm wish, who keeps expressing a desire to see that rat of a boy who deserted her. How could you want to return to him? With a heart, there is much to explore in a brand-new life."

Mina frowned for a second. "You told me life was worthless."

He pulled away, grasping her shoulders, and smiling. "I did, didn't I? Since observing you, I have been thinking. Thinking too much." He lifted a fist, hitting the side of his head. "I should stop. I should keep going about my old ways. If I let you stay any closer"—he let go of her—"then it will all hurt more."

Her breathing shuddered. "What will hurt more?"

"To see you go, too," he said, his voice breaking. He stepped back, chest rising and falling. Dourness overtook him. His head wobbled. He looked at Calin and Amberly, thoughtful. "But perhaps, I could find a new idea. Perhaps, Mina, there are things yet to explore."

Yes, there were things to explore. But she wouldn't find those things if she didn't go to Calin and Amberly, if she didn't get the heart piece.

"Mina," the Blood King said. "Perhaps there can be change in a person. I admire your open thinking to such a thing. A heart would suit you very well."

She swallowed, turning to her friends. *Friends.* But they'd stolen a heart. Her mind whorled. They were also good to her. They deserved the opportunity to remember their true selves and explain what they'd done. Good people would do that. Good people would forgive each other. That was it. Forgiveness. They could forgive.

Racing to her spinning pair of friends, Mina almost tripped on a red slice of fabric as she left the Blood King behind.

"We need to get the heart piece from the Queen," Mina said to them.

They kept spinning.

"We will, we will," Calin said, throwing his arms above his head. Fabric twisted under his feet as he neared Mina. "There's no rush."

"Yes, there is." She ducked out of his way.

Calin's next step took him to a standstill. His arms floated to his sides, and he swayed. "I have no idea what you mean."

Far behind, over Calin's shoulder, the Blood King lingered. Mina's breath hitched. He'd moved so fast without her noticing. Shadows layered his image, his amber irises glowing in them. He met Mina's gaze, flicking his head to the side, urging her to move and a single sheet of black fabric fell from above, dropping in front of him. When it cleared out of his way, he was gone.

"Such a confusing man," Mina said to herself, finding it easier, better, to think of him rather than Davian.

"What did you say?" Amberly shouted. She slapped her mouth and giggled. "Sorry. I didn't need to shout about."

Calin rubbed his ear. "You're right about that. There's no music or speech to shout over." He furrowed his brows. "Wait, why did we dance without music?"

"Because this isn't a marvelous dance," Mina said. "We have to leave."

Hand sliding to his face, Calin rubbed his cheek. "You..." He dropped his arm, shaking out his body. "You're right. We have a trial to get to."

One glance at the twirling young Queen of the Bees said the trial wouldn't happen for certain. Not when she was distracted as she was.

Amberly spun. "I could do this dance forever—marvelous or not."

Calin frowned. "Sorry, you're not going to." Grabbing her arm, he prevented her from spinning again.

She blew a puff of air into his face, her features contorted with anger. "Stop stopping me. I can be the only stopper stopping me. Ever."

"I had to," Calin told her. "We need to help Mina while the Queen is distracted."

"Queen?" Amberly hardened. "Cruel brat. She doesn't deserve such a gem."

"But wait," Mina said. "The Queen isn't so bad. Remember?"

"I cracked my head and do not remember. I bet she doesn't either, just because she's selfish." Amberly squared her shoulders. Mina wanted to stop her and try to explain what her mind couldn't, but she raised her scepter and shouted, "Down!"

The bees fell to the floor in unison, the wind knocking out of them. Amberly led the way through their buzzing bodies, going to the young Queen of the Bees.

"See who has the power," Amberly said to the Queen. "It is me. I can control my size, and the bees."

"And nothing more," the Queen ridiculed. "You're nothingly nothing but wasted time wrapped up into a wrinkled woman."

Amberly pressed her lips together, face falling.

Mina made fists at her sides, shocked by the remarks being made. "You are cruel to speak about someone that way."

"Meaning is found in the highest achievements," the Queen said. Her spine straightened, stinger lifting slightly. She propped her chin up, one long breath leaving her. "We are all nothing without it."

"You're wrong," Amberly cut in. She pointed her scepter at the Queen.

Light exploded from the scepter, knocking into the young Queen. She screamed, falling over, knocking the back of her head against hard ground. The red smear of her lips expanded. Cracks formed over her blank face, black.

Mina expected the Queen to stand and shout for her guards. But the young Queen of the Bees simply burst into tears.

"Having a good heart is what matters," Amberly said. "You'll see it one day when you've gotten into too much trouble." She bent down, plucking the heart piece from the Queen's hair. "I'll be taking this so that a truly kind young woman can have her heart. Yours, on the other hand, must've stopped working."

Amberly handed Mina the heart piece, who stared at the woman in awe. "Halfway there," she said, winking.

Calin waved his hand in front of his face, wiping away the smoke pouring out of Amberly's scepter. "I thought you didn't know magic."

She blinked and stared at the red sphere on her scepter. "I don't." She chuckled. "No, I don't, but maybe..." A smile broke out over her face. "That little practice I did doesn't make me as bad as I thought. If I just focus, like my lessons wanted, calm down, like my lessons wanted, and not hold such an expectation, like my lessons wanted, then I could get us out of here for good."

"That's great," Mina said, finally taking the heart piece into a magic-filled hand.

Amberly spun her scepter up above her head. "I could summon a bit of magic. Hold tight. My mind says we're going to swim out of here."

The red sphere glowed.

Mina stiffened. "I can't swim."

Arm falling, Amberly frowned. "I'm afraid it's too late. Now that I think of it, neither can I."

"Where exactly are we swimming?" Calin asked, scratching the back of his neck..

Amberly pointed behind them.

A heavy flow of water struck Mina right as she turned her head.

SHARING IN A SMILE

"You have more magic on your arm," the Blood King observed, a touch above a murmur.

Mina groaned. She lifted her right arm, watching the magic trail onto her shoulder. Water droplets stuck to the mass. Such small beads created such enormous stings. She hissed a little, reminding herself they had the second heart piece. They were halfway to the full heart. Soon this would all be over, and she would become human. She rested her arm back down at her side. *Soon.*

The damp ceiling of the Blood King's castle floated above her. Or rather, she floated below it. Beaming slashes of glowing crimson stemmed in her peripheral vision. Half numb, Mina drifted in stillness. Distant shivers attempted to prick her. She sensed them rising from her core, trying to strike her shoulders and roll around to her back. She ground her teeth, trying to force them to come to life. They never did.

"I wish this would stop," she said.

"My dearest wish," the Blood King said, "if you could make a wish, you wouldn't be here."

Her fingers curled inward, clasping around the sharp-edged object in her hand. A spark shot through her. She gripped the heart piece, not caring that its contact hurt.

As Mina sat up, the ground splashed and shook underneath her. She tensed. She'd been lying on an orange leaf which floated upon crimson water kept within the round walls of a brick encasing. Nearby, the first heart piece floated. Compared to it, she was the size of a bug.

A bug.

"Oh, no."

Watery magic splashed as she shifted and the leaf nearly tipped her overboard. Mina stilled, holding in her breath. She craned her head up and scanned the room. The Blood King's mirrors sat at the walls. They now seemed much bigger than the buildings in Deamindis, and the Blood King himself, well, he had become a giant standing at the edge of his well. The well Mina floated within.

A nervous laugh drifted over the surface. "At least I didn't drown you," Amberly said from another orange leaf. Her eyes roved over Mina. "You seem finely fine."

"It could have been worse," Mina agreed. They could still be in the hive, and her magic could've eaten more than both of her arms already.

Both arms. She almost tipped over the leaf again. *Both* of her arms were wrapped in violet-black magic. She spread her tainted fingers. Tingling ran over her knuckles. It spread to her elbows, violet lighting snapping to her shoulders. And she was wrong to say it was only both arms. Thin branches crept onto her collarbone and neck, too.

Calin groaned. He rested on his side, leaf spinning lazily, eyes closed. He nestled his head into the crook of his arm.

"Apologies for surprising you with the water," Amberly said, more grave than she'd ever been before. She chewed on her bottom lip. "I got too excited about myself. Me, me, what a we. I never breathe through a thought. You really could have been hurt."

"It's all right," Mina assured her. "We're fine. That's what matters."

Amberly's red lips stretched, blue eyes shimmering. "But I'll remember next time I have a thought, to play it and say it so that we for sure always stay fine."

Mina warmed inside. "That's a nice idea."

"All right." Amberly stuck her hands in the watery magic, spinning toward Calin. She splashed the water at him. "Up, up, up, sleepyhead."

He waved her off. "Leave me alone."

"You would despise me if I did that."

"I wouldn't at the given moment," he mumbled.

A throat cleared from above.

"I would rather you not splash around my hard work," the Blood King said.

Calin blinked wide awake, horrified. Bolting upright, his gaze roved over the deep red of the watery magic. He spat out and wiped the droplets off of himself. "Hey, hey, get this off of me!"

Mina laughed internally. When she shifted her focus to the Blood King, her magic came to life in a way she hadn't felt before. Inside of the thumps, pulses, and stings, it wrapped up tightly, tugging on an unknown sensation of sparks bursting through her stomach.

The Blood King rested an elbow on the well's ledge, placing his cheek in his palm. He tilted his head to the side. Mischievousness danced on his lips.

"I see there is a new little piece of a heart token," he said. "Congratulations, Mina. You truly are a miracle."

She folded her fingers over the heart piece. "Thank you for helping us." She looked around at everyone. "It was an effort from all of you."

Calin sat up, eyes snapping open. "An effort from all of us? The Blo—came and, and, and, distracted us. It was a loose plan."

Amberly beamed. "But it worked. Calin, don't deny that."

"Well…" He frowned. "It did. But next time, I think I could handle things better."

The Blood King dipped a finger into the water, making tiny circles. Mina froze as she bobbed up and down in the wake.

"Calin, is it hard always being the only human around magnificence?" the Blood King asked, bored. "Humans are inherently less magical. Is that why you're so lumped in a grump trying to be tough? As good as us?"

"I'm able to do what I can," Calin said. "That's a lot for me."

"No one is worse or better than anyone else here," Mina said, though she sensed the tiniest waver in her declaration. What of the stolen heart? Didn't that make Calin and Amberly worse in morality?

She peered at the Blood King out of the corner of her eye. If he hated them so, then why did he let them stay here in the mirrors? Why speak so cordially with them? Why let them help her? If he wanted her to get her heart, then it would make no sense to place her in the care of bad people. He did call them that.

There was something off about all of this. Something was missing. Like Calin and Amberly's memories.

"Tell me, are you all—" Mina began.

Amberly cut off her question. "Sometimes, we're selfish. Makes us all as worse as each other."

The Blood King nodded. "Indeed."

Calin scrunched up his face. "Everyone is speaking too loudly." He rubbed the side of his head, face going slack. "Where's my hat?"

From behind his back, the Blood King produced Calin's round hat. It was back to its regular size. Wet fingers dampened the brim.

"Safe and sound," the Blood King announced.

"You," Calin said, narrowing his eyes. "You, you, give that back, hat thief."

A mocking little pout dangled on the Blood King's lips. "Why give it back? It wouldn't fit you now."

Calin folded his arms and glared.

"Don't blame me," Amberly chimed in. "I've accomplished more magic than you ever did."

Silence pursued her voice for a few seconds.

Calin broke it. "I didn't start blaming you for anything."

She shook her finger. "In three more moments, you would have."

"Absurd," he said. "I would not."

A warm chuckle wrapped the air. Mina held her stinging hands together, the heart piece resting carefully between her palms. The Blood King's easy laughter stoked her ears with delight, making her forget her pain for a moment. He stood at ease, setting the hat down.

"Being so small isn't going to benefit any of you," he said to them.

Amberly snapped her fingers. "My magic could fire up a big storm." She shook her scepter. A spark flew out, dying as it hit the water. She frowned. "I guess I spent all my power already."

The Blood King threw up his hands. "How pitiful. It appears you'll stay small and adorable forever. I have the perfect jars to display you in, too."

"Do not dare," Calin said. He jolted up high on his knees, making a fist. Water sloshed under him. The leaf rocked on the waves. His fist shook once at the Blood King before he lowered, hands splaying on the leaf for balance.

Mina sat up straighter. "But..."

The Blood King smirked at her. "I know. I can't. I won't. It is only a silly thought. A jest. You have much more to do than float around in my domain. If you ever want to be a small speck on my magic again, though, please, do let me know."

As the Blood King stepped back, he lifted his hands. All the blood smeared on him lit up. The water shifted, waves returning. They rocked the leaves, tipping them forward.

Mina held her breath. Wind screamed in her ears. She braced for the smash of her face into the water as her head dived forward. Her legs somersaulted over her head, slicing downward. Her feet hit solid ground. The Blood King stood in front of her, a normal size.

She lightly gasped. *"I'm* the normal size."

He smiled and said gently, "Welcome back."

The heart piece returned to normal size, too. She lifted it by her chest.

"Two," he said. "Two heart pieces you have found, and two remain to be found."

More magic crept over her collarbone. The vines evaporated her shawl and blouse. Two more heart pieces would stop it. Then she would go off into a new life.

Back to Davian? she wondered. The idea turned sour, making the sparks in her stomach go from wonderful to bitter.

Whatever she did next, it had to count. For herself. For Calin. Amberly. The Blood King. Once she sorted out their problems, maybe they could leave this place together. Become inseparable as they traveled the world. She couldn't abandon any of them once she had what she needed. She couldn't make a choice like Lumina did to leave Davian behind. Mina needed her new friends with her. She wanted them to feel better. To get along. To solve their problems. Unlike Lumina, she would find a way to take care of herself and not sever people from her life. A heart was flexible. It balanced the things a person cared about. It helped others heal while also healing itself.

Maybe that was the whole purpose of the Blood King's deal. To not only fix him, but help everyone else, too.

Heating up, Mina buried the idea. She needed her heart before she entertained herself with such a lovely future. And besides, even when she got her heart she couldn't be too hopeful for the others. A perfect world full of perfect people would allow for her to have that ideal life. But this wasn't a perfect world, and she wasn't with perfect people. Everything she wanted was too good for her.

"Mina," the Blood King whispered, slightly alarmed.

She found his face, noticing the real care he held for her. The added presence of Amberly and Calin, who also cared and owed a lot to, engulfed her with fire.

"Are you feeling fine?" the Blood King asked. "I imagine changes in body size can be disorienting."

"It's easy to get used to after a thousand times," Amberly said cheerfully.

Calin's brows rose. "A thousand?"

"Maybe a thousand and one."

"The heart piece," Mina said. She handed it to the Blood King.

He brushed a thumb over the heart piece, frowning at it. He placed it on the watery magic. The heart piece floated toward the other, their jagged ends nearly connecting.

The room darkened. Calin and Amberly froze in place, their eyes glowing. Their mouths sealed shut.

Mina shifted. "What's happening?"

"Do you ever think past the heart pieces?" the Blood King asked.

"Of course I do. I can have a life because of them."

"But hearts belong in chests," he said. "I... Mina..."

"What is it?"

"Things just stop working sometimes." He pointed his chin down. At that moment he appeared afraid. "Sometimes it's because of yourself."

"Broken things can be fixed," Mina said. "I'm going to help you. I'm going to help Calin and Amberly, too. There's more to all of this, isn't there? Have you ever considered telling them who they are?"

The Blood King glanced at Calin and Amberly. "They can't be free until you are." He stepped to Mina's side, placing a hand between her shoulder blades.

Fire erupted at his touch. Her magic swarmed to his hand. As he guided her to the mirror adjacent from the first one she went through, she didn't breathe. They stood with their reflections staring at them yet again. This time, frost pooled off the glass, slightly obscuring them.

Seeing herself beside the Blood King gave Mina a lot to think about. She liked how they looked together. Two broken, disheveled beings seeking a heart. They formed their own kind of fractured beauty.

Calin joined them in the reflection. Mina hadn't known he unfroze, his appearance startling her.

"Another heart piece to collect," he said.

"Yes." Amberly joined them. She glanced around. "But I thought there were four. Aren't we supposed to grab four? There are only three mirrors."

The Blood King held Mina's stare in the mirror. "All shall fall into place. I guarantee it. We're getting closer now. Closer to my desire." His hand slid up to the back of her neck. "To you bursting with power."

Fingers squeezing, the Blood King glowered at her. Mina shifted, her magic under her skin running from his fingers, leaving a dull ache behind.

"To you," he said, putting on a weak smile, "bursting with a heart."

Mina inhaled deeply. "And you with yours."

His hand fell away. "I will expect you three back promptly. There's not much time with your magic spreading, Mina." He retreated to the well. "My own magic isn't strong enough to slow the process or end it. I could try, and I believe you'd be willing to let me, but I wouldn't trust my skill."

Calin cocked his head to the side. "But you," he said distantly, "you are all-powerful. Why worry?"

Amberly's shoes clicked as she crossed to the well, shaking her scepter at the Blood King. "You boast your power as the greatest thing to exist."

Confusion swept over Mina. He could slow down her spreading magic?

The Blood King gripped his hands together, white skin cutting through the red stains. "I suppose it is a slip of my tongue. What I mean is that accidents *may* occur. My power, great as it is, cannot prolong the inevitable forever. The heart is the main importance at this moment."

"If you're suggesting you can slow down my magic," Mina said, "why not try? Why not give me a heart now, and I can give you yours after?"

Peril flashed through the Blood King's eyes. "Because that is not what our deal is."

"But—"

"Move forth from your questions," he said, waving her off. "You are wasting time. Unless, that is what you want. Then feel free to argue some more. I am not the one in pain."

Mina wrung her hands. She didn't care about the pain. The sudden change in his mood flared her nostrils for a half second. She didn't want to upset him—or anybody at all. Again, she had no right to probe him about his own magic. He understood it, she didn't. He'd been betrayed before, she understood that, too.

Grabbing his hat, Calin swiftly set it on his head. "We'll get those heart pieces. No worries there."

The Blood King flicked his hand at the mirror. "Yes. Leave."

Behind his face, a battle waged war. Mina wanted to know every detail of what he was thinking. Perhaps it was the fear of saying goodbye. If so, she would tell him that having a heart didn't mean goodbye. She could stay. She'd help him untangle all the mess of his world, including Calin and Amberly.

"I don't understand," she said.

Calin rubbed his hands together, feet shuffling. "A jolly old time might come for us," he said. "I do wonder, Mina, should you need a coat?"

"If I need one, I don't," she said simply, still looking at the Blood King, waiting for him to look back at her.

Amberly huffed, crossing her arms and chattering her teeth as she stared at the frosty mirror. "I'm envious. My poor wings will need to constantly flutter if it's cold there."

"Then I should give you my coat before we go," Calin said.

"I won't need it." She waved him away. "The more I complain about being cold, the faster we'll move."

Green ignited around his cheekbones and nose. "I don't like that idea at all."

"Let's go!" Amberly raised her scepter toward the mirror, grinning. She led the way through, Calin close behind her. Mina shuffled after them.

Crisp wind howled from beyond the glass as they pushed through it. Yes, a normal person would need a coat.

"It's already cold," Amberly said, pouting.

Calin cried out, "Please, not so soon with the complaining!"

They went through the glass entirely, their shoes crunching over the ground.

Mina remained at the cusp of going into the new pocket of time. She moved slowly, hesitating. Vacillating. While her sights wanted to focus ahead, she couldn't stop herself from giving into one last look back at the Blood King.

He watched her. Longing had replaced his anger.

With all the strength she could muster, Mina smiled. She added warmth to it. Assurance. Peace. An offer for friendship. For closeness. She wanted him to know she'd fight for him, and he didn't need to conceal any uncomfortable truths from her any longer.

Mina held onto her aching smile for as long as she could. The mirror's light folded around her. She fought to keep the Blood King in her vision while brightness took over the world.

As she was about to commit the memory of his sad face to the center of her mind, it changed. Quickly, she rewrote his expression, adding the smile he gave back to her.

MIRROR MAZE

A flurry of snow blocked out most of the navy blue sky. It concealed the ground, mounting high on either side of the road extending out beyond the mirror. Orange nebulous glows cut through the weather, bursting off the few streetlamps in the snowbanks.

Amberly pressed back on her heels and tapped her toes together, smiling. Against the snow, her yellow stripes became vibrant, hard to miss. Twinkling flakes shimmered past her light blue wings.

"It isn't as cold as I thought," she said.

Calin unfolded his arms. He set a palm to the sky, catching a pile of snowflakes. "I should be claiming this as a victory against your complaining, but all I can do is agree. The air is closer to warm."

Sharp pings dotted Mina's magic. The cold spurts made her wonder, "How cold is the snow itself?"

"A tad bit," Amberly told her. "Nothing too dramatic or drastic."

If only that were true for Mina. For once, her arms trembled lightly, actually cold to the bone.

"It's not as it usually is." Calin paused. He stuck a finger in the air. "I feel no wind either. Strange."

Lowering her wings, snow trickled to Amberly's feet. "My wings cried to me that they would freeze. They haven't yet."

Calin raised and tapped his chin. "You know, this place feels familiar, but I swear I've never been here before."

Mina ran her tongue over her teeth. "I think there's something you two should know about yourselves."

Twirling, Amberly closed her eyes. Her stinger bounced. "Have we ever known anything about ourselves?" she cheerfully sang.

Specks of snow stuck to Calin's mustache. He stuffed his hands in his pockets. "At this point, I don't think so."

"Then you must know," Mina said. "I have to tell you why you're confused. Who you were before, you both—"

Something hissed in her ear. At first she thought it was the emergence of wind, but it sounded more like someone whistling for her attention. Either way, the sound dug deep into her head, shaking up the magic inside and jumbling her thoughts into mush. Her knees buckled and her teeth clamped together.

When the sky blackened, the snowflakes expanded into little, white pebbles with sharp edges that pelted Mina. She yelped a gargled sound.

Calin grabbed Amberly's elbow, pulling her close to him, and he reached a hand out for Mina. She ran to him. The three of them huddled together, icy chunks hitting their backs and heads.

Mina nestled close into the middle, peering out from under Calin's arm. Every now and again she sensed the hail strike her back, bringing in great relief. The moment she truly felt the slashes, that would mean the ice tore into her, releasing more magic.

As the pieces poured, they thinned, and their surfaces transformed, becoming glass. Calin pulled Mina further underneath him. She bowed her head, tension flooding her body.

Her breath hitched as one of the glass shards struck her hard on the shoulder blade, enough so to make her think it tore her open.

"M-M-Mina," Calin said, sounding far away.

"Mina!" Amberly shouted, resonating everywhere.

Confusion gnawed at her. They hadn't left her. They couldn't have been as far as they sounded.

Yet, when she lifted her head, she stood alone. Calin and Amberly were far from her, but still in view. They also had been separated, and the three of them made a stretched out triangle across a black void. The hailing glass had stopped as well.

Mina reached and felt around the ache on her shoulderblade. Her fingers grazed a sensation she couldn't describe. The lack of angry magic lashing out at her touch told her she hadn't been ripped open. She eased.

Picking up her feet, she ran to the others, calling their names. She ran and ran, only treading in place. She threw up her arms, huffing.

Glass pieces hung in the air. Everywhere Mina turned, her reflection stared back at her, but something was off. Her face bore features too perfect to be hers. Too human. It wasn't quite her face.

"No," she pleaded in a whisper. "No more."

A gale blew on Mina's left, shoving her a step to the side. She knocked a few glass pieces out of place. They exploded into dust when they struck the snowy ground.

"That's not what I look like," Calin said from where he stood. He grew louder, clearer. He felt closer. But he wasn't. "Where's my mustache? Where's my age?"

"You're upset about your lack of age?" Amberly asked in disbelief. "Look at me. I'm young and fresh, but there's something so eerie about my face. Like an evil child."

"Evil," Calin repeated. "My chest is open to me. My heart is charred black."

"All right. Fine. Ignore me," Amberly said. She waited a few seconds. "Calin? Mina? Are you guys even around? Hello? Hello? Where did you go?"

"Amberly? Mina?" Calin called out. "Are you still with me?"

The glass pieces twinkled. The beams of light coming off of them expanded far and wide, blocking out Calin and Amberly.

"I am here," Mina said. No one responded to her. "Can either of you hear me? I can hear you."

The glass pieces moved inward to one another, clicking together and forming larger, various shaped mirrors, some suspended and some touching the ground.

"Can you hear me?" The question died far out in the abyss.

Clenching a fist, Mina's shoulders fell. She sniffled, though she knew that wasn't real. The sound was only a trick. Her mind filled in normal signs of sorrow in places where she could not emit it.

"I'm over here," Calin responded.

"And I'm over here," Amberly said.

Mina spun around. Their answers could've come from anywhere.

"I can't see either of you," she said. "Where are you?"

Faded humming settled in the air.

"Hello?" Mina called out.

The hum died, and everything turned empty. The air curling around her magic blistered colder than ever. On instinct, she crossed her arms, rubbing them to heat herself back up. The sting of her own touch unleashed a squeak from her throat. Fire blazed over her elbows, up to her shoulders—the wrong kind of heat.

Mina approached a diamond-shaped mirror with a wider bottom than top. She observed herself, ratty and jaundiced. The scars on the right side of her face sharpened, hues of violet lying within, brighter than the dull color of eyes.

It was difficult to believe she was a wish. Wishes were spectacular. The word itself filled her mind with streams of gold and grandeur, of sparkles of a happy life, of stars shooting across a night sky, actually able to make dreams come true. She wasn't close to being as beautiful as those things. Not as shiny and wonderful.

Yet, Calin, Amberly, and the Blood King never made her feel ugly or unwanted. They treated her fairly. Right. They saw her existence and didn't fear her, nor want to hide her. Often she found warmth in her chest whenever she was around them. A warmth which opposed the cold she felt around Davian. This warmth made her muscles ease, made her lips twitch more naturally, and made her find beauty in her reflection. Contentment.

Something tapped from within the diamond-shaped mirror. Mina turned frigid. She sensed the presence of Lumina before she saw the woman's face stamped on every piece of glass. She held a cruel grin. Red covered the whites of her eyes, the blood vessels expanded and angry. They sharpened the violet of her irises.

Lumina bared her teeth. "I sense disloyalty."

Mina backed away. She crashed into another mirror, a screech wanting to burst out of her.

"Come now, Mina, don't be afraid to admit to what you really want."

She ran, weaving through the eternal rows of Lumina. Every bloodshot eye followed her, laughter spilling from all the red mouths.

"You can't change your mind about why you came here." Lumina tilted her head. "If you were human, you'd be like me. Davian would love you again. You want to be human for him. You must honor that."

Lumina's visage taunted her, enormous in the glass. Mina threw a hand up by her eyes, trying to block out the perfect faces.

"Say you wish you were me."

Pivoting, Mina frantically searched for Calin and Amberly. She clutched her throat, trying to peel out the words to summon the Blood King. She needed someone, anyone, to free her from this torture.

"This is your real desire," Lumina told her. "Say you wish you were me."

Mina shook her head.

"Coward. How could you deny yourself from what you want? If it weren't for me, you wouldn't exist. If not for me, Davian wouldn't love."

Rejection wanted to spill out of Mina. She choked, trying to force the words out. Her mind kept her from speaking, screaming at her, saying Lumina was right. That she was here because of Davian. That all she wanted was Davian. He was her purpose.

Her head was wrong, though. It had been fooled into thinking she only had one choice in life. That she didn't have another future to find. But she could find a life away from him. She could be truly happy for herself.

Air rushed into Mina's mouth, blocking her denial of wishing to be Lumina. The truth ached in her chest, right where her heart would be placed.

"It would make sense to become me for his love," Lumina went on.

Mina collapsed to her knees, gurgling.

"Be strong enough to admit it," Lumina said. "Say you wish you were me."

Mina opened her mouth. She forced the air up her throat, fighting through the blast of searing pain, stretching through her.

"Say you wish you were me."

A scratch hit the back of her mouth. She pushed the air harder.

"It is what you came for. Say you wish you were me."

"No!" Mina screamed, voice breaking. She fell forward, catching herself on her palms. The impact split lightning through her hands, shaking up her arms. She let out a tiny cry.

Shadows cascaded, covering half of Lumina's face. Her various appearances enhanced in severity. Her lips furled and her brows lowered.

"I wish to have a human heart," Mina said. "For myself."

"A human heart as I have. Me, who you were created after. A heart to be me."

"My heart would define me as Mina. Not Lumina."

"You're still half my name if you choose that life. What point is there to go on like that? You'll always remember where you came from, and it will always cause you grief."

"No."

"What is the point of a human heart? You'll only extend your meager existence and end up as dead. Speed up this process and give your magic to *him*. Save yourself from a life of sorrowful inferiority."

Mina ground her teeth together. She eyed Lumina. The Blood King spoke words close to those once. He was right—life would end anyway. But he was also wrong to think it all meaningless. To be fulfilled, to be happy, kind, that was what made life worth receiving.

"What is the point in continuing on if it won't matter?" Lumina questioned. "Things won't change. You'll keep wishing. Everyone does."

"I want to be a human." Mina stood. "I've had enough of you. There is no 'real Lumina,' only Lumina and Mina, two separate people."

"A human and a wish," Lumina hissed.

"I'll be human soon."

Cracks distorted the images of Lumina, creaking as they traveled over the glass.

"You can't ignore the inevitable," she said. "The decay."

"That's part of everyone's life," Mina said. She glanced at the magic infesting her hands. "Even a wish."

"Say you wish you were me."

"It is not my wish. I will not lie."

"Say it."

"No."

The mirrors exploded all at once. Mina fell backwards, her arms floating forward. One of her feet lifted, arcing through the air. Her other foot stayed firm on the ground. She arched backwards, her head striking the ground. A mixture of snow and black goo splashed up by her sides.

Calin and Amberly fell from above, breaking glass on their way to Mina, joining her in the goo.

The three of them bounced, launching onto their two feet. They stood upright, clean. As if nothing happened.

A starry sky expanded into a navy-blue night with the streetlamps lighting up the long, gray road dissipating into the blackened horizon. Within a few moments of their arrival back on the road, the snow started falling again, blowing in gusts of wind.

"This," Amberly said, folding her arms, her teeth chattering, "is the cold I was expecting."

Calin groaned. "Now you'll complain."

Mina turned to them, relieved. "You're back."

"We are," he said, beaming.

Amberly gushed. "Mina, you look so pretty when you're happy."

Touching her lips, Mina didn't decipher a smile. Nothing about her changed. Not that she expected to. Still, she didn't mind that.

"I'm happy to see you," she said. A tiny jostle of joy illuminated her words, but it didn't stay long. She shifted, putting her hands on her hips. "Now, you must tell me where you went."

Calin glanced at Amberly. "I was with me. The question is, where were you two?"

Amberly threw up her hands, scepter gleaming. "Don't question me. I found myself, and you two were absent. Oh, I wish you were there. My younger self is so stubborn and irritating."

"Did you hear what I said before all this happened?" Mina inquired, ready to tell them about their pasts, even though the Blood King hinted it was pointless. She wanted to try anyway.

No one answered her question, though, for they were interrupted.

"That is quite the truth you speak." The new voice floated through the air, a young man.

They all looked around.

"Who said that?" Amberly asked.

"Me," said the voice.

That was when Mina noticed it. One snowflake, a bit bigger than the others, whirling on its own accord. She lifted her hand. It gently landed on her palm. For once, the touch of something didn't hurt her magic too badly.

"Isn't it nice we've finally met?" the snowflake asked her.

Two coal-colored eyes, very human and very wide, were embedded in the snowflake's face, accompanied by a long, pointy, crooked nose. With human teeth in his mouth, there was something unnerving yet cute about him.

"I hope you'll agree," insisted the snowflake. "For I am Kristofer, and I would like to attempt to help you find a piece of a heart." His dendrites curled inward. "Of course, that is, if you want me around."

Mina peered at the others, trying to find hints of recognition on Calin or Amberly. They were unreadable, however. Disconnected.

"I'm Mina," she introduced. "And these two are Calin and Amberly."

Amberly waved. "Hello, stranger."

She didn't sound as lively as when she spoke to Calin in the bee dungeon, but there was a bounce of glee on her.

"You're all so..." Kristofer squealed, jumping out of Mina's palm. He floated, laughing. "This is so—oh, wait a second or a minute—wait." Spinning rapidly, Kristofer flew away, bouncing harshly. "Help me, please!"

"Kristofer," Mina called out. She hurried over the snow.

"Wait," Calin called after her. "Be careful!"

And right as he said those words, Mina slipped but caught herself from falling. She watched Kristofer fly from her and swallowed as she faced the slick sheen of snow and ice covering the entire road.

ONE DOT IN A STORM

Since Kristofer's dendrites were pointier and his body was bigger, it made seeing him through the blizzard easier. Brisk spinning and fearful shouts distinguished him further.

The problem was the ice. Wherever the snow wasn't, it was there. Wherever the snow was, it was swept aside easily to uncover more ice. Slick, slippery ice.

Mina locked her knees. She sliced her legs back and forth, shuffling. Calin and Amberly managed just as carefully, sharply inhaling and waving their arms overhead at their near slips. The ice slowed them down tremendously.

Mina tried to quicken her pace. Her foot slid from her control and she knocked into Calin's back.

"Gah!" he cried, legs splitting apart. He rocketed forward, palms slapping the ice, knees slamming down. His mouth shriveled and his mustache drooped.

Amberly covered her mouth, shoulders shaking as she angled away.

"I'm sorry," Mina said, holding out her hands. "Are you all right?"

"I'm better than good." The lopsided smile he put on vanished when he planted his foot on the ice and winced. The slickness caught him again, dragging his leg too far to the side. He hissed, shoulders hunching.

"Fanciful display, I say," Amberly said. Her wings fluttered. "Perhaps you are meant to become a graceful dancer."

"Graceful," he grumbled, "is not what I would consider any part of myself."

She clicked her tongue. "It isn't too late to start," she said, winking.

Calin glared at her. "Why don't you fly and catch that snowflake? You're wasting a lot of time and energy doing nothing helpful so far."

Amberly lit up. "A great thought." Her wings expanded outward, buzzing to life. She lifted off the ground, pointing her scepter ahead. "I'll be right back."

"Yes, yes, go," Calin grumbled. He sighed and turned to Mina. "You know, I think she just wanted to see me fall." His eyes darted away from her and he cleared his throat. "Could you please help me up?"

"Of course."

Calin grabbed hold of her arms, fingers pressing into her magic. He pulled himself up, grip tightening and loosening.

Clenching, Mina used all her might to stay upright. Her arms and legs rumbled, balancing herself. She heaved Calin to his feet. By the time he let go, dusting himself off, her throat ached from how stiff it was and her arms turned numb. It took her a few moments to unwind and regain a sense of feeling in her body.

"Well, thank *you*," Calin told her. "At least someone cares for my well-being."

"My pleasure as always." Mina carefully curtsied.

Ahead, Amberly sparkled in the snow. She drew closer to Kristofer, waving her scepter in a circle. The breeze carrying the snowflake slowed, allowing him to gently fall into her palm. Around them, the blizzard raged on.

"Did you see that?" she shouted at them. "I think I used magic again."

"We did see it," Mina called back. "It was wonderful."

"It was," Calin said, ashen. A blue glimmer swiped down his right cheek. "She can do things so greatly if she wants."

"What's wrong?"

He flinched. "What do you mean, what's wrong? I'm up and fine."

"You feel sad."

"I'm not."

"You're lying."

He held in a breath, letting it puff out after a moment. Turning his face away from her, he rubbed the back of his neck. "I haven't really been much help to you after all," he said. "You're the one being more helpful to me."

If she could've laughed, a hearty one would've fallen out of her. "Without you, I wouldn't have the courage to keep going. Once this is over, I was thinking we should stick together—you, me, Amberly, and maybe the, well, you know."

He held up his elbow for her to take. "Kristofer? Maybe. He probably isn't so bad. With my riches, we could go anywhere."

Mina nodded, mouth dry. *Rich.* She'd nearly forgotten Calin thought he was here for a deal. Amberly, too. And likely Kristofer. Magic churned uneasy in her stomach. The Blood King knew they didn't know. All he cared about was his heart. His stolen heart.

Mina should've hated Calin and Amberly for what they had done, but she couldn't help but feel sorry for them. To want them to have better lives. A second chance. If only their minds weren't so decayed and warped by this place, then maybe they could explain themselves and work for forgiveness.

Or maybe Mina was being too hopeful. Maybe they needed to stay here, mindless, because they were awful people.

But the Blood King seemed sad to have lost them. She was here to help them all. The deal was more than she initially believed.

"Now, what's wrong with you?" Calin asked, elbow still hovering.

Mina shook her head and linked her arm with his. "Nothing. Nothing at all."

A barren landscape of snow curved far into the veiled horizon on either side of the road. Not a footprint dented it. Not a house interrupted it. That sort of thing would've worried Mina had they not met Kristofer already. With his offer to help, she could already feel the third heart piece sitting in her hand, sinking a bite into her magic.

Amberly displayed Kristofer on her palm. He stood up on two dendrites at the center, taking up a hefty dose of space, causing Mina to look at one of her hands. Either he was bigger than she thought, or Amberly had smaller hands than Mina. Now that she studied her fingers, she took in just how lanky they were.

"He's the cutest snowflake I ever saw," Amberly declared.

Rosy-red vibrated to the surface of his snowy face. "Stop, stop," he said, waving her off. "This is too kind of you to say."

Mina wondered how his alternative self would appear. Calin and Amberly had both been younger behind their blurry faces. Did snowflakes even age? Younger ones must've been a bit smaller, at least, but that was assuming they were like people and animals.

"But I'm sorry," Kristofer said, sinking. "I've never been a natural at flying. Not like my brothers and sisters are."

"Brothers and sisters," Amberly repeated, eyes crossing. "Are all these snowflakes related to you? Even I, from a beehive, would be overwhelmed and whelmed beyond whelmed. How are you supposed to get personal time?"

Kristofer laughed. "The ones furthest north of the land are my family, not these ones. My family are the best bunch of snowflakes anyone could ever know. You should see, Miss Bee, they fly lovely like you. Perhaps you could teach me."

"I don't believe I could. These wings are different from how it is...you fly." Her chest lifted. "Also, please don't call me Miss Bee. I find it a terrible and unwearable nickname."

"You're right, even if I had wings, I wouldn't grasp the concept better. It's taken me this long to learn, two decades and seven years, and I still do not know what I'm doing. What a fake little flake I am."

"You flew so nice into my hand before," Mina pointed out. "You could do it again."

Kristofer's dendrites fluttered. "Stop being so nice." His red flourished. "It isn't true."

"What is or isn't true can be discussed later," Calin said. "You claimed you would try to help us."

"And I will help." Kristofer puffed out from his center. "As it is known, the Bl—" He gasped. "You all know what you're here for anyway. The old friend of the Bl—is—" He narrowed his eyes, scanning around. "Somewhere in this place."

Calin stroked his chin. "Excellent deduction skills."

"Mister Mustache, don't speak in glum. This place may be bigger than you think, but if we all put our heads together, we can figure out where to start. I'll go first."

Kristofer tapped a dendrite to his mouth. He held it in place, deep in thought. They waited, leaning forward as the volume of his hum grew louder and his eyes brightened with a thought bubbling to his face. Dendrites stretching out, Kristofer ripped open his mouth.

"I—" he started.

Everyone leaned in even closer.

His dendrites fell and his expression dulled. "I don't know."

Calin let out a long sigh. "So you have no thoughts at all?"

"That's a rude thing to assume," Amberly chided him. "There are thoughts. They just aren't...coming."

"Sadly, he is correct," Kristofer said. "But it is also a happy thing that I have nothing. Imagine I did come up with a thought. It could have been a horrible plan, or worse yet, a silly little impossible thing. We would have failed, then I would be blamed, and I would be ashamed more so than I already am."

Amberly nodded. "You are smart for thinking of that possibility."

Kristofer smiled, so sincerely. "Thank you."

"I could rip my hat in half," Calin muttered. "Time grows thinner. We can't *not* come up with ideas. Kristofer, where are you?"

The snowflake blinked. "I'm here."

"And where have you been?"

He blinked twice. "Everywhere."

"Perfect," Calin said. His shoulders sank. The whites of his eyes reddened, growing glossy. He sounded different. Younger. "A perfect a-answer."

Mina tilted her head. "Calin?"

Amberly groaned. Her eyes changed, too. A shade above Calin's. On her hand, Kristofer blankly stared at her fingertips.

"Is everyone all right?" Mina asked.

"Do you ever think about it?" Kristofer said. "The moment where decency left and foul laughter came. Every day I think of what happened. What could've happened instead."

"Instead," Calin said.

"Instead," Amberly repeated.

Calin grabbed his cheeks. "Grandmother's face keeps reflecting off every surface. I look at Oldest Son and myself, wondering why I am wrong now."

"The young Queen of the Bees does not care." Amberly's voice deepened into a haunting melody. "She enjoyed herself too much, for she was in the place she thought she could only be—at the top, at the top, at the top. Only the top, never to think of a possibility below."

Mina shuffled backwards. "You remember yourselves."

Blank white eyes turned to her, with her reflection in each eyeball, twisting between her broken self and the perfect image of Lumina.

"Not again," she murmured. "I don't want you here."

"Who have you been?" the three of them asked in unison, Lumina underneath. "Who are you going to become if humanity isn't enough?"

Mina's back hit a streetlamp. Snow shook off the top, dumping onto her. It sliced her magic and got stuck in her hair.

"I'm not wishing to be you any longer," she said. "So leave me and my friends alone."

"But I'm your greatest friend," Lumina said solely, pouting in the eyes.

"You never were a friend. I never knew you."

"Say you wish you were me."

The cracks around Mina's right eye expanded sharply. She clawed at her face. Magic crawled onto her scalp, blackening her hair. The other ends reached her jaw, the strands of violet-black roping around her throat, slivers connecting to the mass on her shoulders and chest, electrified. Her hands flexed, aches encasing her.

Mina held onto the streetlamp, trying to remain upright.

In the blank eyes of her friends, twigs of blood seeped along the edges, going to the centers, tainting their irises.

"Please," Mina begged. "Come back to me. I need you."

Three deep breaths flowed through them. They each blinked, the red retreating. Back came the gray, blue, and black of each pair of eyes. Back came the warmth. Back came life.

"What happened?" Mina's voice radiated over the icy road. More snowflakes flew in front of her, shielding the others from her view. "What happened before the mirrors existed?"

The snow dwindled. A couple of stranded flakes floated to the ground. Mina faced her friends in clarity. She touched her temple.

"Why did you steal the heart?" she asked.

"I know where to go," Kristofer announced, not hearing her.

Frustration entangled Mina. She'd been so close to answers. Or had she? Lumina came again, just a trick. That's all these mirrors could be at points..

"Every year the snowflakes march for the fallen," Kristofer explained. "We could join their tradition and nab the heart piece from the Jewel of the Knights."

"The Jewel of the Knights?" Mina echoed softly, still reeling in from what she'd witnessed.

"Yes, he's the one put in charge of the other snowflakes." Kristofer spun on Amberly's palm. "We will need to go straight ahead on this road."

"I could've guessed that," Calin said, puffing his cheeks. He shook his head, brows flicking up. "It's the only road here."

"Yes, but I know where the March is *exactly*," Kristofer told him. "You would miss it easily."

"Miss the March easily?" Calin touched his chin. "How so?"

Kristofer shuddered. "The entrance is in a place the living try to avoid."

FORGETTING HOME

*A*mberly flew at the front of their line. Kristofer stood on the same hand she nested her scepter in, the handle in the curve between her thumb and forefinger. She kept the red end pointed ahead. Calin held onto her other hand, sliding on the ice. Mina gripped his wrist. The touch hurt much less than the harsh snowflakes pelting her exposed magic.

Mina shuffled over the ice, constantly slipping. Whenever her foot got away from her, she'd fasten her grip on Calin, yanking his arm.

"I'm sorry," she had said each time.

"Listen," he finally told her, "this road is long. If you apologize every time you lose balance, you'll have no voice to go along with your new heart."

"All right. I'm sorry for being...sorry."

He smirked, playfully shaking his head.

Another slip nearly caught her in its clutches. Calin's arm went taut at her pull. Mina pressed her lips together, burying the apology. She thought about how much abuse his poor arm socket endured. If only she could walk on her own. Her body, however, ached and pleaded for rest. If she did let go, she'd never make it anywhere. The wind was too strong for her. The pain was too much.

Her fingers loosened.

"Mina?" Calin looked at her, concerned. "Are you fine?" He swallowed. "Amberly, I think we should stop."

"Got it." Amberly's wings slowed. Her toes touched the ground.

Mina tightened. "Don't."

Calin lifted his brows in concern. "You seem tired, though."

Kristofer shimmied. "The storm won't let up any time soon, and we still have a little ways to go."

The flakes pecked Mina, keeping alive an excruciating eternal fire. Her magic whined in the lashing wind, burning her hands, arms, chest, and the right half of her face. They spread around her sides, reaching her back, caressing her shoulder blades. The blotches on her scalp wiggled in irritation with her hair bouncing all over the place.

"We can't rest," she said. "I'll be fine."

Calin's mustache swirled in the wind. "A quick moment wouldn't hurt."

Amberly clicked her tongue. "He's righty right, you know. Being too tired makes it too hard to move."

"We don't need to stop," Mina insisted.

"Your magic," Calin said, mellow, as if afraid to mention it, "is flaring with more purple than usual."

"It's angry," Kristofer added, turning pale blue.

Rivers of dread rushed in Mina. They twisted in her stomach, making it hard to breathe. Hard to think. A moment of rest would've been nice.

"It is angry," she said, biting her bottom lip. "It all hurts."

A tear inched out of Amberly's eye. "We should get you out of this storm."

Mina lowered her chin. "I'm sorry."

"For what?" they all asked in unison.

"For everything. For always needing your help."

Calin's lips twitched up. "We've gone over this before: everyone needs help sometimes."

She met his eyes. "You included?"

He faltered, turning his gaze down. After a moment, he slowly nodded.

"All of us," Amberly said. "We need to be there to help each other relax."

"And keep sliding forward." Kristofer beamed. "Straight to the heart pieces."

Forward. They would go forward. Together. No more questions or doubts. Mina sturdied herself.

"You're drifting away from me again," a murmur curled over her shoulder.

Her eagerness dropped. "Davian?"

"Yes," the voice said.

Fingers grasped Mina's shoulders, tight on her magic. Inside, she winced.

"Don't touch me," she whispered.

Calin, Amberly, and Kristofer turned to stone, mouths pressed tightly shut, eyes glazed over. Three separate hums drifted out of them.

"Lumina told me you upset her." She sensed Davian's smile. "I'm glad. I let you go like the silly boy I am. I thought you'd abandoned hope in me, but you left Lumina in the glass, just as I have. Through all these mirrors, I've been searching for you. Hoping to bring you home with me."

"To Virvin," Mina said.

"You could either stay here and fail, or you could come home with me. End my agony of losing you."

"You didn't lose me. You gave me up."

"I wished for you. I've searched for you."

"You're not actually here."

He dug his fingers deeper into her shoulders. She buckled. "Wish for me back," he demanded.

Wish for Davian?

"It hadn't occurred to me before," she said to herself, "to wish for my own version of you. It couldn't have happened anyway, though I suppose I could've asked for you instead of a heart as part of my deal with the spirit."

"There needn't be any of that. Make your wish for me, and I will take you home."

And if she went, everyone would suffer. Davian with his wish, her with him, the Blood King with no heart, and the others in these mirrors, confused forever. Getting the Blood King's heart meant making him feel whole again. It meant a chance at freeing her new friends. It meant a second chance for everybody.

She adjusted her grip on Calin's hand, holding him tighter. "I don't want to go back," she said over her shoulder. "I don't live for you."

Davian leaned closer. "You're being selfish for leaving me. Even with a heart, you'd feel nothing. I know it."

"Yes, *you* would know," she said. "You live that way each day."

Mina took a step toward Calin. He and the others blinked, awakening. The hands left her shoulders.

STRAIGHT PATH DOWN

*K*ristofer shouted above the howling wind blowing against them, "Keep going forward! It is clear that we are almost near."

"You said that three clear almost nears ago!" Calin shouted back.

"Ah, but Mister Mustache, that means this is an even closer clear almost near."

"That is soundly sound logic," Amberly added, hoarse yet bubbly.

Mina clung to Calin. He grunted every now and again, his knuckles and veins bulging out of his hands. Bright red blotches covered his and Amberly's cheeks. Mina probably had some red on the portions of her real skin, too.

"This March better be coming soon," Calin said. "I don't know how much longer we can go like this."

When Mina opened her mouth, the wind sucked the words out of her. Its strength worsened against them. Back in Virvin, the weather never got this bad, and while she never felt a chill, she understood through Davian's frosty breath, his terrible chills, and constant complaints, that winter air was less than favorable. There was no possibility he would've survived this world behind the mirror. The idea of him whining like a baby about it made her lips twitch up.

"I see it!" Kristofer exclaimed.

The snow blurred the world too much for Mina to make out the world ahead. Amberly's sigh of relief, however, wrote a good note on Kristofer's words being true.

Magic coursed in gallons through Mina's legs as she worked harder. She focused on sliding her feet, trying not to notice the magic crawling down to her stomach, eating half her blouse.

"We're close," Kristofer said.

The buzz of Amberly's wings heightened. She put her head down, scepter lifting an inch higher. A groan escaped her. Calin sped up, and in turn, so did Mina.

"There!" Kristofer called out. "It's there."

The wind died down. Kristofer's voice and Amberly's wings grew louder, Calin's hat, which somehow managed to stay on his head, wiggled less, and Mina's hair fell to her shoulders while her skirt flowed freely around her legs.

Navy-blue light flickered in the sky. Red broke through the cracks, taking over the surface and casting a hue onto the snow. Against it, black clouds plumed, long and skinny.

The ice thinned and they stepped atop pure snow. Mina wanted to cry for joy when she stepped without slipping.

Amberly landed on the ground, face burned bright as a cherry. She swooned. "It's over."

The right side of Mina's face, full of magic, blazed. She tapped her cheek. A spark shot onto her fingertip, electrifying.

Calin bent over, holding his knees. "I've never been so glad to see snow." He chuckled. "Snow. Of all the worst things in the world. Better than ice."

Kristofer narrowed his eyes. "Watch what you speak, Mister Mustache."

"Not you, not you," Calin said. "I mean, as in, I don't like how cold snow is." He straightened. "Snowflakes themselves, I've never met a mean one."

Amberly beamed, twirling. "But a bee can be…" Her face fell flat and she gestured ahead. *"This* is where you've taken us?" she asked Kristofer, trembling. "Is this a funny dunny way of telling us about something?"

"No, Miss Bee, not at all," Kristofer said simply. He hopped in place on her palm, rotating to face the same way as her. "This is it. The entrance to the March of the Snowflakes."

Mina assessed the entrance, agreeing that no living person would ever want to enter this place. The road led to a literal dead end.

The cemetery reminded Mina of the Herre house. Both guarded themselves with a pointed fence along their perimeters. Unlike the Herre's fence, the pickets of this one shot straight up and sat close together. Their sharp ends twinkled in the pieces of red light bursting through the black clouds. A craggy diamond-patterned lattice hooked the pickets together, actually keeping someone out.

The gate to the cemetery squealed as Calin opened it. Cautiously, Mina stepped through the threshold, finding something to distract herself from death.

She used the sky, specifically the crimson radiance blanketed underneath the puffy clouds. Snowflakes drifted down, bright white against the black and red. They sparkled a little, more so shooting stars than snow.

"Beautiful," she murmured.

Amberly choked, contorting in disgust. "Beautiful? I suppose for the dead it is a nice place to sleep, but being alivey live, I think this place is ultra-terrible."

Adjusting his coat, Calin nodded.

And Mina supposed she agreed, too. It was quite gloomy here.

Tombstones disintegrated into the smooth snow. No particular order arranged them. They scattered about in different graying shades, angular shapes and sizes, and lonely names. A few scraggly bushes, clumped up like tangled brown hairs, accompanied the dead, and they tried clawing their way out of the snow.

At the center of the cemetery was a mausoleum. Stone bricks built the square base, and extended into five sharp pillars at various heights. Snow fell off the roof, lodging in the cracks. It reminded Mina of a miniature castle. She was certain the outside of the Blood King's castle was similar—black, sharp, and full of decay.

One thin path of packed down snow wound between the graves. Mina walked on it. Death was the only constant for anybody. People, animals, plants, wishes. Any one of them could die.

She ran a hand over the curve of one of the fractured tombstones, wondering who rested there. Behind the mirror, it might've been nobody at all.

She crouched by the grave. Cracks broke up the once smooth surface. The rock could've used polishing, and maybe a flower to lighten it up. It could've used anything at all.

Feeling along the bottom of her skirt, Mina found a loose, green thread. She ripped it off and laid it across the rock.

Tipping her head forward, Mina placed her fingers against the tombstone, rippling her magic. Inside, she mourned for every lost soul she did not know and bloomed with appreciation for the ones she did know—Calin, Amberly, Kristofer, the Blood King. Despite their faults, they made her feel human.

In a strange way, she was even thankful for Davian and Lumina. They gave her the greatest gift of all: freedom.

"Mina," Calin said. "Are you fine?"

The tiniest smile danced on her lips. It hurt. "I am, thank you."

"We have the March to get to," he reminded her. "You better come quick."

Nodding, Mina got up. She brushed the snow off her and gave the grave one last glance. She bid it a silent farewell.

Amberly and Kristofer stood in front of the mausoleum, peering curiously at her as she joined them.

Darkness spilled from within the structure, hiding whatever lay inside far from view. Not even the red sky could penetrate a hole in it.

"You're certain"—Calin cleared his throat—"the March is inside there?"

"I am for sure for certain," Kristofer said. "Where else could it be?"

"A friendlier place, I would've hoped," Calin said. "Maybe something bigger."

Kristofer twisted, looking side to side. "Tell me another place in this barren wasteland of snow where you'll find the March? I've seen nothing. Have you seen nothing?"

"Yes," Calin said with a sigh. "I've seen nothing. Let's just go inside then. It's freezing out here."

Amberly fluttered her wings, pointing at him. "Ah, now listen here, and let us witness who the real complainer of the cold is."

Pulling his coat to his chin, Calin put his head down, grumbling his way toward the mausoleum's entrance.

Another smile sprang up in the distance of Mina's mind. It bubbled close to the surface of her lips, never getting close enough to touch. But Amberly shared a mischievous grin. Even Kristofer giggled behind two dendrites.

Ahead, Calin glared at them over his shoulder, but the corners of his lips twitched up, and he jerked his face away.

They crunched the snow, going up the three steps to the entrance, facing the thick darkness within.

"Don't be so hesitant," Kristofer said, voice shaking. "I'm not leading you into a trap."

Calin rubbed his chin, peeking at Kristofer out of the corner of his eye. "Nobody has mentioned a trap, Kristofer. Nobody except you now."

Kristofer smiled with all his teeth, waving a dendrite. "Oh, you think so highly of me. I could never be smart enough to plot a trap, so why would I try? I know what I know and avoid doing what I don't know."

"You're too hard on yourself," Mina said. "While you have no reason to trap us, I do think you could make an excellent trap under the right circumstances."

"If you need advice, mine is to use honey," Amberly said.

A blush overcame Kristofer. "So sweet you all are."

"And you're too sweet to trap anyone." Calin jerked his head. "Come on. Everyone grab hands."

They shuffled. Calin took Amberly's free hand and Kristofer stayed on her other one. Mina took Calin's other hand gently. A sliver of pain rumbled in her knuckles, but his grip was loose enough for her to manage.

Inside the mausoleum, the dark laid too heavy to see through. Their shoes scuffed the floor. That and the linkage of hands reminded Mina she wasn't alone. Her urge to scurry back to the entrance, to the light, eased away.

Going back would've been pointless anyway. The entrance disappeared.

"I should've expected that," Mina murmured.

"If I'm to be believed," Kristofer said, voice bouncing off the unseen walls, "we keep going straight ahead. Soon, the marching will thunder in our ears, and then we'll know we're there."

"Is it that simple?" Calin asked.

"Thank you," gushed Kristofer. "I knew I could make a coherent plan."

"I asked a…" Calin trailed off. "Yes, thank you, Kristofer."

He shuffled. Mina followed, attempting to make out any shapes around them. There wasn't anything to latch onto. She wasn't even sure how far she was from the ceiling or the walls, or how far the floor extended forward.

"We'll move slowly," Calin said, "and then—"

His hand clamped around Mina's. A giant tug ripped her arm, unleashing a horrible slash of pain up to her shoulder. She cried out. Calin let go immediately and a thud resounded throughout the room.

Amberly scuttled. "Here, here, Calin, where are you?"

She screamed. Her wings buzzed, but they stopped abruptly with another thud. She moaned, sliding away.

Kristofer shouted happily, voice traveling downward as he exclaimed, "Just keep going forward!"

Getting on her knees, Mina inched forward, feeling the ground. She hit an edge and ran his fingers over it, concluding that the floor broke off into a steep incline. She flipped onto her backside and extended her legs down it, knowing an abundance of pain would hit her once she slid onto it. But there was no other choice.

"One, two—" Palms hitting the ground, Mina pushed herself down the incline.

MARCHING SNOWFLAKES

In the darkness, violet lightning flashed. The storm lit up on her hands, her arms, as she pawed for something to grapple onto and slow her down. The constantly changing world couldn't be trusted to take her to the same place as the others.

From the midst of her mind, the Blood King's visage floated, begging her to call upon him. He was the only one who could help her if she ended up alone, but she bit down on her tongue, withholding herself. Even if the world twisted and separated her, she could manage her way back to the others. She had before. A string connected them. A bond that drew them across any distance.

The ground shifted, evening out into flatness. Mina came to a stop, sitting upright. Aches popped and seethed all over her magic.

A glowing white speck drifted from above. It fluttered and landed on her nose. She followed its path as it swiped off her, erupting into an enormous white light that exposed the room she'd landed in.

Slushy snow with dirt and grime in it clung to the walls and ceiling. Chunks melted and splattered onto the snowy, footprint-ridden ground. For finding the Jewel of the Knights at what sounded like a grand event, Mina expected a place more akin to the Wishmaker's home—icy and decadent. Here, it didn't surprise her that the spacious, dirty room was under an abandoned cemetery.

But that didn't matter. Not when she saw the people at the center of the room, lying on their sides.

Kristofer floated above Calin and Amberly. "Rise, rise, rise," he sang. "We made it. I told you that the path was right ahead. You didn't believe me. You should have believed me. I was right. I was so right. Right, right, right." He frowned. "But I shouldn't gloat. Today's smartness can't be tomorrow's."

"Being helpful now makes up for it all," Mina said. The sound of her voice lit Kristofer up with sparkles. "You offer more than you think you do."

"Like newfound back pain," Calin said, rubbing his back as he sat up, his face dotted with purple. "I can't break away from hitting the same spot."

Amberly stretched out her arms, smiling as she sat up. "Wasn't that slide too, too, too fun? I would do it again." She pulled her arms back into her sides. "But it's not there anymore."

The room had indeed closed off from the rest of the world. Only the slushy walls surrounded them with nowhere to run.

Mina tensed. An initial spurt of panic knocked at her door. She fought not to let it in. There would be a way out of this room. She trusted there would be. The others would also fight to stay right beside her.

Thunder boomed. The room vibrated.

Kristofer gleamed, spinning in place. "There it is," he said, turning to the wall the sound sat on the other side of. "The March of the Snowflakes."

He lurched forward.

"Wait," Amberly said, jumping up. "What are you doing?"

"We have to break the wall," Kristofer told her.

Calin winced as he stood. "You suggest that as if it'll be easy. We have no tools."

Kristofer bounced into the wall, using all his might. He ricocheted off of it, repeating the process all over again, huffing and puffing. "They're on the other side. You have ears. Listen. Little chitters, chatters, giggles. The trumpets will blare soon."

And as if Kristofer were the conductor lifting his baton, the trumpets blared at his cue. Brassy high and low notes conjoined to create a melodic sound, one fit for marching.

"Every time I mention them, they like to start," he said, puzzled. "Say, don't be lazy now. Use your hands. Break the wall. It's fun for all."

Calin strolled to the wall, lifting a brow. "Break it with our hands," he mused. He cupped his fingers, digging them into the slush. "What? Like this?" He scooped out a pile and flung it to the ground.

"Yes," Kristofer said dryly. "What other way?"

Calin quietly dug out more snow. Amberly and Mina joined him. Kristofer kept bouncing, somehow crumbling a bit of slush.

It took Mina the longest to scoop the slush. Her hands flexed, numb from the cold. Light gasps filtered through her lips. She didn't understand how the others could do it. Frost marked their hands, and yet they kept pulling. She on the other hand had to pause between each scoop, reeling in from the excruciating scrapes of crystallized snow across her magic.

"Are you fine to keep going?" Calin asked.

She didn't need to see him to know his question was for her.

"I can manage," she said, jabbing her hand into the wall.

"You don't have to do this if it hurts too much," he said.

"I'll be fine," she assured Calin.

"If you say so."

Kristofer hit the wall, hardly breaking off any slush. "You and me, Mina, we're doing a much finer job than them. The wall will be gone in zero time—well, not zero time, as we're past zero time already, but quick time, yes."

Calin and Amberly made a huge dent in the wall already, which was much more progress than she and Kristofer did combined.

The hint of a smile touched Mina anyway. "I think so."

Kristofer laughed, spinning all the way around.

Chunk by chunk, the wall thinned. Calin formed the biggest pit, so they turned their attention to his spot, working to deepen the hole. They stuffed themselves inside, bumping each other. The trumpets got louder on the other side of the wall.

Mina glanced at her companions—giving each one a couple seconds of regard—glad it was them helping her. That they chose to do so, despite their past endeavors. They helped her regardless of whether or not they thought she'd fail. None even suggested making a deal with her for their help. Not like the Blood King had.

Mina's chest ached. They were so unlike the Blood King. The Blood King latched onto her to make a deal, and she latched onto her friends for help with the self-promise to pay them back one day. She would have called herself more commendable for that aspect, but it was the same as the Blood King promising her a heart in the future—they both took and planned to give later.

Later, however, didn't mean never, and once later happened, things would be better for them all.

Maroon light penetrated through the thinning wall. The music sounded even louder. They worked harder, scraping the rest of the slush away. Calin used his heel to knock the bottom out, crumbling the rest of it down. The oval opening gave way into a blizzard-filled room. Snowflakes floated in circles, covering the air. They moved on their own accord like Kristofer did, or, rather, tried to.

"There it is," Kristofer said, jumping and sailing out into the room. He yelped, unable to control himself. Amberly caught him before he drifted too far. He rested on her palm.

"Thank you," he told her, blushing. "That was a now good choice."

"I tend to make a lot of now good choices," she informed him.

Calin snorted.

Amberly narrowed her eyes at him. "I didn't say *always*, just a lot."

Taking off his hat, Calin turned it upside down, shaking the snowy dirt out of the brim. He placed it back on his head, examining the room. "So where would we find the heart piece? Do we keep tearing apart all of this slush?"

"We need to wait a second for the Knight to show up," Kristofer answered.

"Which one would he be?" Amberly flashed a look around. "A bigger one? A mighty mightier one?"

"Just wait," he sang to her.

They did as Kristofer commanded and waited. The snowflakes kept flying in a giant tornado, never hitting the ground.

"It's a time for belief," Kristofer whispered.

The trumpets, which were nowhere to be seen, stopped playing.

Dendrites elongated on the flakes. They pulled their bodies into tall shapes, resembling human arms and legs. More human features popped out of them, eyeballs, long noses, full lips.

Mina slackened, feeling like she was back in the Wishmaker's home. The snow globe of a room became a globe full of icy people dressed in uniform. Navy-blue coats with silver tassels adorned every newly formed person. Each strand of hair on each head frosted upward, colored in varying degrees of white. Blue lips stretched into smiles as they acknowledged each other, shaking frosted hands.

Amberly let out a small cry. Kristofer trembled in her hand, his eyeballs stretching and bulging. He flung himself off her palm, twisting in the air. He shook and reshaped as the other snowflakes had, becoming a straight-backed, pleasant-looking man. The youngest-looking between Calin and Amberly, but perhaps having a year or two over the Blood King.

Kristofer grinned. His overly long nose wiggled. Frost covered his blue-hued skin. He patted his coat, the same as the ones the others wore.

"Surprised?" He shook out his hands. He stood around the same height as Mina. "I, too, change under the March."

His lips twitched. They were more blackened than the others. He bowed and shot back up, puzzlement creasing his brow while he scratched his frosted scalp.

"Why are you all staring at me?" he asked. "Should it actually be surprising? I jested about surprise. Look at the others. Why should I not change?"

An excellent point. Mina closed her gaping mouth.

Calin cleared his throat. "It's not a surprise. It's..." His shoulders fell. "Fine. Perhaps I'm a little surprised. Though you should've surprised us sooner when we were breaking the wall."

Kristofer tapped his chin. "I didn't think of that."

Amberly giggled. "You're such an adorable little man."

"Was I not an adorable snowflake?" Kristofer trembled, eyes going wide.

"No, no, that isn't a meaning I meant at all," Amberly said. "I remember a different image. It seems as though my expectations of you as you were and you as you are now are different."

Mina's head spun. She was too tired to overthink what Amberly was saying. If she asked a question, the subject would've been changed or something would've popped out to distract them all. The world behind each mirror had a mind of its own, throwing a new problem at them at the most inconvenient time.

Kristofer patted his chest. "I'm glad I'm fine. I have to admit, some of the others don't seem that way." He gestured to the human snowflakes. "Observe, the Knight."

The snowflake people formed a circle, facing the subject in the middle. Even if he wasn't in the spotlight, the Knight would've stood out anyway. Extra shininess covered his shoes, his coat was longer, and, of course, he possessed a blank sheen over his face.

"The March of the Snowflakes," the Knight said, a tad bit awkwardly. "It is tonight. A night where the cold drops furthest and we honor the fallen."

Pairs of heels clicked together with metallic pings. Chests lifted, backs straightened, eagerness blossomed for the first step.

Calin spoke from the corner of his mouth, directly at Kristofer. "Where do we find the heart piece?"

Kristofer only laughed lightly, shrugging in response. Mina's confidence dropped for a second.

The snowflake people stomped. They clumped together, marching around in a circle and chattering as if they were at a grand party.

The Jewel of the Knight lifted his knees high. He rotated clockwise on his spot in the center, matching the direction everyone else moved in.

"It appears," Amberly said, "as a start, we should march, too."

"Probably a good idea," Mina said. Exhaustion pricked her muscles and joints. Magic clutched her stomach, crawling on her back. The last thing she wanted to do was move. "Kristofer, you said we have to get the heart piece from the Knight. How?"

Sucking back a breath, Kristofer shrunk. "I thought we should ask him to give it to us."

Calin shook his head. "It's not *that* easy."

"What if he's rude?" Amberly asked. She hummed, rubbing her chin. "I don't think so, but sometimes thinking so can be a bad so."

Mina opened her mouth to join the others in criticizing the plan but stopped short at Kristofer's burning cheeks and glossy eyes.

"Forget it," he said, hoarsely.

"No," she said. The marching droned on. Mina surprised herself by speaking over top of it, not a syllable hiding underneath the beat of the steps. "Maybe the answer can be that easy."

Calin slid his gaze to the Knight. He swished his lips. "My plan for the first piece was simple, too, until *things* got in our way."

"And getting the second piece turned simple," Amberly added. She hit the end of her scepter into her palm. "Trying simplicity first wouldn't hurt."

Mina forced her lips to go up.

Breaking the air with waving arms, Kristofer made an anguished sound in his throat. "No, don't listen to me. Please, you're right to think my plan is silly. I think it is silly. We shouldn't do what I say, because I never know what I'm saying, and worse yet, I don't understand if I even speak, what I speak. Speak? See? I already lost my head."

"Be calm," Calin said, patting Kristofer's arm. "We always think too much, so we'll try to be simple."

Kristofer nodded.

Mina gave Kristofer her best attempt at a warm look. "You never know until you try," she said. He shivered, smiling back.

"The best outcome," Calin said, "is that he gives us the heart piece. The worst outcome: I can't possibly imagine what it is, but whatever it could be, we'll be on the alert when we go to him."

Mina looked at the Knight, stiff and subdued in his steps. His arms fluttered in a similar manner as Kristofer's dendrites. She guessed some aspects of a person didn't change over time. Something she would know; Davian never stopped pining for Lumina.

"I don't think we should bombard him all at once," Mina said. "I'll go myself."

"No," Calin said immediately. "We won't leave you to an uncertain doom. I could go with you at least."

Touching his arm, Mina shook her head. "I don't want to overwhelm him. Let me try to speak to him. Alone."

"She would be more easy weasy for the Knight to speak to," Amberly said.

Calin crossed his arms. "I don't like it."

Kristofer stepped up. "Maybe I should go with you, Mina. It is my idea. It would hurt me if you got hurt because of my plan."

"I'll be fine." Mina took a solid stance. "You'll all be close anyway. Nothing will hurt me."

"If you're certain, then," Kristofer said, puffing up his chest and snapping his fingers, "then I'm certain, then."

"So am I." Amberly set her scepter on her shoulder. "I quite enjoy marching. It moves me more. I could use some improvement on my step."

She and Kristofer linked arms. Their bodies canted toward the herd of marching snowflakes off in their own world. Kristofer put out his other elbow for Calin to take. The latter hesitated, giving Mina a questioning look.

"I'll be fine," she whispered to him, adding all the reassurance she could. Though, she didn't need to work hard to convince him of her emotions. He already saw them. Everybody saw them.

Calin swallowed and took Kristofer's arm. The three of them began marching on the outside of the snowflakes, leaving Mina alone.

ONLY ONE CONVERSATION

*M*arch or be trampled. Those were the only two options. Once Mina joined the snowflakes, she wouldn't be allowed any rest, for they didn't slow. They didn't stop.

She marched in place for practice. Her knees didn't rise as high as theirs, and she couldn't tell if she'd be able to match their speed. Pounding jolts in her magic reminded her there wasn't any time for hesitation. She had to get moving.

Calin, Amberly, and Kristofer moved along the edge of the circle, a good idea for her, too, just to get an extra feel for how things would be. They'd already rounded once past her. From how tight the snowflakes packed themselves together, barreling straight into the crowd wasn't a choice anyway. They marched shoulder to shoulder, chest to back.

Mina placed herself next to a stranger, her shoulder hugging him. Her stomach twisted and her legs struggled to carry her. She slowed just the tiniest bit and brushed the arm of the snowflake directly behind the one she marched beside.

"Carry yourself," the snowflake hissed.

"Yes, sorry," she heaved and picked up the pace.

Mina tensed all over. She couldn't march. She couldn't reach the center. She shouldn't have sent the others away. Everything spun so fast in her head. She was bound to fail this task.

But when she touched her temple, she realized she wasn't the one spinning. It was the room itself. The slushy walls crumpled silently. The ceiling unfurled from above their heads, the chunks spitting out into the slopes of the crater they marched inside. A hazy, navy night hung over them.

Mina looked to her left. There were a lot more snowflakes than she had anticipated. All were a similar height to her and Kristofer, making it easier to see Calin and Amberly's heads bobbing over the March on the other side of the circle. The Knight remained difficult to make out at the center, however.

Chest burning, she tapped the snowflake beside her. "Excuse me."

The snowflake choked on whatever he was saying to the one on his other side, whipping his head to face her. The tip of his long, pointy nose nearly struck Mina's.

"What was that?" he asked.

"Excuse me," she repeated. "I need to get through."

"Get through?" He flicked his temple and then tapped the shoulder of the snowflake he'd been speaking to. He gestured toward Mina. "She wants to get through."

The second snowflake gasped and clutched his throat. "Get through? How do you get through?'

"Get through where is a better question," said the first.

The second snowflake crossed his eyes. "Oh," he said, keeping his lips pursed. "That is a good question."

"I mean to get through to the center," she said.

"Of your mind?" asked the first.

"Your heart?" suggested the second.

"Of the March," she told them, flicking her hand toward it.

They looked at each other, mouths going wide. A long-held note seeped out of them, subsiding when they finally understood what she meant.

The first snowflake stuck up a finger. His mouth stayed open, but he said nothing.

"Ah," the second said, shrugging.

"If you want to get to the center," they said in unison, looking at Mina, "then go to the center."

Drooling exhaustion settled and soaked deep within her. She would've given anything to lie down and not move for at least a month.

"You are correct," she said, "if I want to get to the center, I need to go to the center. However, in order to do that, I would need to shuffle past you. It is difficult to do that with the lack of space, but if you make a tiny bit of space, I could slide by and be on my way."

"Do you think that makes sense?" the first snowflake asked the second, tugging on his sleeve.

"I think it does make sense," the second said, head bobbing on his neck.

They angled themselves, giving up a little room. Mina sidestepped, squeezing into the March. Her magic thumped hard at the contact with the snowflakes behind and in front of her. As she settled into her new spot, one she was sure hadn't been there before, the thumping increased. When she glanced at the kind pair of snowflakes, she noticed the first snowflake had taken her spot on the edge of the March.

"Thank you," she said, sending as much gratitude as she could their way.

They tipped their heads toward her, teeth sparkling as they smiled. They returned their attention back to each other and continued with their previous conversation.

Turning to the left, Mina confidently tapped the next snowflake's shoulder. "Excuse me, but may I get through?"

"What was that?" the snowflake asked. Her nose hit the tip of Mina's.

"May I please get through to the center of the March by shuffling past you?" Mina asked.

"Get through?" The snowflake turned to her partner. "She wants to get through."

"She wants to get through," the snowflake said.

"Get through?" asked her friend. "How do you get through?'

"Get through to where is a better question."

"Oh. That is a good question."

Mina cut in. "Get through to the center—"

Their questions raced out.

"Of your mind?" asked the first.

"Your heart?" asked the second.

"—of the March."

Deflated, it dawned on Mina that she was going to have to go through the exact same conversation as before, hitting all the same points of confusion and explanation no matter what she said.

So she repeated her initial question, and they repeated everything the first two snowflakes said, again.

Eventually they made sense of what she was getting at. Eventually they let her go by. Eventually she tapped on the shoulder of a third snowflake.

"May I shuffle by you, please, in order to get through to the center of the March?" she asked, hopeful this time would be different.

The snowflake whipped his face to meet hers. His nose hit Mina's cheekbone—on her right side with all its magic—and her nose. Her breath hitched.

"What was that?" he asked.

"Could I please get through to the center of the March?"

Even with clarity, the snowflake went through the same script with her and another snowflake, word for word, question for question.

"Be thankful," Mina whispered to herself, despite her agitation, as she finally shuffled past the third snowflake pair. "At least there is a script to keep you going."

Looking to the left, however, her mouth grew dry. There were *a lot* more snowflakes than she initially thought.

She lifted her hand to tap on the fourth snowflake's shoulder. "Excuse me."

Another nose struck her, followed by another series of the same sentences, questions, which all resulted in another set of bodies letting her by.

She tapped more shoulders. Got smacked by more noses. Repeated the same script. Again. Again. Again. Then some more. More. More. More.

Mina lost count of the number of snowflakes she spoke with, making the same inquiry and shuffling by.

It all paid off, for in time, she made it to the center and nobody blocked the Knight. She could've squealed with joy and danced in circles if it weren't for the main purpose of her coming here still needing to be accomplished.

The Knight's back faced her as he marched in place, still going in the same direction as everyone else. Luckily, he remained alone, and he seemed to have taken advantage of that since he marched slower than everyone else.

Before she approached him, Mina glanced around to see if she could find her friends. Calin and Amberly's heads still stood out near the March's edge, Kristofer blending in with the other snowflakes. Knowing they were still there gave her enough strength to go to the Knight. At every step, she expected someone to shout at her, accusing her of doing something wrong. A few snowflakes shifted their eyes her way. None of them, however, seemed to mind her. After all, she wasn't and didn't intend to be a threat.

The Knight kept marching. He rounded toward her as she got near him, his face blurry. For a moment, she thought he looked directly at her. She expected him to say something, but he simply rotated away from her.

Mina marched around him in a circle, practically within his line of sight. She weakly cleared her throat. She stared right at him, giving him a tiny smile that begged for him to address her first.

"Hello?" she finally said.

He screamed.

She waved her hands. "No, no, don't! I don't want to startle you."

"But y-y-you did," he told her, wiping his blurry forehead.

"I am sorry," Mina said. The words came out sounding too fake. She cleared her throat, trying to add legitimacy to her voice. "I am sorry." Now she seemed slightly sarcastic and uncaring. "I mean I am sorry," she hurried out, sounding as flatly fake as her first attempt.

She gave up. He'd feel her grievance over the incident anyway.

The Knight lifted a hand, swinging his fingers down. "I do not deserve an apology. My head was drifting off to the far places. But you don't care. I mean, as in why care for me? But as in, who wants to listen to a ramble by a stranger?"

"I do care." *You're Kristofer.*

The blank blue of where his mouth would've been brightened as though he smiled. "Your name?"

"Mina."

"Mina. Nice name. Been on a long walk?"

"I have," she told him.

"An enjoyable walk?"

"Most of the time, yes."

"Glad for it," he said. "I'm glad for it."

Marching without a cluster of snowflakes on every side of her rested Mina's muscles. The slower pace allowed her to think clearly without worrying about keeping up.

"These places you go to in your head," she said. "Tell me about them."

"They're silly," he answered, quickly. Swirls of red entered his cheeks, little roses.

Her tone evened out, more convincing in her truth. "I don't believe that."

"If you liked hearing silly things, I'd tell you."

"They're not silly, and even if they were, I would like to listen. In fact, I used to always listen to a man who told me about his grand adventures with his friends. Sometimes he exaggerated his stories into silliness. I liked listening. I still like it, just not from him."

"But these aren't stories," the Knight said. "They're thoughts all strung out together. Kind of like...stories."

"Go on," she softly urged.

He clapped his hands together, rubbing his palms. "Well, it's—well, it's—I am a good Knight in a good palace. A big palace. Icy, yet warm. Warm, yet icy. Have you ever met the Wishmaker?"

Mina almost tripped over her own feet. "I am a wish he created."

"A wish?" the Knight repeated. "Oh, on my ways, you *are* a wish. Congratulations. It must be so nice to be born a grand being."

"As the Jewel of the Knights, you would know."

His jolliness blew over, taking off the smeared blush. He hunched his shoulders, and the area around his lips grayed. He tore his face away from her.

"I wasn't born so grand," he said. His knees popped up and down, up and down. "I am the oldest disappointment. All the brothers and sisters after me are much more naturally gifted in mind and body. They all deserve to be where I stand, so grand. My only luck in life was being born first. It took me much longer to learn how to fly compared to them, and I still struggle. They got it down the first time; me, however, the noble Knight, I am actually a fake noble. Nothing special at all under the gleam."

The Knight rushed as he spoke, welling up. He burst into tears and clutched his face. Little chunks of ice fell from his chin, hitting the ground.

His sobbing rumbled over the March. Snowflakes cast critical inspection upon Mina.

From inside the crowd, a man's voice sounded. Mina didn't catch exactly what he said, it sounded like Calin.

"The Knight is extremely happy about the March," Mina told the nearest snowflakes, "whilst also being sad for the fallen. He is proud of all and wants no attention on him right now."

Hard faces still stared at her. Mina's stomach fell into her boots.

Kristofer sniffled. "She's right," he squeaked out.

Bodies loosened, removing a heavy level of scrutiny off of her. Slowly, the snowflakes returned to their chatter, satisfied by the lie for now. All it would take was one snowflake to grow too suspicious for rationality, though, and then she'd be in real trouble.

Mina lowered her tone, voice cracking. "Why are you crying?"

"I'm emotional," Kristofer said.

"There's no need to be. This is a special event, and I wish to speak to you. It would be hard to hold a conversation through tears."

One last piece of ice fell from his chin as he lowered his hands. "You want to speak with me?"

"I firmly do."

"Why?"

"Truth is," she said. Her chest twisted. "I need something."

"So many do," he said sadly. "They walk here only on a mission."

"I'm sorry, but I also do like speaking to you. Honest."

Something told her he was examining her deeply. His stiff shoulders untangled and fell, making him breathe easier.

"What are you searching for?"

"A piece of a heart."

"The Bloo—" His voice cut off. "I do know." He chuckled. "Look at that. I know something."

"So you know why I am here."

"Like so many others."

"You know I want to be honest."

"Not like so many others."

"I care for you."

His shoulders rose and fell with the sweep of a heavy sigh. Shiny slivers of ice pierced through the blank shield over his eyes.

"Don't cry again," she pleaded. "It's not a bad thing."

"For anyone but me," the Knight said, "it isn't. But for me, it is. My whole life I've been pitied, not out of care but just... I want people to speak to me because they want to, not because I'm a sad little Knight."

"You're wrong about yourself. You're very noble, brave, and helpful."

His chin lifted. "I don't know if I should believe for a second anything you say. You only want a heart piece from my pocket. The token of true friendship."

Token? She didn't consider stolen pieces of a heart a token of anything but cruelty. But it did strike her as odd because the Blood King had referred to the second heart piece as being part of a token.

"Isn't friendship a sign that you're good enough for someone to talk to you for *you?*" she asked.

Gray flickered over the top half of his face. A blink.

"I think you're hard on yourself," she said hurriedly. "As a wish, I feel that way, too."

"A wish," he said. "Tell me about that."

"I was wished upon to fill in for the place of someone else. Naturally, I could never be someone I am not, and I could never force myself to do so. I think the better way to go about these things is to accept what we are and strive forward as who we can be." She cleared her drying throat, stunned by how distinct and hearty it was. "Does this make any sense?"

The tilt of his head from side to side synced with the rhythm at which his feet marched. "So and so."

"Better than no," she told him.

"I suppose so." He angled the top half of his body away from her. "I also suppose you did work your way here to speak to me, even if you do need something. And you've stayed long enough. I appreciate that."

"It would be nice not to need something," Mina said. "I would have liked to speak with you without the subsidiary reason."

"Perhaps, you have," said the Knight, the gray slinking off his face.

At their feet, his icy tears melted into the ground. He stuck up his neck, head positioned to look over his shoulder. Mina followed where she thought his gaze led to, finding Kristofer at the outside of the March, somehow having grown a touch taller than the other snowflakes. With him, Calin and Amberly marched. He kept his eye on Mina, the tiniest, warmest smile on his lips. For a snowflake, such a smile should've melted him. But an icy-cold body didn't need to melt because of the warmth inside. That warmth was natural to all living beings. Choosing it pumped the beat into a person's heart—or sometimes, a snowflake's beating heart. A bee's. A spirit's.

Mina put a hand on her chest. A wish?

"Do you know who you really are?" she asked the Knight.

Digging inside his jacket, the Knight produced the second-last heart piece, jagged edges glinting on both of the longer sides. Sides that would connect perfectly with the others.

"I know you've only come here for this," the Knight said, "but *his* smile, in your short while of acquaintance, tells me enough to know you will be a good friend."

"How do you feel about Kristofer?"

"I am similar to him. He is similar to me." He hummed. "Oh, I don't know if anyone knows. Not when you're a reflection of a mind."

She touched her bottom lip, stunned. "You know more than the others did."

He shrugged. "Maybe."

The world pulled away from Mina. She stared at the faceless snowflake, closely examining the shape outside. The frosty hair. The thinly square shoulders. The timid manner of standing. A lack of self-belief.

She marched.

Clack. Clack. Clack.

Then there was the young Queen of the Bees. Her massive, messy hair. Her squealing, energetic voice. The longing for a life that once was, not knowing how to live without it, but that young Queen had been forced to learn. She'd regret not being kinder one day, but at least she would see it. She would be better.

Clack. Clack. Clack.

Oldest Son. A man always lost from his memories—ones forced away from him. Someone who was propped up to become special but lost the light of it because he wouldn't accept a helping hand. But his eyes were brighter now. He recognized that what he once thought was bad, really wasn't at all.

Clack. Clack. Clack.

Mina glimpsed her friends. Calin, Amberly, Kristofer. They fit together perfectly.

Only, together they had done a deplorable deed to another. A friend of theirs. Mina braced herself. The answer as to why they took the heart may have been worse than what she wanted it to be. What if they got their memories back and changed into unforgivable thieves? How would she help them if they fell into darkness? She needed to help them get those memories. She needed to help them no matter what.

"I think you need this more than me," the Knight said.

The heart piece sat in his palm, easy for the taking.

She looked into his missing face. She couldn't envision him being capable of stealing a heart. Believing such a thing was wrong. Too wrong.

"Kristofer."

"Please, take it," he said.

Glancing down at the magic on her hands, Mina watched the lighting strikes of violet over the black mass. In a way, she had to admit, it was beautiful.

She lifted one hand, still staring at the other. Her fingers went for the heart piece but stopped when they encountered something that didn't seem like glass. Her brain must've been malfunctioning. It made her feel something different. Something squishier. *Warm.*

Her magic had felt things more truly than what touched her skin.

A bloody hand took her by the wrist, tugging on her. By some miracle, the touch did not bring any pain. Mina stumbled, hair flinging into her face. Her chest collided with another. Both lacking heartbeats.

The Blood King peered down at her with more fire in his eyes than what was usual. The blood all over him glowed.

"I didn't call for you," she breathed.

He shifted so they were side by side, snaking an arm around her waist, a soothing wave washing all over her. "I know," he said. "I just wanted to see you."

TURNING IN CIRCLES

*M*ina seized, magic pulsating. She couldn't believe it. The Blood King walked with her. The Blood King had his arm around her. The Blood King was here. Without her call, he was here.

She heard his voice, she stared into his soul. Nothing dispelled her from believing he was here. Here for real.

He took her into the marching snowflakes, away from the Knight, away from the heart piece. The snowflakes around them spread away, giving them sufficient room within the crowd.

"Why?" She hardly heard her own voice over beating boots everywhere.

"I told you," he said, smacking his lips together. "I wanted to see you."

"Why?" she repeated, louder.

"Envy." His eyes sharpened. He pulled her closer to his side. "I wanted to be the one to march with you."

Blood-drenched blond hair piled neatly on top of his head, a singular piece sitting above the bridge of his nose, the end stabbing into the corner of his left eye.

"I don't understand," she told him. She itched to take the hair out of his eye. "This is impossible. You said you couldn't come here."

"But I have over and over," he pointed out. "I will not enter of my own free will, I told you. It does not mean I can't."

Stomach tightening, Mina wanted to kick down another slushy wall. How could she be so blind? This whole time he could've shown up whenever he wanted, none of the ridiculous summoning required.

"You made it sound like a rule," she said feebly, knowing she couldn't come up with any solid excuse for her presumptions.

"Any rule can be disregarded." He tapped her good cheek. "Don't feel so dour. I thought you would have liked to see me."

She glanced at the Knight rotating in place. The heart piece glinted off his palm.

The Blood King frowned. "Ah, yes, but your quest. Do not worry. I've come to discuss exactly that. I had a spell of deep thought, and I've decided to make you an offer you might enjoy."

She considered his words. So much about the mirrors confused her, the Blood King included. This happy walking and talking might've been a trick. Perhaps he was a faux manifestation like Davian and Lumina had been. Accepting whatever he offered might lead to her downfall. Magic branches already reached the bottom of her stomach and curled like ribbons onto her back. Once the gaps filled in around her torso, only her legs and the left side of her face would remain to be eaten. With two heart pieces to collect, that didn't instill much confidence. The magic moved sporadically, making it hard to judge when the next heavy growth would be.

But maybe she was overthinking everything. Maybe the Blood King was being genuine. Then again, his brain got warped behind the mirrors. He told her and displayed that fact as true.

Across the circle, a pair of eyes gazed upon her. All the snowflakes had varying shades of colors, ranging from light blue to dark, stormy gray, but these eyes, however, stood out from the rest, pitch-black on a pale face.

Kristofer's lips trembled as he watched her. Sharp looks threatened to knock him over as he pushed through the crowd to get to her. The snowflakes grew stubborn. Angry. Glued to their spots as they blocked him.

At different points along the circle, more voices shouted. Calin and Amberly also tried tearing into the crowd, greeted with more stubbornness.

"What's happening?" Mina wondered, insides shaking.

"This March is nice," the Blood King said.

She fixed her gaze on him. "You stopped me from grabbing the heart piece."

"I did? Oh, I didn't realize." He drummed his fingers on her waist, the touch blasting soothing warmth into her. "It will never happen again. I promise."

"It was right in front of your face."

"No, it was right behind my back."

Mina clenched.

He must've noticed her stiffness under his hand. He swept his face away from her, muttering a short, "I'm sorry."

He sounded genuinely apologetic. It made sense for him to be. He did say he wanted her to get her heart.

"Mina," he said, "this offer I wish to make—"

"We already have a deal," she interrupted, "and I'm going to fulfill my end of it. You should prepare to fulfill yours."

"Please."

Her eyebrows twitched. "You told me your head gets messy behind the mirrors. Unless all of that is a lie." Her throat grew dry. "Have you been holding me back on purpose? Do you use your magic on me?"

"Never," he said. "Never, never. My magic has created this place, but I don't put my hands in your mind like I do the others. The others which you so strangely care about. You know how being heartless feels. Stealing a heart is deplorable."

Everywhere, all around her, silence ensued. Mina sucked in a breath. "Put your hands in the minds of others?" she questioned. "You changed them? They could be unchanged then?"

The Blood King wouldn't meet her eyes. "It's too late for that."

"Why?" she asked.

He blinked. "I can't tell you."

"Why?" she pressed.

"Because you'll hate me."

The March went on endlessly. In it, Calin, Amberly, and Kristofer shoved through a couple of snowflakes, sweating and puffing with red tints on their cheeks.

"You ruined my chance at getting the third heart piece," Mina pointed out. "I should already hate you for that. I should've hated you when you interrupted me in getting the second piece."

Coolness smoothed over the Blood King, changing him completely. "I did it unintentionally. Both times."

She didn't believe that for some reason. "Don't you want me to succeed?"

"Ease off your worry, dearest wish. You are not going to fade." He smirked, eyes darting to the right side of her face. "You're brightening."

Through the crowd, scuffed noises drew closer behind them. Mina spotted Calin's hat moving above the snowflakes as he tried to get to her.

"Let me go," Mina said, "and you'll have your heart back."

"Why the rush to get away from me?" the Blood King asked off the heel of her sentence.

"I'm not rushing to get away from you. I'm rushing to get our hearts."

"How considerate." The Blood King sulked.

Confusion wrapped around Mina, digging deep in her. She didn't care for the Blood King's change in demeanor and the severity of his face. It made him become the spirit the Wishmaker warned her about, twisting her with doubt. Doubt that he wanted a heart at all. Wanted *her* to have one.

No, she was overthinking his intentions. His head was warped in the mirrors, he acted differently because of it.

"This is our deal," she whispered. "You should want what's yours."

"I can't hear you," he said, and it might've been true. The footsteps in the crater grew louder.

"I can help us."

The high-pitched voice of Amberly rang close behind, calling, "Mina!"

The Blood King eased his grip on Mina, eyes pulling to the ground. Up close it was easier to see how thick his lashes were, and how even they had blood on them.

"I'm afraid of what comes next," he admitted. "I did come here to stop you from grabbing that heart piece, but only because I have a better deal. One where everyone wins."

Cold. In the back of Mina's mind, she grew cold. "Why does someone lose at all?"

Calin shouted her name. He was close. So very close.

The Blood King shot a worried look over his shoulder. He pulled Mina into his side, virtually carrying her as the marching picked up speed.

Somewhere in the midst, Kristofer shouted for her.

"I wonder if you'll hate me soon," the Blood King said. "Or if you'll stay as kind as you are. Whatever you may choose, Mina, you must know, you're my favorite person."

"I'm not a person. I'm a wish."

"Makes no difference what you are. You're still my favorite in the life that I know."

She tensed for a moment, unsure of what to make of the sparks in her stomach, so opposite to the dark cloudiness in her mind.

The marching sped up some more. The Blood King lowered his head, taking Mina forward. If not for him holding her, she wouldn't have been able to keep up.

Shouts and gasps flung through the crowd. Snowflakes slid and lost balance. The Blood King was the only one able to navigate fluidly through the crowd. His speed sat on a steady line. If he was about to collide with someone, he moved around them in the nick of time, racing through the circle.

"Mina," Calin said, her name ghostly in the fold.

"What are you doing?" Mina asked. Every face blended into the next. In the corner of her eye, a red line blurred horizontally all around from the center of the circle.

"I don't know," was the Blood King's response.

"Please, don't be clueless," she said. "I want to help you."

He halted. Everyone froze alongside them.

"I don't know how to act anymore," he said, "because I don't want to be what I am."

Mina placed her hand flat on his chest. "I can help you."

"There's something." He pressed his lips together, falling into a silent stare. When he broke out of it, he shook his head. "I see hopes for a future I can't have. Not as long as this deal continues. What I see goes against what I set out to accomplish long ago. You are different from what I have ever planned. I don't understand it. I don't understand it."

"You're making no sense."

He took her hands and squeezed them. Where she expected pain, she found relief. For the first time since Davian gave her up, she felt like she might live to become human.

"There is a heart for you to give," he said.

"For you."

"No, for you."

His hands left hers. He grasped her shoulders and spun her around.

If energy allowed it, Mina would've generated a powerful scream. Frustration and confusion would've crafted the bulk of it, no fear at all. Nothing about the Blood King made sense. Not his words, his face, nor the way his hands cradled her shoulders so tenderly.

He leaned close by her magic-covered ear, lips inches from it. "Or perhaps, you can give up and come back with me. I wouldn't fault you for doing so." He pressed his face against the side of hers, breathing heavy, easing the pulse of her magic. "Forgo the hearts. I would help you in other ways. I don't want you to hate me."

Her chest grew cold. His grip tightened on her and then released. He stepped back, wincing, and held out a hand to her, blood glistening across his palm.

He hardly dug the words out of his throat. "Come with me and live."

"I need to complete the deal," she told him, focusing on the glinting heart piece sitting on the Knight's hand. "This is for you and me. Once we have our hearts, everything will be better."

The Blood King lowered his hand. Despair glazed over him.

She distanced herself, pushing through the frozen bodies, making sure she wasn't harsh to them as she made her way to the Knight.

"Kristofer," she whispered to the Knight, wondering if he showed any hint of recognizing his own name under his blurry guise. She placed her fingers on the heart piece, gently taking it. "Why did you steal this in the first place?"

"Mina," the Knight said. Kristofer said. "I can't remember."

The blurriness washed away, turning him into the human form of Kristofer as he was today. Calin and Amberly emerged from the crowd, standing on either side of him, their cheeks rosy and eyes holding regret. The three turned as still as statues.

Around them, the snowflakes turned back into little white dots and faded into shadows seeping from the sky and covering the crater.

Piece by piece, the world behind the mirror vanished.

SPEAKING STATUES

The red ripple of the Blood King's watery magic brightened the brick room in his castle. It layered over Mina's own magic, which started curving onto her back. Everything but her legs and part of her face dissipated into the mass of violet-black. Needles pricked into every portion consumed, digging deeper and deeper at every moment.

Calin, Amberly, and Kristofer stood on the other side of the well. Speechless. Blank.

She broke the silence. "You never knew, did you? About who you are?"

After a long while, right as Mina went to repeat her question, Calin removed his hat. He held it to his chest. "I had an inkling after speaking to Grandmother. There were all these flashes of a boy long gone, but every time I felt close to the right thoughts, they slipped away."

"Speaking to the young Queen," Amberly said, caressing her scepter, "made me want to explore the past and find out how bad I really used to be. I tried, but I found nothing over and over."

Body melting, Kristofer's limbs shortened as he spoke, transforming him back into a snowflake. "I knew. The magic didn't want me to admit it. My past self is as pitiful as my present self. Forgetting is a necessity to ease despair."

Each one of them shifted. Amberly's wings buzzed, Calin tilted his head, and Kristofer spiraled in the air.

"You're the Blood King's companions," Mina said. "You helped me find the pieces of the heart you stole. Why?"

"That's all we can do," Amberly answered. "All we want to do."

"Since we were trapped," Calin added.

Trapped.

"All we can do is fumble for memory," he continued. "Somewhere, we knew we needed to help the person who might change things. Who could listen to the right story."

"A brave knight who could march through the unbeatable," Kristofer added.

"And a ruler of their own life," Amberly finished.

The third heart piece weighed heavily in Mina's hand. The smooth, red glass meant another step closer to humanity.

One more piece. The only thing in the way of her heart. One more piece.

"Do you feel guilty about what you did?" she asked.

Her three new friends, the first ones she'd ever made, did not move. Cloudiness accumulated in the air around their heads, graying their faces. None of them uttered a syllable. It didn't appear like they would soon.

"Tell me something," she demanded. "What is your side of the story?"

Nothing. The clouds thickened.

Mina swayed. She battled for air through a closed throat. As she thought about her friends, she grappled with who they were and what they had done. Worst of all, she thought of her old home. Of Davian and Lumina swaying together, deeply in love. Deep in their own, hopeful future. They had a happy ending, and they weren't perfect people. Mina wanted that chance, too, for herself and her friends.

A breeze blew from behind her. Fog curled around her skirt. Rigid, Mina kept the heart piece by her chest, turning to look at where the breeze came from.

The Blood King stood by the wall that never had a mirror on it. The one with the only door to let them in and out of the room.

"Don't let yourself worry," he whispered, beckoning her with a finger. "There is plenty of time left."

Unlike the pleading man at the March, he had turned serious, much paler beneath the blood. Fire, bright and wild, wove into his amber eyes, blackness pooling underneath them.

Mina's impending disintegration carried her forth. Aiding her decision was the sacrifice of her friends. They spent their time helping her when they didn't have to. Thieves or not, she held a high degree of gratitude for them and would always consider them friends in a strange sort of way.

The Blood King plucked the heart piece from her hand. "There is only one left. Do you truly want to collect it?"

"Yes," she said. "In another pocket of time." She glanced around. "But all the mirrors are gone. Where—"

He set his fingers on her lips, hushing her. Stepping aside, the Blood King uncurled his arm toward the wall. The bricks glowed, rumbling downward and unveiling a long hallway on the other side. A hall unlike the one she'd first walked through to get to this room. First coming here felt like it happened years ago.

"At the end," he said, "you will find the last heart piece."

A moment passed and Mina grew weak. Her hand lingered near her chest. She could already feel the beating from within.

The Blood King crossed to the well, sticking his hand in the magic. He pulled out the first two heart pieces, cradling them. He sauntered to her.

"Take them," he said, holding them out.

Mina did. Their sharpness scraped her magic, squeezing pain into her.

Across the well, her friends wore blank expressions. Despite that, she sensed their encouragement. Sensed their pride in her.

Clenching, Mina almost didn't move. She didn't want to leave them.

The Blood King grabbed her wrist. "Mina," he said. "Are you sure you want to go through on *this* deal?"

She met his eyes. "I do."

"Then go on," he urged, softly gazing upon her face. He let go of her. "There is only one stretch between you and your fate."

SIX GEARS AND A GLASS HEART

*F*og obscured the ground and climbed up the walls in the new hallway. It puffed around Mina, wrapping up her legs and going as high as her shoulders. One stray string reached her face, tickling the magic on her cheek. The lack of pain took her by surprise. She must've been getting used to it at this point.

That prospect died after seconds ticked by, and then came the pain, fierce and deep.

When the fog swirled off the walls, it revealed decayed brick beneath, gray and filled with moss in the cracks. The heel of her boot landed inside a gap in the floor. She jolted downward. The heart pieces clanked together in her hand. She held them close by her stomach, constantly running her thumb—splicing pain on the tip—over each edge, counting them.

One. Two. Three.

Lifting her foot, Mina bent, clearing the fog away with her hand and finding the floor underneath. A floor made of bricks that had gaps between each edge.

She proceeded carefully, boot clicks pinging off the walls and screeching into an empty pit below the brick's gaps. She covered her ears. A zap surged from her right palm, shooting into her right temple. The shock rocked her body and her arms shot down, vibrating. Magic shifted over her, pulsing onto new areas, filling into the remaining spaces all around her torso. It curled around her hips, coming with electrical pierces off the surface.

The floor shifted, rumbling. The bricks rose, taking her higher along with them. As they moved, the fog cleared out of the way, allowing her to view the entire hallway and how the floor changed into an alternating pattern of sections protruding up and inching down. They shifted and formed six giant circles all the way to the other end of the hallway. Circles with teeth interlocking and pushing against each other to move.

Her breath hitched. *Gears.*

Metal pipes ran up the walls, emerging from far below her feet. Their harsh noises banged on Mina's ears, tearing up the magic inside her head. They gleamed as though they sat in the sunlight. An impossibility for there was no light source here. Just the glowing white of the fog.

When the rumbling stopped, Mina rested. She recounted the heart pieces, turning her sights ahead. Being higher allowed her a better view of the other end of the hall where she spotted a red twinkle. A connection to the red in her hands.

Her chest thumped. The last piece of the Blood King's heart.

A whistle blew. Steam hissed out the sides of the gears. The floor moved. Mina's legs stiffened. The high part of the bricks she stood on, the platform, started to circle forward, carrying her straight into the next gear.

Mina counted the heart pieces. *One. Two. Three.*

Ahead, the last heart piece kept taunting her. *Want me?* it seemed to say. *Come and take me.*

The gear kept moving. Mina kept still, mind ticking away.

Staying on the teeth of the gears would make it easier to navigate. Though, unfortunately, doing so would be impossible. The teeth were too far apart for her to jump from one to the other. She'd need to go on the lower parts—the gaps between—and she'd have to climb the brick back up to the higher platforms.

Jumping would still be required of her to get onto the next gear. Both weren't her strong suits, and she didn't like—

"Who cares what you like?" she told herself. "Just go!"

Mina's feet pushed off the brick and she leapt forward, slamming into one of the second gear's gaps. Aches splayed across her. Her mouth opened wide, no sound able to come out.

The heart pieces cut into her magic. Pops of violet-black liquid oozed from her hand, stormy as they bubbled.

The gear carried her backwards, toward the first. She didn't have time to catch her breath as she hurried to the short wall of bricks, placing the tip of her boot into the open spaces, climbing up to the top of the gear's tooth.

At the top, she wheezed. *How are you going to manage the rest of the way?* her mind screamed.

"I don't know," she snapped back. "But I've managed impossibilities before."

Shuffling over the tooth, she slid down into the next gap. Fatigue weathered her muscles. The gears groaned against each other, unstoppable. Mina crawled her way to the third gear, leaping onto it. The gear took her forward, allowing her a moment of rest, which she desperately craved. Everything ached and begged her to stop and abandon this folly, telling her she wasn't strong enough to do three more gears.

But the three heart pieces in her hand were enough for her to ignore doubt. The edges pressed into her, the red of the glass reflected onto her magic, a blood stain.

As the gear's tooth neared interlocking with the next, Mina stood up. She clenched the heart pieces tighter as she jumped onto the fourth gear, not slowing as she climbed the tooth, went into the gap, and repeated that up and down process two more times before she landed on the fifth gear, where she found another place to rest.

The heart pieces morphed to become one with her hand, blending in with the violet-black light. Mina numbed. She hunched over, ready to collapse.

Drops of magic splashed onto the brick, landing in circular puddles of marbled violet, red, and black. She pressed the clean side of her head against the wall, panting. Her body begged: *rest, rest, rest.*

The fourth heart piece sat closer than ever.

Hauling herself to her feet, Mina faced the sixth and final gear. She bent her knees. Right as she jumped, a scuff from a pair of shoes from behind snagged her attention.

On top of the first gear, the Blood King stood sturdy like a tree, emerging out of the fog. He remained on the gear's tooth, arcing toward her, flowing so easily. The blood on his skin glowed.

Mina's left foot scraped the edge of the tooth she'd aimed for. Her legs split apart, pain blaring through her hip. She lurched forward, slapping her hands on top of the tooth, her magic sparking. On her way down, her chin hit the brick's edge, teeth clamping together, a high-pitched crack pinged in her ears. Splatters of black dots split up her vision and she fell into the gap on her back. The gear took her away from the heart piece.

Ridden with tension, Mina struggled to her feet, fog and brick spinning everywhere. Her body wobbled, shaking rapidly. Her eyeballs strained, wanting to blink. Arms flailing to help her balance, she sauntered to the wall, aware she was moving too slowly. Weakly, she set her hands in the gaps of the bricks, wedging her toes in as well, climbing through the abundance of painful ocean waves crashing from the top to the very center of her body.

Pulling herself upward, the stars in her eyes increased, streaking the world together into a mess of nothingness. Her muscles whined and burned.

Moving became an arduous task. Mina's speed went on a steep decline. She couldn't get off this gear. Like a snail, she slunk up and down each tooth and gap, seemingly going nowhere. She climbed up the same wall over and over, getting stiffer and slower.

Her face lacked sweat and eyes lacked tears, but her body cried inside, engulfed with the greatest fire she'd ever known.

Head lolling forward, she paused at the wall of one of the teeth, not caring if she fell into the abyss below. If she got her heart at all.

She was too tired, in too much pain, to try anymore.

All the work she'd done, all the hope she had, it came to nothing.

She thought of Davian and Lumina. How they wouldn't care about her demise. How the entire town of Virvin would never miss her. The whole world would never know she, a wish, wanted to become human.

No. That wasn't true.

Calin, Amberly, and Kristofer flooded her mind. They'd helped her so much. No matter who they were, who they became, she wanted to help them, too. To let them have a second chance.

And the Blood King. Whatever he'd done, whatever he planned, she still wanted to honor her deal with him. The original one they made, for he needed to regain his heart. To settle in peace.

If she failed, she'd let everyone down. She'd let herself, the hopeful girl who wanted to live, down.

Cold decorated the inside of her throat, stabbing like knives all the way into her chest. It reminded her she was still alive. She still had a chance to continue her life. That she had to try for that chance until the bitter end.

Anything was better than giving up.

Mina rose through her pain. She climbed the rest of the bricks, biting through the searing tension radiating through her.

She climbed up the tooth, and then she lowered into the gap.

The depths of her core grew brighter with a sizzling sensation.

The heart pieces sawed through her hand. Magic spilled everywhere.

She climbed. She lowered. She counted the pieces.

One. Two. Three.

She climbed. She lowered. She counted the pieces.

One. Two. Three.

She climbed. She lowered. She counted the pieces.

One. Two. Three.

The ground stopped moving.

Mina collapsed onto her side. The blast of pain striking her was nothing compared to the blazing in her hand, the tightness her knees endured, the dull pressure built up behind her eyes, radiating along her jawline.

Her fingers unfurled from the heart pieces. Chunks of curdled magic stuck to the sharp edges.

Opaque puffs of fog swooped from above, pressing a chill into her. Not in abundance, but just enough for her to feel. She rose.

Mina limped to the red glint of light sitting upon a rectangular, black rock, fog bushy at its base. The last heart piece's upward swoop at the top resembled how a human heart was. It's one jagged edge begged to connect with the other pieces.

Setting the heart pieces on the rock, Mina trembled all over. She fit the edges together, creating a flat slab of glass with four cracks in it.

Mina stepped back. A whole human heart.

The cracks glowed.

Pale light spread from deep within the glass, washing over the red. The heart floated. Strings of light wrapped around the shape, tying it together. A final burst filled in the cracks, making it a smooth heart-shaped token.

It clanked back onto the rock.

Mina picked up the token, running her fingers along its smooth edges. The whole thing was a few inches wider and taller than her hand, a flat token of red glass only shaped into a human heart, bound to be more than it seemed.

She buckled.

An abundance of stinging trickled down her hips in angry ferocity. Her magic delved over her thighs, calves, and shins, tearing at her ankles and the tops of her feet, eating her boots along with them. Her skirt disintegrated into her legs, making her appear naked underneath the magic sculpted onto her.

Soon the left side of her face would be the only human-like thing about her. But that didn't matter. Not anymore. She had the Blood King's heart.

Spinning around, she came face-to-face with him.

"I have found your heart," she told him, puffing with pride.

She presented it in its full, healed glory. A little bit of her magic smeared across it, one string of violet flickering on the black.

Faraway amber eyes turned to the red heart. Gently, he took it from her, examining both sides, running his blood-laced fingers over the surface. In his hand, the heart shrunk and lost some of its vibrancy.

He raised it above his head. In one swift motion, he hurled his heart against the ground, smashing it into tiny pieces.

PERSISTENT COMPASSION

*S*omething worse than defeat plagued Mina. Death itself slowly fastened around her, ready to drag her away. And she couldn't even cry over it.

Mina crouched and scooped up what was left of the heart pieces. Her magic wrapped around the toe of her boots, circling painfully under her feet. Only the left side of her face remained intact. She sat back on her knees, not knowing where to look—at the glass in her dead hands, or at the spirit who sealed her end.

She chose the latter, filled with a fury she'd never felt before. A coldness she didn't even hold against Davian, her true murderer. She'd forgiven and held the benefit of the doubt for her friends, for the Blood King, but this, *this*, couldn't be overlooked so easily. She grew tired of trying to think of reasons for his behavior.

The Blood King remained blank as he kept his head high, eyes peering down at her. He'd become the embodiment of the fear in the Wishmaker's voice during his warning, yet a few tears glistened off his gaze.

One of the glass shards fell out of Mina's hands, further breaking. "Fix it," she demanded, shoving the pile towards him. "Use your magic. Make it beat like you said you would."

He tried to turn from her.

She shot up. More glass fell and shattered. "I trusted you."

"And you were warned to not do so." He peered at her out of the corner of his eye. "That is the price you pay for naivety."

"Naivety?" she repeated, aghast. "You lied to me so easily. I put trust in you because I wanted to believe you were good."

"No, it was because you wanted something. You should have listened to me when I wanted to change the deal. It was for the better."

"And when would you have told me that *this* deal would end badly for me?"

He clamped his mouth shut.

"I didn't want to forgo the hearts," she said. The rest of the glass fell to the floor. She didn't care when she stepped on the shards, the crunches thunderous to her ears. "Yes, I wanted my heart, but I also wanted yours. All I could think about was the life we could share if I helped you, if I helped the others. You treated me fair. You made me believe I had a chance. Now you call me naive because...for having...for..."

"For what?" He turned to her, a brow cocked.

"For having a heart."

She turned her chin down in shame, wishing he'd disappear. When she spoke again, her voice came out low and hoarse, hardly recognizable as her own. "My whole existence, I gave everything I could to one man, and I was nothing but dirt to him. For once, I tried to give myself something, and I'm still dirt." Her face sunk further down. "I wanted you to be good."

"Goodness is deceit."

"For you, yes." Mina curled her magic-covered hands into fists. She winced a little. "I had faith in you."

"A mistake," he whispered.

"I relied on you."

His voice cracked. "A second mistake."

"You told me to find the heart pieces. You encouraged me to do it. If this isn't what you wanted—" A choke cut her off. She put her hand over her icy chest, emotions welling inside her. She knew he could see them. She hoped he feared them. Regretted causing them—her despair, her anger, her turmoil. "If you wanted to prevent this from happening with a second deal, why didn't you tell me this was a ruse? You left this option open to me. You let me have hope."

"I asked if you wanted to finish this deal. You did, so I let you."

She couldn't believe what she was hearing. Her jaw tensed. "That is no good reason. Oh, I must be the silliest thing in the universe! I should've known when I caught the first lie that you'd have more. That *everything* was a lie. I thought you were in pain and I could fix it. You acted like you cared about all of this...about me. I wanted to finish this deal for your heart as well as mine. So where is it?"

"Mina," he said, "even if I told you the pieces were useless, you still wouldn't be able to find my beating heart."

Oh, he was cruel. Crueler than anything she'd ever known. At least Davian told her the truth of why he let her go. At least Calin, Amberly, and Kristofer had reasons for not being able to tell her who they were. The Blood King, he had no excuse for his lies.

While he was a liar, she was plain stupid. The fact he had no heart endeared her to him, despite all warnings. Their similarity made her want the best for him. It made her draw incredible conclusions as to why he'd acted strange so often and made her take in his words as truth.

But he tricked her. Lied straight to her face, sending her on a journey that never had a victory. Everything he did wasted her time. Now her magic would win, and in the end, as per their deal, it would now belong to the Blood King, granting him more power than anything human blood provided.

Studying his full bloody form, Mina wanted to scream and pound her fists on his back.

"You wanted me to fail," she accused. "This entire time."

The Blood King's lips parted and then snapped shut. His glossy eyes fell to the floor. The etchings of misery on his face should've spurned her with hatred beyond comparison. It was he who wronged her—she should've been the miserable one. Not him.

But Mina, poor and naive as she just discovered, could not feel the full hatred she wanted to. All she could find was pity. Pity when she observed the rise and fall of his chest. His empty chest. She placed a hand over her own.

Maybe he was born without a heart. Maybe he ripped it out himself and discarded it.

No, that couldn't be true. None of it. He'd shown glimmers of kindness, the gentleness of a touch, of genuine care floating along in a sentence or two—things someone with a heart could do.

However, nothing beat in his chest. Where would it have been then? How would he have displayed a few good qualities without it? And her? What about her? How did either one of them have good qualities if they had no hearts?

The Blood King finally lifted his eyes to hers. He trembled. "Mina, let me show you my real story."

Mina took a step back when he raised his hand to her. Glass crunched under her magic covered boots, and as she'd suspected before, walking on magic dug sharp knives into her soles, crumpling her insides. She sucked in a hiss, blistering all over in excruciating pain.

His face strained. "You don't need to be afraid." His other hand went to his chest. "I cannot lie to you anymore."

White wax slithered like snakes out of the room's fog, creeping across the ground. Certain points of the lines broke off in two. The wax hit the back of the Blood King's shoes, seeping in a puddle around his heels. Slices ran up his legs, ribbons curling around him. They crawled to his torso, spiraling down his arms and pooling at his hands. He brought his palms together, cupping the wax between them. Light exploded inside the space, flickering orange.

When he removed his left hand from his right, he revealed a candle to her. It sat on his palm, one sliver away from being completely melted.

"Take it," he said. "It'll give you enough light and comfort if you choose to leave this place."

"My magic will take over me before I—"

"It won't." He struggled to speak. "Mina, I have become utterly attached to you."

A tiny burble of laughter popped out of her. She didn't know where it came from or how it happened. It must've had something to do with the confusing warm stab in her chest, which went against the anger she tried to hold onto.

"Take a walk with me, and I will show you all that I have hid for so long," he told her. "There isn't an apology I can give you for what I have done—what I have done to others. The best I can do is start by exposing my wrongs in the hopes that one day forgiveness will allow you and I to have something more."

Mina touched her chin. She observed his empty hand, thinking of all the deadly possibilities that might come out of taking it. Sincerity trickled from his voice, and it interlaced his face. This was no different from how he strung his previous lies and truths, thus getting her stuck to him in the first place.

Turning inward, Mina tried imagining what would happen if she didn't go with him. Her body might melt like the wax in his hand. Flames might burn her into a puddle of watery light waiting to be added to the Blood King's well.

"Does the Wishmaker know?" she asked quietly.

"I believe so," he said, drained of any emotion.

"To what extent?"

"He knows enough to have warned you."

"And he can't get rid of you?"

"No one can get rid of a spirit," he said. "Not one like me."

Cracks of loneliness and regret rested on the surface of the Blood King's skin. Mina remembered his gentle shock when she'd once asked for his name. No magic in the world may have compared to his. But perhaps something more powerful than sheer magic existed. Something human.

She'd spent so long wanting to give Davian a second chance. She wanted Calin, Amberly, and Kristofer to have theirs, too. She even knew she wanted the Blood King to have one. It might've been beyond naive to even think of going with him, to continue to want the best for him, but that naivety, she supposed, was just a part of her nature. And she'd never truly get rid of it.

Mina placed her fingers on the Blood King's empty palm.

FINAL PATH THROUGH GLASS

*M*ina's fingers stiffened on the Blood King's palm while his stayed flat and away, never truly conjoining their hands. If she wanted to, she could've slipped off.

He led her back through the hall. The gears had gone and the floor was normal. The gaps between the bricks weren't there anymore. Fog fled in fear from each one of the Blood King's steps. He brought her back to where his well of magic should've been. Calin, Amberly, and Kristofer didn't stand where she'd left them, either. The foggy hallway sealed shut behind her, plunging the room in darkness.

The bottoms of Mina's feet blistered. Violet flashes radiating off her body shone on the broken statues ahead, their faces warped. It was like someone melted them, stuck their hand in the goo, and mixed it in a circle. When the statues hardened they were left with swirled messes for faces.

Mina shuffled backwards a little. The Blood King finally ran his thumb over her knuckles. The warmth stilled her.

"Mina," he said her name softly. He gazed at her, determined and sad. He took in a quick breath, as if to say more, but he didn't. In the flashing of her magic, he turned his face away from her.

At the turn of his other palm to the ceiling, the center of the room shifted. Bricks rubbed together and shifted, moving down to form an open circle in the floor with cloudy gray and white blooming out of it and evaporating as it traveled too far from its place of origin. Through the obscurity, a glassy surface twinkled.

"I have never entered this path," the Blood King said hoarsely. "Not since living it. These mirrors I created, they are extractions of the mind. The others have lived in their pasts behind glass." He lowered his chin. "But I added the blurriness to their heads, so they'd never know. I placed the heart pieces with their past selves. Those pieces were only a split up token from our friendship, nothing more.

"The mirrors don't only change around a specific mind, but all minds. They only resemble one mind the most because that one mind has been affecting it the longest. It's why you saw where Calin grew up, where Amberly ruled, where Kristofer marched, but also why you saw your own thoughts seeping into reality."

"Davian and Lumina," Mina murmured.

"I'd told you before, so long as you kept letting him back, he'd stay. And that goes for Lumina, too."

"What about the others?"

"Calin, Amberly—"

"No, the others who made deals."

The Blood King took his thumb off her knuckles. "There were many deals. Years of deals. I—only one person has escaped me, but that was when I was very young, and that boy was the first. He had people who wanted to save him. Since then I've been careful. Only the lonely may be near me. Only the desperate may enter the mirrors. While no one has truly gotten stuck behind the mirrors, they have all failed." A broken smile touched his lips. "You see, Mina, I've taken a lot of drops of blood at the start of my bargains. I've tampered with a lot of minds at the end of each failure to make them think they needed to give more blood. You would've been my first natural death."

Despair. Deep, dreadful despair washed over Mina. Her throat closed off and she could not look into those amber eyes any longer. Her fingers itched to rip away from his palm, and her legs itched to carry her far away. But what would it matter if she ran? Death had its grips on her wherever she went.

The mirror embedded in the floor glowed brighter. The click of Mina's boots against the floor hit her ears before she realized she was moving. Inside and out, her magic grew hot, coursing all over in pulses of adrenaline.

"This mirror," the Blood King said, taking her to the puddle of glass on the floor, "holds my own mind."

HEARTLESS DISINTEGRATION

*T*he Blood King clasped his fingers around Mina's hand when she stiffened upon seeing where he'd taken her.

"Nothing will hurt you here," he assured her.

Mina wasn't so certain about that.

Tree roots broke out of the patchy mix of dirt and grass. She lifted her foot, avoiding their pointy ends as they angled at her like snakes. And where the ground held danger, so did the air. From the roots, enormous trees sprouted. Weapons dangled off jangling chains that strung between the leafless trees as though they were streamers. Knives, scalpels, scissors, every sharp object imaginable rattled off the chains.

A sizzle of heat burned behind Mina's eyes. It pummeled, circling her throat, stomach, legs, and toes. It grated against her, barbed wire pulling too tightly. With only a piece of herself free from magic, Mina only had a little sense of relief. One spot, on the left side of her face, where she could find comfort, as difficult as it was to do so.

"You are safe, Mina."

At the touch of the Blood King's fingers, her magic subsided. The stinging beat into a steady, unnoticeable rhythm. But while her physical pain left, heaviness weighed upon her soul.

The Blood King had the power to heal her from the start and she knew it. While playing the part of a good spirit with a missing her, he'd allowed her to go through the mirrors knowing she was in pain. If he were considerate, he would've eased her, or at least tried to, like he'd mentioned before. Instead, Mina did exactly to the Blood King what she'd done to Davian for years: make excuses for his selfishness and allow herself to suffer in the wake of it.

Her insides curled in a blend of emotions. Hatred for the Blood King and the blood he wore whorled in her. Hatred for his lies, for giving her false hope. Hatred for the fact she still had a piece of warmth for him.

"Mina, you can trust me," the Blood King told her. "You can believe...you can..." He bowed his head. A tear slipped out of the corner of his eye.

Reaching up, Mina wiped it with a magic-filled finger. The Blood King held still. Violet lightning flashed around the tear. It bubbled and steamed. She brought it to the remaining skin on her face, drawing a line from the corner of her eye down to her jaw. Her mind couldn't make out how the tear felt on her real, beautiful skin.

"Mina," the Blood King said.

She interlaced her fingers with his, nodding. The Blood King swallowed and then carefully took her through the roots and rusted blades. He kept his word about her safety, his blood smears lighting up. Every root, every blade, moaned, turning away from his presence as if he were a disease.

He stopped, gesturing ahead to dense smog covering the rest of the desolate forest. In the smoke, two people walked, only appearing as shadows. The smaller figure, who must've only been a child, limped next to someone taller with long, flowing hair.

The smaller shadow paused, turning to the taller one. They pushed an arm out. Something burst out of their hand. A bouquet.

Taking the bouquet, the taller shadow knelt down to eye level with the other. At first, Mina thought they were going to embrace, but then the taller shadow lifted the bouquet over their head and smashed it to the ground.

The smaller shadow collapsed to their knees, hunching over to pick up the flowers, as the taller one stood back up and unveiled a knife from their hip.

"No!" Mina cried as the taller shadow raised the knife and plunged it down into the smaller shadow's shoulderblades. She hurried to run and save the child. Her hand slipped from the Blood King's. Without his presence, however, the roots hissed at her, turning their sharp ends her way, and the blades shifted, threatening to slice off her head. She froze.

Crying flowed out of the smoke. A young boy's weeping. The smaller shadow fell forward as the knife was removed out of them and the taller shadow held up the dripping knife, words of an unknown language floating out of them, loud and clear. As the syllables pricked Mina's ears, her magic livened. Some sort of spell was happening.

The knife lowered and the taller shadow turned their head down, cocking it to the side as they looked at the spot where the smaller shadow certainly laid.

They bent down.

A root cracked.

The smaller shadow burst upward, hands grabbing the taller one's throat and leaning forward to bite into the flesh. While the taller shadow screamed and struggled, the smaller shadow did not let go. Like a wild animal, they kept their teeth in the flesh, head shaking side to side. Finally, they broke away. The taller shadow clutched the wound, stumbling backwards and falling into the smog, vanishing forever.

Breathless, Mina stared at the small shadow. They turned toward her, a twig snapping under a step as they drew nearer. Piece by piece, the human behind the smoke came into full transparency.

Glowing blood covered the boy. His mouth pressed into a firm, raging line, contrasting his big, round eyes. His amber irises glistened in fright.

Mina turned to the Blood King, questions stuck in her throat.

"People sometimes use each other to test the limits of magic," he said. "Even loved ones can hurt each other."

A new wind whistled, swinging the blades and carrying orange and yellow leaves from a far-off place on their surface. They tumbled by the young boy's feet. Mina shifted. Right before her eyes, the boy and the leaves changed. As the latter's color altered, getting brown and wrinkly and then suddenly bursting with healthy, green life. Meanwhile, the boy stretched taller, older. He grew into his face, developed a broader chest, and had trouble standing straight since his right shoulder stuck up a sliver higher than his left. His legs were different lengths.

Mina glanced at the Blood King's shoes, noticing that more heel extended off his left boot, evening him out. She chided herself for not seeing it sooner.

Three faces peeked from behind different trees, disintegrating the swaying blades into dust. That dust seeped into the soil and blades of bright green grass grew. The empty branches now sprung out tiny bulbs to grow fresh leaves.

Mina warmed inside at the slightly younger versions of Calin, Amberly, and Kristofer.

Calin seemed close to thirty, mustache bushier than ever and eyebrows a bit thicker. His run-down clothing hung off him at every joint, too big and tattered on the ends. He held a cracked cup in his hands, gold coins clanking inside.

Amberly slouched more than she did now, a touch over thirty. Her stinger had greater shine, and one sliver of gray entered her hair. Black streaks ran from her eyes, thinning over her cheeks. An indent sat on her head in the same place where her younger self, the young Queen of the Bees, wore her crown. Her scepter wagged in her hand. Despite her dripping tears, she smiled, lips bright red as always.

The youngest of the three, Kristofer, looked as boyish as he did now in his human form. He shivered and sucked on his bottom lip. Frost cascaded off his simple, black cloak, stitched together with white thread. It trailed the ground after him. He kept the hood up, hiding his face underneath it.

"Friendship is sacred," the Blood King said. "Honesty makes any relationship stronger, but while these three wanderers, fresh away from their homes, trusted each other, they were about to pluck and try to blossom a flower out of a weed. To take a lost young man and help him find a home."

Calin, Amberly, and Kristofer tapped up on their toes from behind the trees, joining together. Sunshine, real sunshine, strung through the trees. The sky above cleared of any fog and turned into a light, crystal blue.

The young Blood King smiled as the other three formed a semi-circle around him, their backs to Mina. She propped up, trying to peek at what they were doing.

A few clouds started to creep into the sky.

"Spirits have purpose," the Blood King said, resentful. "The Wishmaker is our best example. He lives so happily, so freely, so loved by everyone. Our world is filled with meaningful spirits. But created spirits have no grand purpose."

Electricity exploded from ahead. Calin, Amberly, and Kristofer stepped back, giving applause to the young Blood King and his smoking hands.

"Magic is intriguing," the Blood King said. "It can grant people every desire they want, but they grow bored and then want something else. The only way to stay is to be better than what anyone desires. You understand that."

"I do," Mina said.

"It hurts to not be kept."

"Yes. But you still have yourself."

Gesturing to the scene, the Blood King took in a breath. "Great power is my specialty. It delighted them, made me important to everyone I ever came across. They knew I was a powerful spirit, but being a created spirit has its limits. I must take from others in order to stay the idea I've become."

His younger self spun. Flashes of fire and lightning flew off his arms. The others clapped and cheered in delight, congratulating him on how marvelous he was.

"The well of magic is what fuels the mirrors. The blood on my skin fuels me. I can't exist without it." The Blood King's muscles tightened. "I need it. Always, always, always."

The world behind the final mirror faded into shadow as shame riddled his face. He turned to Mina. Red light illuminated a piece of the room; his well of magic. *Stolen* magic.

"Since you are a wish, I knew I needed to take the opportunity to have what's yours," he told her, hunger etched on his features. "You are crafted from pure magic. An abundance I couldn't pass up."

Harsh sharpness slashed straight across Mina's chest. She didn't like the way he stared at her.

He must've sensed her new fear, for he blinked and his face relaxed back to normal.

"What about the others?" she asked. "You found friendship, this I know, but what made them steal your heart?"

"They never stole a thing. They only discovered I was making these deals and stealing magic," the Blood King said simply. "That meant they discovered I wasn't a natural spirit, so I stuffed them in the mirrors and scrambled their minds to keep them from telling. Not even the Wishmaker knows as much as he thinks he does."

Mina could hardly hear her own voice as everything hollowed out inside her. "You didn't need to lie to them. They would've accepted you as you are."

The Blood King's blood dimmed. "I know," he murmured, serene.

"If you cared for them, you should free them."

He laughed a little. "You're about to be nothing at all, and what you're thinking about is helping people you hardly know."

"It would release you from your own pain if you let the truth out," she said. "Your chest feels empty not because you lack a heart, but because it doesn't work." She went to him and placed a hand on his chest. "Everyone's heart beats for something. Sometimes it takes longer to recognize what it beats for."

"I ask for no forgiveness, Mina," he said. At the mention of her name, something moved in his chest, pumping against her hand. "I have been wrong, to you and so many others. All I want is to give you your heart. There is a lot to value about you. I would hate to exist anywhere when you don't at all."

On the other side of the room, Calin, Amberly, and Kristofer lingered, barely visible in the red light as Mina peered over the Blood King's shoulder.

"With a heart," Mina began, "I could do anything. I could run around the entire world. I could rest on a bed of leaves. I could float on the sea for as many hours as I'd like. There are many people I could speak with, many whom I'll know for moments, and more I may know for the rest of my life."

She removed her hand from the Blood King's chest and looked him right in the eye. "You once spoke about how pointless living is. You were right. Nothing does matter. Not the friends I've made, or the experiences I've had. The near smiles, the missing tears. None of that will matter in a great while from now when we're all dead. But it doesn't feel pointless right now, and that is what makes me want to keep living."

She turned to the well and swept her hands over the magic's surface. "There is nothing I regret. I'm glad to have had the chance to see life on my own."

"Mina," the Blood King said. "Please, let me help you."

She shook her head. "I don't need you."

Magic constricted around her, biting her, eating what remained of the skin on her face. The Blood King watched in silence, shoulders slouched, defeated.

"A heart must be given." Her hands closed over her chest. "So I will give myself a heart."

The room faded as the well's light died out. Darkness swallowed everyone away. Mina stretched her left fingers, isolating her index one. She examined the spot where she'd first been cut by one of the many cards sent to Davian.

He once thanked her for teaching him to let go. Mina thanked him in return.

"I have a heart," she said, curling her fingers into a fist. "I've always had one."

And the magic ate what was left of her.

HUMAN

Shallow breaths dipped in and out of Mina. She laid on her back, atop something cushy. She couldn't tell exactly how the cushy fabric felt against her skin, her sense of touch evading her yet again.

Hues of red curtained over her eyes. She shifted her head, unsure of what to make of the sight. She'd always thought people saw pure darkness whenever they closed their eyes.

Closed eyes.

Mina twitched. Then she stilled. Her eyes were closed. She'd been asleep. For how long, she did not know, but she was alive, and had been sleeping. She was too busy relishing in her closed eyes to notice the deep ache on the left side of her face.

As she became more aware of herself, her muscles awoke, shocked to life. Her breathing deepened. Stinging shot around her joints, warming them up so that they may twist and bend.

Fingers wiggling, face swishing, Mina embraced the sharpness searing into place. She tightened her jaw and found that a smile still hurt her. Lifting her brows was still a bit painful, but as she worked her muscles, tensing and letting go, she noticed they relaxed a lot easier. The frustration that once grew at what she lacked did not appear.

Thumping beats drummed at certain points in her body—behind her knees, underneath her wrists, in her throat, at the crux of her big toe—hitting against the inside of her flesh, pushing up and down.

The most intense pulse came from her chest, beating a sliver to the left. She held a palm down over it, entrapping it so it wouldn't burst through her flesh.

Incomprehensible voices touched the air. Mina strained, trying to make out who might've been speaking, or if she mistook a different sound for the voices.

When she couldn't decipher anything, she sat up.

Tingles sprang to her head, raining down to her arms in little pecks. Touching the right side of her face, Mina found the cracks circling her eye. She felt around to the other side, determining she was properly covered in skin again. Everything seemed the same as before, except for the intense pulses in her and the red behind her eyelids.

Closed eyes.

A blood-curdling scream broke through the air.

POP!

Mina pried her eyes open, blinded at first. She hovered an arm by her forehead, shielding her gaze from the overbearing sunlight.

The voices grew louder, jumbling together into a bigger mess.

In the Virvin courtyard, a cloudless, bright day bestowed itself onto an event that had everyone in the village gathering together. An event with wooden chairs lined up on the grass, food on tables against the back wall, and lanterns hanging from the rafters, though they were quite pointless. The sun was so bright already.

At first, Mina suspected everyone was here for a happy event. Except, the perplexed faces and screeches of terror didn't add up to any happiness.

Mina tilted her head. She struggled for an expression but still found a blink. A twinge echoed in the movement. It wasn't enough to discourage her from trying to blink again.

"Why is everyone upset with me?" she asked, pushing some gray and brown hair off her neck with a jaundiced hand. Her voice didn't make it over the noise.

Orange flowerpots—round, tall, large, and bursting with healthy light pink and white carnations—sat on both ends of the small wooden stage the chairs pointed toward. The place everyone directed their terror at. The stage, furnished with acorn-brown paint, was the place where Mina laid on.

No, *in*.

Over it.

She was in a box. A long, rectangular box with a red cushion inside. A lid propped open on the other side of her, putting her on full display. Nobody had gathered here for a happy event. Not even close.

"Mina."

Davian stood on the grass with his hands behind his back, slick with sweat. He looked so different from how she used to picture him. Silver streaked the brown waves of his hair. Wrinkles crept onto his face, crinkling mostly around his eyes and near his mouth. The tired puddles that had always been under his eyes disappeared, enhancing the green in them.

For the first time, Mina saw how aged he'd been. Aged but more lively than ever.

"You're awake," he said.

Mina blinked again. She couldn't stop. "Of course I am."

"But you weren't waking up." He scratched behind his ear.

Someone burst through the crowd, her face aged and similar to Mina's.

Lumina's radiant eyes, as cold as ever, stared Mina down. One of her brows lifted, the perfect arch. "What? Two weeks asleep, barely breathing, and now you're up at your own funeral."

Mina's breath hitched. "Funeral." She glanced around at all the stunned faces. "How did you get everyone to come?"

Davian cleared his throat. "A lot of people cared."

She didn't believe it. Davian strained too much. Besides, all the people here didn't know her before. She never had that chance.

"What is going on?" someone asked. He was a tall goat, a man-goat—top half goat, bottom half human. Mister Delegade. He always made bread in the morning, filling the streets with the most decadent smells, as people always said. "I thought we were here to get together for this one." He gestured to Mina.

Davian cleared his throat, addressing the crowd. "Just give us a moment to take care of her, and then we can celebrate her...not being dead."

Tension pulled through the crowd of faces Mina had seen her whole life. They turned to each other, grumbling about wasting time and whether they should start eating or not. She couldn't wait to leave Virvin.

Davian turned to her. He opened and closed his mouth.

"You left us without saying a word," Lumina said evenly, chin raised. "We thought you were gone for good."

"How long have I been gone?" Mina asked.

"A while."

Mina swallowed. "How long is a while?"

Davian and Lumina shared a look.

"A month and a half," Davian finally said.

The old Mina, the wish, would have exploded into hysterics upon hearing that. Being so far from Davian for so long would've tormented her. Now she shook in eagerness to be parted again.

"A month and a half including two weeks being maybe dead?" she wondered.

"No," Davian answered.

"Well then. Time moves quickly when you're busy," she said.

"What *have* you been doing?" he asked, lifting a brow.

Mina propped herself up so she could climb out of the casket. She waved off any help, slowly lowering one foot onto the stage and then the other. Her clothing had changed. A sweep of white hung around her legs, a long nightgown to put her to rest.

Davian stepped back onto the grass. He glanced nervously at Lumina, as if to ask her for help. "We..."

"We worried about you," Lumina finished for him, to which he nodded in agreement.

"Don't lie to me," Mina said. "It's fine that you didn't."

"That's not..." Davian pressed his lips together. She never noticed how bad at lying he was. All that love she thought she had really blinded her.

"What were you busy doing?" Lumina asked. She scanned Mina. "You feel different."

Davian stroked his chin. "You do feel different. I wonder if it has anything to do with that man."

"Which man?" Mina asked quickly.

"The one who brought you here," Davian told her as if she should've known. "He carried you here. Brought you in his arms right to my door."

Lumina shivered. "He seemed so familiar. Evil."

The beating in Mina's chest quickened and her stomach tied into knots. Blood rushed into her ears. She wanted to claw at it, pry it out.

"Did the man say anything? About me? About himself? Was he covered in blood?"

Davian's upper lip curled. "No, thank goodness. He was a clean young man. He felt very, very familiar."

"It was like he held a spell over our heads," Lumina added. "I felt like I was forgetting something."

Davian nodded. "He wanted us to tell you he's thankful for you. He mumbled something about how he brought you here because he didn't know where to put you, and told us he hoped you'd leave. Said there would be some friends waiting for you when you did."

"A strange man all around," Lumina added. "I don't know what sort of friend you made—if he is one—but I wouldn't even stand five steps near him if I could help it. I remember thinking that if he spent any longer at our door, I was going to scratch his face off."

"I would've helped you," Davian said.

Mina slipped off the stage. "I have to go."

"Go?" Davian echoed.

"Of course."

"Where?"

"I don't know where, but I'll be happy."

"For how long?"

"Forever," she told him. She hurried forward. Davian and Lumina moved out of her way. Incredulous looks simmered between the pair.

Mina paused, turning to them. "Oh, I wanted to thank you for teaching me something," she said. "Good luck to the rest of your lives. I hope you'll be as happy as I am."

When Davian had given up Mina, it had been easy for him to do so. She never understood why it was easy until now. Until feeling fully free. Without a second thought, she walked away from him, the thudding in her chest jumping for joy.

"Teaching you what?" Davian called out. She didn't bother to look back.

The crowd that gathered for a funeral didn't pay attention as the corpse left. Not that she cared. The world was full of different people. She'd find the right ones to care for.

Mina skipped out of Virvin. The pulse points in her body hammered in aching drawls. The skin under her feet pulled too tightly at each step, making her legs stiff. Every few seconds, lightning shocked new parts of her body. Awakening a new version of herself. One she'd happily get used to.

Entering the forest outside of Virvin, Mina thought of who she was when she first walked through it. The heartbroken wish, lost and terrified. She laughed at that version of herself. The forest wasn't so bad. Neither was being alone.

Still, she longed for her friends. Calin. Amberly. Kristofer. They were good people, framed for a crime they didn't commit. Sentenced to a fate they couldn't control. And even though they still weren't perfect, she loved them anyway.

She stroked her chin. "Where could they be?" she murmured, thinking of what Davian said about friends waiting for her when she left Virvin.

As she walked deeper into the forest, Mina wondered what happened to them in the two weeks she slept. Were they free? Were they with the Blood King?

She soured. Thinking about the Blood King stabbed her with confusion. Part of her hated him. Another part simply pitied him. She hoped he'd walk out of his lonely castle one day and help himself into a better life. In that life, she hoped to run into him, and wanted for both of them to have changed so much that they'd have to reintroduce themselves to each other. From that point on, they could have a second chance together.

But for now, she'd keep walking on her own path.

Up ahead, heavy footsteps knocked the dirt on the road. Mina caught the shape of a rounded hat bobbing up and down as the person accompanying the footsteps jogged toward her.

"Calin?" she whispered. She pushed up on her toes for a few seconds.

It was a trick. A mirage. She thought him to life.

He ran to her, his mustache as thick as ever. The hairs bounced as he moved. He was real. Real. Just like she wanted him to be.

"Late-night traveler," he said, coming to a stop, panting.

Mina laughed inwardly. "It's daytime."

He looked at the sky, frowning. "So it is. My mistake. I'm still readjusting to the real world. I may need a little help in doing so."

Launching forward, she wrapped her arms around him, catching him by surprise.

"Oh, Calin," Mina said. "You're here."

"I am, I am," he said, patting her back. "And you, you look as lovely as always. Very rosy on the cheeks."

She cupped her cheeks. "I am?"

He nodded. Then shouted, "She's here!"

Buzzing came from within the trees. Amberly flew over the grass, scepter in hand.

Mina perked up.

Amberly's eyes brightened, and her complexion shone. "If you need royalty," she said, pushing her scepter over her head and twirling around. "Then I might do as the trick for you."

Mina rushed to meet her. "I'm so happy to see you."

"And I you." She descended, wrapping an arm around Mina's shoulders. "You know, I had a deeply sleeply, and you were in my dream."

"Was I there, too?" someone asked from Amberly's hand. Mina knew exactly who it was.

"Oh!" Amberly exclaimed. She uncurled her fingers from around him.

Kristofer popped out his dendrites, coming to full size and grinning.

"Mina!" He jumped off Amberly's palm.

"Kristofer," Mina said. She reached toward him. "Watch out. You'll—"

"No, don't worry about me," he said, tapping her cheek. "I've been dedicated to control recently. It's not the best, but it is there, and little by little, it'll—"

He bounced a little too hard, gasping and spinning rapidly. In the nick of time, Amberly caught him and kept him safe in her hand. She clicked her tongue against the top of her mouth.

"Get better?" Mina said.

Kristofer blushed. "I'll try."

Mina tapped one of his dendrites. He blushed deeper.

Everyone looked healthier than before. Sunlight brought out the natural beauty of their faces. Their voices were fuller, and they presented themselves with more confidence.

"So, Mina," Calin said, placing a hand over his chest, "how does it feel?"

Kristofer bobbed. "Yes, yes, how's it feeling?"

"I don't feel too different," she explained. "My body has a bit more sensation, and I slept for the first time ever, but my mind still operates in its usual manner. I'm mostly the same in mind and appearance, but that doesn't bother me. It can't. Not when I have something important I want to do. There's a farm nearby that I'd like to visit if that's okay."

"Okay?" Amberly put on her brightest grin. "Of coursely course it is. We'll go as quickly as we want. My magic can carry us there." She snapped her fingers. "You know, I used to visit a farm close to my hive."

"Really? Could you tell me more about it?"

"I will."

Calin extended his elbow. "There will be lots of time for stories. But right now, there's a whole world waiting for you to arrive, Mina."

"With us by your side," Amberly declared.

"If you want that, of course," Kristofer added.

"I want that more than anything." Mina took Calin's elbow, glancing at each one of *her* friends.

Calin moved his arm. He looked down at her hand and gasped. "Mina, you're bleeding."

She glanced at her hand. A red slice ran across the end of her left forefinger.

"I hadn't noticed," she said.

A smile tugged on her lips. She lifted her gaze to the world ahead and picked up her feet. In her chest, her heart beat at a steady rhythm.

ACKNOWLEDGMENTS

Mom. Papa. Thank you.

I could write a whole novel about how grateful I am to have you as my parents and how much your support means to me, but I think it would be very difficult to see what I'm writing through my tears for that long. The whole thing would be an incomprehensible mess by page ten.

You two, and the two beautiful dogs who graced our lives, are the brightest stars in my life. Every time I wage war against myself, you pull me through it. Every time I stray from happiness, you guide me back. You have made my own wishes come true. For that, I endlessly thank you.

Thanks to Clara Abigail for your hard work in editing this book. I greatly appreciate the timely and constructive manner in which you helped me edit this book. You were so patient and kind with me. I'm so thankful for you.

Aimeé Fôrémar, thank you for giving this book such a beautiful cover. Book covers help the story come to life even more and you brought my vision to life better than I ever imagined it. I am so happy to have your beautiful work on display. Thank you!

And finally, dear reader, thank you. Knowing you're here with me in the acknowledgments, whether you flipped on a whim or read to the end, fills me with tremendous honor. Getting this book to you has been quite the adventure. It features a lot of high emotions, a lot of doubt, a lot of snacks, and, of course, a lot of words being written and torn apart.

Thank you, thank you, thank you for choosing *Heart of the Wish*. I wish every one of you all the happiness, safety, and health.

ABOUT THE AUTHOR

Maggie Alexandrite is a Canadian author who lives with an emergency bag of chocolate for emotional support and the constant flow of music, which inspires her writing but is also a huge distraction (there are just some songs she *has* to sing along with). She is always wishing to life her next story idea, often discovering the most extraordinary plot points, haunted houses, and lively characters in places like the cheese section.

Heart of the Wish is her debut novel.

www.ingramcontent.com/pod-product-compliance
Lightning Source LLC
Chambersburg PA
CBHW071554030726
47593CB00001BA/152